"*Have you ever met someone with so much passion and charisma, such an uncanny lust for life that it scares you, motivates and inspires you, all at the same time? People like that you admire. Their company you don't want to be without. Their characteristics can go unmatched for a lifetime. They are respected, loved, and never forgotten. ... For me, her name was Veronica Tomez- Ronni, and as I sat there watching her sleep, I knew that some promises had to be broken.*"

She Rode The Bus

By

Akil Victor

Akil Victor

2004

Chapter 1

They say that marijuana slows down reaction time and impairs judgement. That may be true, but any frequent user will tell you that it also improves your ability to focus on whatever you're doing at the time. Although, you may have a one-track mind.

We were traveling north on La Brea, in Inglewood. By *we*, I mean me. I go by Kay, and my right-and left-hand men, Slip, the solidly built light-skin brother with close-cropped hair and a goatee in the passenger seat counting money, and Will, the dark complected one with cornrows seated behind me. Like Slip, he also had a love affair with weights, and was currently fogging up my car with smoke from a chronic blunt. Purple Kush, some of the best California has to offer.

All three of us had on black matching attire, from shirts to Converse All-Stars. Robbery outfits. Although, the crime had already been committed successfully twenty minutes ago and three cities over with no way it could be linked back to us. We were surgically careful. It's what we do, one of our jobs. Even though we only got a little over $3,500 each this time, it was still a good job and only took a minute and twenty seconds to make. Most people don't even make that much in three months where we come from.

I glanced in the rearview mirror at Will and then over to Slip. Both looked like they should be playing college or professional football. Actually, Will had an athletic scholarship to USC but blew it before the first season ended. He was caught selling drugs on campus. He even sold to a couple of his teammates, almost ruining their chances as well.

Slip was a former Inglewood High School star, but fell wayward living around the wrong influences. He started drinking and smoking more than he went to school and practice, eventually dropping out, choosing to gangbang instead. At the age of sixteen he was arrested for a gang-related shooting and served three years in Youth Authority. In the process, waving away any athletic chances he might've had.

Me, I was just an aspiring rapper working on an album called '*Hustle Mentality*,' which was two years in the making now. I didn't always have adequate studio time like I wanted, or the pleasure of making disposable demos at my leisure to distribute on a regional scale. It required money—more than I'd make working some retail job full-time, which seemed like the only positive option there was at the moment. Instead, I chose to skip what was referred to as the "sucker's way of living." I was trying to make something out of myself the easy way, because in my opinion any other way was just a waste of time.

So all three of us decided to rob and sell whatever we could get our hands on in the meantime, hoping that one day we'd come across enough money to open up a business or put out a record. Which isn't uncommon, seeing as how one-third of people in all of the inner cities throughout America look at life this way. We were just part of a trend—no, an epidemic, because when you're living a life like this, there are two major outcomes: incarceration or an early death. But some were fortunate enough to make it out of a lifestyle like this to cross the threshold into opulent abundance. That was our plan: to become some of the fortunate ones.

I was coasting through the palm tree and business-lined street in a black, 2003 Chevy Impala SS on 21-inch DUB Esinem floaters wrapped in run-flat tires. The interior, cream, complemented with wood-grain trimming, ash grey leather seats, and three TVs, one in the dash and one in each headrest. I usually didn't allow smoking in my car, but having money was always a reason for celebration.

"Ay, Will, pass that. You been hoggin' the blunt too long," I said, reaching my hand back over the seat while still focused on the road.

"Here," Will said, taking his last pull before placing the blunt in my hand. "Ay, watch out. -Oh shit!" Will yelled suddenly, grabbing my shoulder, making me drop the cigarillo in the process.

I saw it as well, at the same time as the basketball rolled into the street and the little kid darted after it.

I stomped on the brake, causing the tires to squeal from the sudden reflex, followed by a *thump*. The car didn't stop quickly enough. The kid was knocked at least six feet into the crossing intersection of La Brea and Arbor Vitae.

"Damn," Slip breathed, hand braced hard against the dashboard. "Come on, B, we gotta go."

"Nah, I can't leave him," I said, half panicked, stumbling out of the car.

It seemed as if time had warped into slow motion, cinema-like. I couldn't hear anything beyond the pounding of my heart. The light was green ... then yellow.

The kid, a Hispanic boy of about seven, lie prone on the ground. I ran to him and scooped him in my arms. His left leg was visibly broken with blood seeping out. His eyes were half-lidded, rolling back.

"Shit," I thought out loud. "Damn." Centinela Hospital was just down the street. I could hurry up and get him there. I turned to run with him back to my car, oblivious to everything but the task at hand.

Hooonnnk-skuuurrr. An older-model blue pick-up could not stop in time, and I was unable to get out of the way quickly enough. I turned to the side to ensure that I would take the brunt of the hit instead of the kid.

The truck had to be doing about thirty-five when it made impact with my side. Not hard enough to send me flying, instead lifting me on top of its hood with the child still in my arms. I slid off 180 degrees, landing hard on my back with the kid on top of me.

My head was spinning. I heard sirens in the distance, saw the lights. There was a bus, the number 40 bus. It stopped, the passengers hopping out to run in our direction.

A woman with a book bag on stooped beside me mumbling inaudible words. Will was standing nearby. I turned and saw Slip running down the street, and then everything went black.

"Excuse me, Mr. Anthony ... Mr. Anthony." It sounded like it was coming from heaven as I slowly opened my eyes, seeing the fuzzy overhead light. *This must be heaven; surely I'm in heaven,* I thought. But it was a nurse. A Caucasian woman of about forty, who called my surname with her hand on my forearm.

"Mr. Anthony, can you hear me?"

"Hmm," I mumbled, only understanding half of what she said.

"Mr. Anthony, you were part of a car accident. You were struck by a car," she said, as if speaking to a five-year-old.

I was beginning to regain consciousness. "The kid, the little boy," I said inquisitively, trying to rise out of the hospital bed, but I was stunned by a sharp pain on my left side.

"No, Mr. Anthony, you must stay down. The little boy is fine, just a broken leg. You saved his life, from what I hear."

Yeah, and I almost took it before then, I thought but did not say, relaxing on the bed once more. "Ouch," I groaned, pressing my padded left side.

"Hurts, doesn't it? Your left side is bruised from the impact. One broken rib, one cracked, and you have a little bump on your head. But you'll live." She smiled. "Be right back." Another smile before trotting off.

I took in my hospital room surroundings, which was no different from any other community hospital room. White tiled floor, cheap wood and cushion furniture placed neatly around the room with a somewhat sterile look and medicinal smell.

The door was open. In the hall stood a police officer questioning a woman whose back was to the room, leaving only a view of half the officer's face beyond the long curly hair that draped the top part of the backpack she wore. Probably the child's mother, I figured as she walked off and the cop entered the room.

"Kaeshon Anthony, right?" he asked upon entrance.

"Yeah."

"Have you had anything to drink before you got behind the wheel today?"

"No, sir," I replied, quite sure I was in for a breathalyzer test soon.

"Use any drugs?"

"No again," I lied.

"Okay, because I found a marijuana joint in your vehicle during a search following your accident."

"It wasn't mine."

"Okay, your friend, a William Bryman, admitted to it being his. You corroborate with this story, right?"

"It's the truth." Partially. Will was a good homie, willing to take the rap, knowing I was the one behind the wheel. He didn't mention anything about guns or money yet, so I knew that Slip had ran off with all incriminating evidence in tow.

The cop, a young white male of maybe twenty-five, looked at me skeptically before continuing. "Okay, as I'm sure you've heard, the kid you hit is going to be alright. Scarred for life, but alright. His mother blames herself for not keeping a close enough watch on him." He looked down at the sheaf of papers pinned to the small clipboard he was holding. "Two witnesses, your buddy and a Veronica Tomez, who was riding the bus at the time, both claim that the light was green, giving you the right of way." He looked back up at me. "Which is good for you and the fact that you stopped, which means that no legal action will be taken today—as far as you going to jail. But you and your insurance company can and probably will be sued by the child's mother," he said nonchalantly[A1].

"Okay," my simple reply to end the conversation.

"Have a nice day," he said, turning to exit. "Oh, by the way," He said, turning heel to face me once more. "When you got out of your car to grab the kid, you forgot to put the car in park after braking, so it hit a street light. Not pretty, you might want to get that fixed," he said with a smirk.

"Pig!"

Chapter 2

Two weeks later.

"Man, where the hell is this bus at?" I asked to no one in particular.

"This bus always late," Will replied to the undirected question.

The time on my cell displayed 6:32 p.m. It seemed as if the sky was growing darker with each passing minute on a canvas of mixed blues with navy conquering the lighter hues.

We were standing near the bus stop on the corner of Hawthorne Blvd and Rosecrans, waiting on the number .40 bus that would lead us closer to our apartment destination in Inglewood.

"There it go right there," I said, pointing at the approaching bus behind several cars.

Neither one of us was in a rush, but hated to wait.

The bus pulled to a stop on the side of a 7-eleven that had walls adorned with artless graffiti from a number of various Los Angeles gangs.

"It's about time yo ass got here. You thirty minutes late," Will said upon entrance.

"Yeah, we got shit to do," I added.

"Like what, be home before the street lights come on?" The bus driver, a heavy set Black man in his mid thirties asked with a sneer.

"Nah, like be at yo house before you get off work," Will replied.

"Fatboy," I finished.

Since it was practically dark out, the inside of the bus was well lit by an overhead row of lights and half full with a mixture of working class people, teenagers, and a few other stragglers on their way home from the mall, jobs, or other unknown activities. I quickly scanned the sea of expressions on the faces in view as we made our way across the rubbery floor that was dotted with unidentifiable spots and old chewing gum as hard as cement. We stopped at the final row of seats; the thug section, in the very back, just like old times when we use to ride to and from school, securing spots next to an old woman and teenage girl.

It's been four years since I last stepped foot on a bus. I hated public transportation, everything about it, the bumpy ride, the smell, the passengers. But I had no choice until my car was out of the shop in two days.

"Man, I can't believe we back on this joint again," Will said, nodding his head. Although he never had a car of his own, which was by choice because he had the money to get one. However, he chose to rely on me and other people for rides, something he's been doing for about three years now ever since he graduated from high school.

"Might as well make the most of our trip ... Ay dawg, I bet you can't get her number," I said with a nudge in the direction of an attractive Hispanic girl who was seated on the side bench, two spaces across from us listening to a CD player.

"What you wanna put on it?" Will asked, accepting my challenge.

"Twenty."

"Bet," he replied, shaking my hand. "Ay, excuse me," he said in the young woman's direction. "Ay mamacita." This time with a tap on her arm.

"What?" She asked, clearly annoyed, pulling down her headphones.

"Damn, like that? I'm just tryna holla at you mama," Will said with a grin.

"I'm not your mama, and I don't like being holla'd at," She said, placing her headphones back on.

Her reply and the smile that faded from Will's face was too funny to contain. I started laughing out loud with the elderly woman and teenaged girl next to me.

"Yeah whatever, she prolly a lesbian anyway. Here go yo twenty dollars," Will said, slapping the bill he'd just dug from his pocket into my hand. "What you laughing at grandma?" He continued on the older Black woman.

"Boy, you fellas just don't have a clue these days," she remarked, revealing a denture smile.

I looked at the young woman who had just shamelessly turned Will down. She was in her own world, lost in the music she was listening to. Her eyes were closed as she slowly moved her head to the melody as if it had a spell on her.

She was by far more attractive than I'd initially thought. She had the face of a print model, smooth butternut tone skin, almond shaped eyes set perfectly above a little fairy nose and full heart shaped lips touched lightly with lip gloss. All of which was draped by long raven curls that sat listlessly on shoulders covered by a tight, long sleeve, black beatnik-style shirt. This shirt, although dark and plain, did nothing to draw attention away from the contours of her ample breast that sat arrogantly above a flat stomach and small waist. Add that to tight stonewash jeans and small, suede, black Timberlands.

For some reason she looked familiar to me, but I couldn't recall where I might have seen her. But I was sure that we've never spoke to each other before. Although she looked at least twenty, she had a black and brown backpack between her legs on the floor. She probably went to college, though one never could tell nowadays, she could just be a mature sixteen year old.

She opened her eyes and noticed me staring. To my surprise, she smiled.

"What you listening to?" I asked.

"Huh?" She asked in return, pulling the headphones off once more.

"What're you listening to?"

"Beautiful Stranger," She replied.

"Thank you. My name is Kay," I said, half smile, extending my hand knowing that song title was the perfect opener.

"Not you," she said, smiling as well, with her hand in mine.

"Ouch. That's embarrassing. So I guess I'm the ugly stranger, huh?" I kidded.

"No." She paused to study me. "You're cute."

"Thanks, and your an angel. Can I know your name?"

"Ronni."

"Nice to meet you, Ronni," I continued. "So, what does that song sound like?"

"Great, it's my favorite, come here," she said, patting the seat next to her which I filled without hesitation.

She took the headphones from around her neck and placed them on my ears. "There you go, listen," she said while securing the headphones over my head.

"NA NA NA NA, NA NA NA..NA NA NAAA Beautiful Stranger,' Madonna crooned as the song's melody played. It was hypnotic.

"That's a nice song," I commented after a moments listen, handing her back the headphones.

"I know, I love it. She's my favorite singer."

"Yeah, I might have to buy that. She makes some good music."

"Like you know," she said, rolling her eyes. "You probably only listen to rap."

"As a matter of fact, I know a couple of Madonna's songs," I declared.

"Name one."

"Umm ... Umm. What's the name of that song?" I pondered out loud. "Will, name a Madonna song."

"What?" Will said, looking at me as if I had lost my mind. "I don't listen to that shit."

"Okay, I got one! American Life," I said, triumphant.

Smiling, Ronni said, "you only know that one because she raps in it."

"She do?" I asked unbelievingly. "Get out of here, Madonna can't rap."

"Okay, so you know one Madonna song."

"Now I know two, and I dedicate that song to you."

"American Life?" She raised an eyebrow.

"Beautiful Stranger," I replied smoothly, watching as she slightly lowered her head to blush.

"Thank you, but I should be dedicating

that song to you ... Oh, this is my stop," she announced, looking out of the window at the darkened street while yanking the overhead wire to signal her stop.

She got up to stand next to the last set of doors, holding on to the railing.

"Hey," I said, rising to stand with her. "Maybe I can get your number and we can continue this conversation later." The bus stopped and the doors opened on 118th and Hawthorne. "What's up?" I asked, hands overturned as she began to step off.

"See you later, Kaeshon," she smiled, exiting the bus.

The doors closed, separating our worlds, as I stood there in a daze watching her sashay down the street.

"I can't believe you just had a conversation about Madonna," Will said as I returned to my seat. "And you still didn't get the number." he continued, nodding his head as if in disgust. "I could have won twenty dollars my damnself."

Ignoring Will, I stared blankly for a moment recounting the last words Ronni spoke to me.

"Better luck next time, young man." The old woman seated next to me said as she got up, using my shoulder as a brace before walking towards the doors for her exit.

"Will, she called me Kaeshon," I said, looking in his direction.

"So."

"Dawg, I told her my name was Kay, I never said Kaeshon."

Thinking for a moment, Will replied, "You right. She do look kinda familiar now that I think about it. Maybe we went to school with her or somethin'."

"Yeah, maybe."

Chapter 3

Hawthorne boulevard turns into La Brea once you cross Century into Inglewood. We got off the bus at La Brea and Florence heading north on La Brea, making a right on a very ran down Beach St. Our destination was the corner of Hazel and Market St. Where Will shared an apartment with his uncle, and where I stayed as well part time. We made it to Beach and Market when a silver Cutlass rode by, passing us at first, before zooming back quickly in reverse.

"Who's that?" Will asked with his hand under his shirt as if ready to brandish a pistol for an oncoming shoot out.

"Don't know," I said, putting my hand under my shirt in the same manner.

We both had weapons on us. I carried a five shot gunmetal Walther .380- well, actually it was a six shot including the one I kept in its brain- and Will, I knew possessed a hollow-tip filled 9mm.

We always had to be careful in this neighborhood, although two blocks west of Florence

Akil Victor

we considered our own. Hell, even this far across we considered our hood partly, even though there's an Inglewood 13 Mexican gang that occupies certain blocks it was still in between Piru's and Bloods. The majority of whom we associate, or are familiar with. But one never could tell, there were Crip gangs right up the street on both sides of the neighboring West L.A. and South Central. In addition to all sorts of other out of bounds gang members from who knows where, that crept around these parts either for women, a business transaction, or trouble. Which made me think of the latter as the reversing Cutlass pulled to a stop in front of us, the tinted passenger window slowly rolling down.

"West," Slip said, fingers twisted to form a 'W', as the window slid down far enough to reveal his face.

"You was about to get shot," Will said, walking up to give him a handshake.

I did the same.

"Neither one of y'all was gon buss," Slip replied.

"Who that?" I inquired, peering through the window at the driver whose head was facing toward his side mirror.

"Big Reck," the driver barked as he turned to face me.

"Oh shit, what's up big homie?" I said, walking around to the driver's side.

He rose out of the car casting an eclipse-like shadow over me. He stood well over my six feet, with a build powerful enough to be wrote off as a modern day Paul Bunyan. He was a formidable looking guy with a bald head, flawless goatee and piercing green eyes that stood out because of his plum colored skin.

Everything always seemed perfect with him. From the plain white-T that clung to his mountainous shoulders, to the plain grey sweatpants, down to the plain white Air Force 1's he wore. Everything, just ... perfect.

It's been six years since I'd last seen him. He was recently released from the Feds on appeal for racketeering and some other charges I couldn't recall or dare ask. He was also filthy rich from any kind of illegal activity a vast mind could think of. Which was no secret to anyone affiliated with street life.

"What's up boy? I ain't seen you in years," Big Reck said with a crescent grin, giving me a bear hug. "You getting big. What they been feeding y'all?"

"Dog food," I replied jokingly.

"Will, get over here," Reck continued.

"Kay," Slip called out to me, holding the door open, gesturing for me to get in.

Will got in beside me and we drove back towards La Brea.

"A grand a piece. I need y'all to do something for me," Reck said, turning the wheel to make a left on La Brea to travel south.

"Sounds good. What you need?" I asked eagerly.

"ES, at a strip club in Lennox right now. He owe me some money. I want y'all to go to the strip club and enjoy y'all selves and give this phone a ring when he get up to leave the club," he said, holding up a cell phone for us to see.

"That's it?"

"That's it, and y'all a stack richer."

"Who he with?"

"ES a gangsta, he by himself. Prolly got a girl or two that work in there," Big Reck replied, his green eyes on mine in the rearview mirror. "I got a girl that's going to meet y'all in the parking lot. Her name Gina. Y'all gon hang with her, buy drinks and get dances, but keep ya hands to yaself. Understood?"

"Okay," I replied to his stern rule.

Chapter 4

Ronni entered the door of the one bed-room apartment she shared with her fiancé Ricky and his seven year old daughter Melissa. The apartment was dirty, as usual, which irritated her because of the cramped quarters in which they lived. She felt there should be no problem in keeping the house clean.

"Look at this place," she sighed, placing her backpack on the side wall next to the dinner table.

The walls were filthy yet again, she had just washed them three days ago. The carpet was full of clothes, scraps of paper, and any kind of food crumb you could name. Dirty dishes were piled high on top of one another in the sink like a Tupperware, glass, and porcelain mountain. The dinner table had food crusted on top of it as if it was part of the design.

Melissa's homework was scattered across the dinner table as well as the living room coffee table and floor next to it. Which was the only thing Ronni wasn't upset to see out of place. She scooped up the loose pages, scanning over the first sheet on top: Math; 9 + 7 = 12. Nearly all of the answers were wrong.

She walked over to Melissa, who lay sleeping on the floor three inches away from the older model 19 inch television that sat on the carpet to the right of the room.

"Melissa, honey, wake up baby," she said, gently lifting the child to a sitting position.

"Huh ... Hi Ronni," Melissa said waking, in a whisper, giving Ronni a hug around the neck.

"Hi baby. You wanna help me clean up? And then I'll help you with your homework," Ronni said, smoothing Melissa's back.

"Yes, but we gotta be quiet because daddy's sleeping," she said, still whispering.

"Okay, come on."

They started in the kitchen. Ronni washing dishes and Melissa drying them beside her, standing on a chair.

"Daddy's been drinking again," Melissa spoke in a hushed tone.

Hearing what Melissa said made Ronni cringe at the thought of Ricky in an all too familiar inebriated state. She lost grip of the glass cup she was holding over the sink, causing it to fall back into the shallow water with a loud clank. She hated when Ricky drank. Which he did often now that he was on disability leave from his contracting job. He became verbally and physically abusive to Ronni and Melissa both. Seemingly much worse with each passing day.

"VERONICA," Ricky yelled from the bedroom. "VERONICA, IS THAT YOU? GET IN HERE."

"Ronni," Melissa whined, grabbing her arm as she began to walk in the direction of the bedroom.

There was fear in the child's eyes. Fear for Ronni more than herself. She'd seen time after time how cruel her father could be towards Ronni. Especially after consuming alcohol. She regretted having to tell Ronni the disturbing news that caused her to drop the cup, but she had to give her the warning so they could keep quiet as long as possible while her father slept off his drunken stupor. With him being awake she knew they were in for trouble.

"VERONICA," Ricky yelled more fiercely this time, making his way through the bedroom door. He walked with a slight limp, which was caused by his accident. An accident that left him with a slipped disc in his left hip after tripping over loose wire then slipping into a clumsy slide on a nail that was flat on the floor of a bale house he was building six months ago to the day.

Helping Melissa down from the chair, Ronni started towards Ricky with Melissa unshakably in tow, who chose to squeeze her hand tightly. She would not let go.

"Did you hear me calling you right now?" Ricky asked out loud with venom, stopping to brace himself on the door jamb with a pillow

Akil Victor

gripped by his side.

"I was on my way," Ronni replied timidly.

"Bitch," Ricky growled, throwing the pillow as hard as he could in Veronica's direction.

Ronni ducked out of the way, the pillow barely missing her face as it flew by to hit the window blinds behind her.

Ricky's anger surged, he charged, seizing her in both hands around the collar.

"Stop it, stop it," Melissa wailed with tears in her eyes.

"When I'm calling you, you don't ignore me," he said, forehead to forehead with Ronni, spittle escaping his mouth, the smell of cheap vodka on his breath.

Veronica turned her head to the side to avoid his challenging glare. The last time she decided to keep her light brown eyes on his to have a stare down, he choked her. He choked her using all the strength his hands and forearms could muster in his intoxicated state. Which was far less than what it would've been had he been sober. He choked her near unconsciousness, possibly death. A thought that wasn't unwelcome to her in that moment. It wouldn't have been a problem to fight him off, to knee him in the groin or poke him in the eye. Instead she chose to let him overpower her, hoping he would cross the line, serve the purpose of a vessel through which she would exit a miserable life. Teach him a lesson in his volatile despair, hopefully he would

28

learn that some mistakes were incorrigible in the event of her demise.

It wasn't until Melissa woke up during the commotion and ran to Ronni's aide by jumping on her father's back, clawing at him, pleading with him to release Ronni from his grasp. Begging him to let her go. It was then that she realized that she had more to live for than herself. Even though she wasn't Melissa's biological mother, she loved her as such and knew she couldn't afford to hurt her, to scar her like she had been scarred herself.

"I was on my way," Ronni said more clearly this time.

"Stop it, let her go," Melissa cried, hitting her father's leg.

"This is how you're going to act in front of your daughter?" Ronni asked, eyes fixed on his, hands on his wrist. She didn't expect an answer in return.

He let go. Took a step back to look at them both. Still enraged, he picked up a dirty wineglass from the counter and hurled it at the stained refrigerator, shattering glass all over the kitchen floor. Ronni and Melissa both flinched at the clamor made from his pitch. Stalking back to the bedroom, Ricky slammed the door hard enough to wake the entire building.

"Be careful around the glass," Ronni said as she began to sweep up the shards while Melissa held the dustpan. A routine that wasn't foreign to them.

Chapter 5

It was an attractive L.A. night, I thought to myself as we rode down La Brea on our way to the StripJoint. I took in the sights of the various businesses passed, gas stations, private clubs, car dealerships, fast food restaurants. Each paying contribution to the night's prismatic illumination.

We were riding in Big Reck's dark green H2 Hummer, with Slip following close behind in the Cutlass we were previously in. We had stopped for a moment to change our outfits. With the exception of Reck who was now dapper in a black Sean John suit with a matching black button-down and shoes, me and Will had on nothing spectacular. Just regular block wear with a couple of pieces of jewelry to enhance our plainness. Slip chose to keep on the same beige Tims, beige Dickies and white T-shirt. He looked like a clean construction worker minus the hard hat. But it didn't matter since we had a job to do.

"So, how much money does ES owe you? If you don't mind me asking, big homie." Will spoke up, breaking the silence we rode in.

"More than you can count. And I do mind you asking. What, you work for him or somethin'?" Reck asked, still focused on the road.

"Nah, he got his own crew."

"And they usually be with him," I added from the passenger seat.

"See that's the problem, not sharing the love. He must not be paying them enough. When a person is not paying enough to his fam, his own crew, then he putting his neck on the line. Because not only are the outsiders going to want what he got, but the people around him too," Reck said matter-of-factly.

This struck me as odd, because I've admired ES, studied him from afar and have dealt with him first hand on a few occasions.

When I was thirteen, I had my first encounter with him. He was on my block sitting in a blue five series BMW listening to some rap artist I've never heard of before, while waiting on a neighbor.

I walked by his car and peered in, as a nosey kid would, to ask what he was bumping. He let me know who, and his business in the recording industry. I wound up rapping for him, an unimpressive flow at the time. But, he told me to keep at it, he'd see what he could do for me in the future and gave me $300 so I could get some better clothes and shoes than what I had on at the time.

A couple of years later, he gave me and Slip $500 to beat the shit out of some kid who refused to stop sitting on his car when he wasn't around. And more recently; a year ago, I asked him for a large loan. While he didn't give me the money directly he arranged for me to receive something else.

"Look, I'm not going to give you two G's with hopes of you paying me back, because if you need it now without trying to work for it, chances are you're going to be needing it for the rest of your life. I'm not going to give you no fish, but instead, a fishing pole and bait. If you grind diligently you will be fruitful and multiply, making way more than what you asked for. Setting yourself up to keep making money, ya heard? Oh, and for future purposes, don't ask me for nothing else. When you become needy people like you less." ES told me that day, words I would never forget.

An hour later, a large Samoan hand delivered a pound of chronic and an ounce of dope to me personally.

I wasn't part of ES's crew but he didn't hesitate to help me out when I needed it most. I was quite sure that his crew was well fed and he didn't owe Big Reck any money. Especially when he had just as much money, if not more. And what reason would he have for not settling a debt, if he had any. Especially knowing the infamy Big Reck had attached to his name. A much

more aggressive guy than that of ES who pre-
ferred finesse over muscle.

Chapter 6

We entered Lennox, a predominately Hispanic sub-city on the southwest side of town. Also where the StripJoint was located. We parked on the right side of the locale, on 106th and Hawthorne. Slip kept driving by. More than likely on the near impossible task of finding another park on this street.

"Damn, who's that?" Will asked, lustfully, looking out of his window at an approaching, extremely attractive, light-skin Black woman in her mid-late twenties.

"That's Gina, my wife! Y'all get out and hold the door open for her so she can get in that seat," Big Reck said to me as I started to step out.

"Thank you," Gina said in a songbird voice as I held the door open for her in the manner of a chauffeur.

"Damn, she got ass too!" Will said as soon as I closed the door.

"Yeah, she a dime piece, but we both know that's off limits," I replied, knowing exactly what Will was thinking.

The small parking lot was filled to capacity with just about any kind of up-to-date car one could name. I scanned all of the vehicles in view, looking for the most expensive one. The one I knew ES would be driving.

"There," I said, lightly elbowing Will, pointing in the direction of a candy painted, burgundy, Escalade with limo tint, 26 inch rims, and a license plate that read, 'EDABOSS'.

"There what?"

"There go ES whip." I spoke, approaching the SUV with Will for a closer inspection.

"This how I'm trying to roll right here," Will said enthusiastically, pointing to the Cadillac's rims.

"What y'all doing?" Gina asked, walking in our direction.

I peered around her noticing that Big Reck had driven away.

"Just checking out this truck. What you think about me picking you up in something like this?" Will asked with a grin.

Looking him up and down before rolling her eyes, "N-E ways, we got something to do," she said.

"Hold on, we waiting for the homie." I stopped.

"What is that your boyfriend? He's gone. Let's go."

"Ay, you work here?" Will asked, still checking her out.

"Do it look like I work here?" She asked, hands on hips, seemingly offended with a sarcastic attitude.

Looking at the softballs she called breast nearly busting out of her tube top, I almost laughed as Will and I both answered, "Yeah," in unison, nodding our heads.

She turned, disgusted, and stormed off towards the entrance. "I hope you two nut-heads didn't touch that car," she yelled back.

The strip club was shaped like a very small industrial building. It looked like one as well except for the flamboyant name advertising its business in neon letters on the side. The entrance was double door, in which only one was open. A large Warren Sapp looking bouncer stood in front patting would be patrons down and granting them entrance upon the satisfaction of his search. Behind him, another bouncer collected the entrance fee and behind him was the curtain leading to the boom-boom room.

"Damn, it's some fine bitches in this joint," Will commented over the thunderous music.

The place was live.

"Hell yeah dawg. I'm about to enjoy myself, pleasure before business," I said, rubbing my hands together, securing us a table not too far from the stage.

The place was dimly lit with black lights. The stage, the same, with a neon glow to it and golden pole in the middle backed by mirrors.

On the stage, a beautiful chocolate sister and gorgeous Latina, both topless, were dancing seductively with one another, rubbing up and down each others private parts. It looked like a soft-core porn movie with better music and finer actresses.

"So, where is this ES dude at?" Will asked as soon as he was seated, scanning the club.

"Back there with all those hoes around him." Gina replied, not looking in the direction in which she spoke.

ES was sitting at a table in the back of the club with the company of three women. All attractive in bikinis or lingerie. Exotic dancer garb. Each laughing at every word that came out of the man's mouth like he was an expensive comic strip in a navy blue designer suit with maroon lining. Not to mention the glow in the dark jewelry that was sparkling like mini disco balls off of his neck and wrist.

"Him ... Him? Man that's Shemar Moore. What he doing here?" Will said to Gina, looking silly attempting to be serious.

"That's not Shemar Moore ... Put your arm down," Gina said, lowering Will's pointing arm.

"He look like Shemar Moore. What ES stand for? Evil Shemar." Will continued foolishly.

"I'm going over there," I declared, getting up from my seat but was stopped short by Gina's hand around my forearm.

"What're you doing? Don't go over there."

"What you mean don't go over there. That's my homeboy."

"Then why are you here?" Gina asked as she stood up, searching my eyes quizzically.

The way she looked at me in that moment revealed the tragedy that would take place as soon as that man got up to leave this place. It would be more than him being shaken up for money owed. There were personal feelings involved. A bruised ego. Which I figured had to do with a woman, more than likely this woman in front of me.

I pulled away from her and made my way to ES's table.

"He said what's the point of having a watch if you can't tell the time on it ... I said it's a watch, and I like to watch everybody expression when they look at it and see nothing but diamonds sparkling in their face." ES said over the music, holding up his wrist to reveal a white and canary diamond flecked watch big enough to be worn on Flavor Flav's neck. Receiving a wave of forced laughs from the company of women he shared the table with.

"Should I put on some shades?" I said, using my hands to shield my eyes as if the timepiece was blinding me.

An enormous smile creased his face as he stood to give me a handshake and hug. "Damn it's good to see you. How you doing man?"

"You already know. Surviving. How you?" I replied.

"Take a look around," ES said, gesturing towards his company. "It only gets better when they're naked in a hotel suite."

"Tell me about it."

"Oh they'll tell you themselves. Grab a seat, scoot in between ... Ladies," E said, snapping his fingers as if to remember their names.

"Havana." Said a bronzed Hispanic woman with tight eyes, long silky hair, and D-cups in a purple satin two-piece bikini, with a Cuban flag tattoo on her left breast.

"Barbie." Said the long legged blonde with enchanting aqua greenish-blue eyes, but too much make-up on her face, that did resemble that of the popular doll.

"Mahogany," Answered a caramel complexion woman with light brown eyes and an amazing body, who was probably the most attractive woman in the place two times over.

"I'm Kay," I said, placing my seat in between Barbie and Mahogany. "So, how are you meretricious ladies doing tonight?"

"Fine," Havana and Barbie replied with smiles in unison.

"Meretricious, a prostitute, showy, a person who's attractive in a vulgar manner." Mahogany recited the word definition.

I was impressed as she sat there snaking

her head and neck in an attitude fashion.

"Meretricious? Did he just call us hookers? I thought he said delicious." Barbie announced, dumbfounded.

"Santa Monica college baby." Said Mahogany, once again rolling her head as she seen the shocked expression on my face.

"That's right girl, gon wit ya bad self," I said, putting out my hand for a low five that she accepted with a gleam of self-pride.

"Ladies, could y'all excuse us for a minute," ES chimed in.

"Bye Kay," Havana said, sliding her hand across my shoulder as she got up with the others heading towards fresh customers in the room.

"For now."

"What's it been, about six months?" ES said, more seriously now.

"No more than seven."

"How ya money look?"

"Not bad, it's growing. I'm a better fisherman now. Tryna catch bass."

"Glad to hear that ..." He paused to study me for a moment, reflectively. "I ain't never seen you in here before."

"I didn't know this was your spot."

"I'm a silent partner. Every once in a while I go through the tapes to see what kind of guys we get in here. Usually a lot of cholos, maybe an Islander or two," he said before sipping from a glass filled with dark liquor. "You want a drink?" He offered, tipping the glass my way.

"Nah, I'm good. Just came to enjoy the view, maybe spend a few."

"Looks like you brought a view with you," he said with a nod in Gina's direction. "I never took you for the type to bring sand to the beach."

"I'm not. I thought she work here," I said, looking from Gina back to ES to see if he would take the bait.

"Nope, I ain't never seen her before," he said, squinting his eyes in Gina and Will's direction, who obviously looked like a couple flirting with one another.

"Yeah, that was a joke, she with my boy," I continued, figuring I would get little to no information out of him.

"You should try stand-up," he said without humor. "You sure you don't want that drink?"

"No thanks."

"Well I don't know about you, but I'm about to get drunk and make sure that uh ... a few of the employees are working right," ES said, rising out of his chair extending his hand to be shook. "Enjoy your night. It's on me."

I looked at the money he placed in my hand during the shake. A small stack of crisp hundred dollar bills. "Damn," I breathed to myself regretfully as I placed the money in my pocket. It would be an insult to give it back.

Chapter 7

"There are certain things you have to do in life in order to get where you wanna be." Big Reck said to Slip, who was in the passenger seat of the Hummer alongside him.

"Right, right." Slip's simple reply, not wanting to challenge the seasoned game being spoken to him.

They were on Prairie and Century. In the rear of the Hollywood Park Casino's parking lot. Its glamorous lights dancing off of the hoods and windshields of the sea of cars before them.

"You want to get from the block with 40s and blunts, to suits and cigars. And that's just an expression. You get what I'm saying?" The large man asked.

"Yeah, I got you," Slip answered. And he did get what he said. In the last week since Reck had been home from the pen, Slip had become a sponge, soaking up every detail Big Reck had placed before him. Watching every movement and habit alike. In his eyes Reck was a pure street legend, he had been through the fire and back, through the fire again and had emerged through the rubble and ash unscathed, powerful and rich. He was the epitome of everything Slip aspired to be.

"Now, I'm going to put you in a position," Big Reck continued, speech slightly slower than normal due to the marijuana smoke that wafted from the ash tray, lingering in the car, "to be somebody. You feel me? I'm going to do you a service by letting you work with me."

"Ay, I appreciate it OG. I really do." Slip said, focused on Reck.

"You can't appreciate something you haven't got yet ... But take care of this business and you will appreciate me."

"A'ight, I won't let you down."

"You bet not," Big Reck concluded, more seriously than Slip would ever know.

Chapter 8

ES, short for Eric Stanan, staggered out of the StripJoint unsure if he could make the drive home but willing to take the risk. "Damn, I drunk too much," he mumbled to himself. "Oh well, Ladera just down the street." He sighed this thought as if the little angel and devil had spoken from his shoulders.

Pulling out his car keys and stopping short of his two week old Escalade to read the license plate, 'EDABOSS', the corners of his mouth began to curl, "Damn right," he smiled to himself.

And he was the boss. He had $90,000 worth of jewelry on, the best clothes money could buy, had just spent $2500 in the bar, still had $5,000 in his pocket, had just been reminded of the meaning of fellatio by two beautifully talented women at the same time with a promise of more to come at his place in 30 minutes. Add all that and his trusty .45 on his hip, then according to the standards of the streets he was most definitely considered a boss.

An older model Oldsmobile pulled up on

the side of the small parking lot. ES noticed it immediately because it reminded him of an '85 Cutlass he had owned some years back. The driver stepped out of the car in all black, from boots to beanie, walking towards ES who was forty feet from the club entrance. Having been from the streets all of his life and a former master at jacking, he could smell a potential robbery from a mile away.

Fingering the gun under his shirt for re-assurance, moving closer to his Cadillac, ES said, "What's up black?"

Without replying, the would be assailant, whose head was lowered to avoid his face being seen, continued walking past Eric towards the StripJoint's entrance, raising his head to reveal the beanie was now a ski mask.

He won't get far, ES thought, sensing the threat was not directed at him, continued to open his car door. Averting his eyes to this task would be the last mistake he made in life.

'Wham.' Out of nowhere he was pistol whipped. Mixed with being drunk, the blow was hard enough to knock him off of his feet.

The assailant straddled him, pressing the silencer equipped 9mm to the left side of his chest. Focusing in and out of consciousness, Eric settled his eyes on the enhanced barrel of the gun. He knew this was no ordinary robbery, if one at all, but his fear was a pleasure he would give to no man. Through his grogginess he noticed that his waist was lighter, meaning that his pistol had slipped off when he fell. His eyes did a quick peripheral scan for it but turned up nothing. He looked back to his attacker's eyes. The only feature he could see on the masked face, they looked vaguely familiar.

"You wasting time if you're going to rob or kill me," ES spat, telling himself how stupid he was for slipping like this.

His attacker reached up with his free hand to reveal his mouth through the self-made ski mask. Looking up at a neatly trimmed goatee, he now knew who his soon to be killer was.

"MMM," was the last sound he made before the muffled bullet entered his heart.

"I can't believe how bold some people are," Detective Shaw said to himself after receiving the coordinates of the recent murder on his scanner. 106th and Hawthorne Blvd. The StripJoint's parking lot. The place was only two blocks from the Lennox Sheriff Station, on the same street. Which was the reason for his comment.

Standing on the scene, he noted the time at 1:15 a.m. A dark Wednesday morning. The parking lot was filled with uniformed officers, club patrons, and scantly dressed exotic dancers. He made his way to the spot where the crime took place and was greeted by a young deputy whose facial expression said he was on the scene of his first murder.

"Detective Shaw, I'm deputy Rodriguez," the young officer said, extending his hand.

"Okay, brief me," Shaw said.

"The vic is a Black male, with an ID that reads: 6 feet, 185 pounds, 32 years of age, and a Ladera Heights address."

"Hmph," Detective Shaw grunted, "Must've been doing well. Any witnesses?"

"Well, there are no witnesses to the crime, but that woman over there," he said, gesturing toward a woman amongst the onlookers. "Said she knew him and came out to discover his body on the side of his car and called it in."

"Thank you deputy," Shaw said, walking towards the woman in the crowd.

"The hater coming over here. You sure you wanna talk to him?" I lowered my tone and asked Gina as a cop approached.

"Look, you did your job, now I have to do mine. Get away from me so he don't ask y'all no questions with me," Gina said through teeth, without making eye contact with me nor Will.

We moved to a smaller crowd of gawkers that included the women Havana and Barbie, who were initially sitting at the table with ES when I first approached him.

"Excuse me Miss ..."

"Gina," she said, finishing his greeting.

"I'm Detective Shaw. You knew the victim and called in the crime?" He asked, noting her appearance. She was about 5'6 with three-inch heels on, a small waist, shapely hips and natural looking breast that were a cup size too big for her small frame. Her face had light make-up, the eye shadow enhancing her sensual eyes, with her hair pulled into a long whipped-curl ponytail. She would be considered attractive by any mans standards.

"Yes I did." Gina answered him. "His name was E..I mean Eric. I met him before, you know when I was out clubbing. He was a cool guy, real popular with throwing his money around. He usually has a lot of guys with him, but not tonight."

"Anyone out here you notice hangout with him before tonight?" Shaw asked.

"No," Gina nodded.

"Thank you for your time," he said, figuring what she knew would get him nowhere, and took down her information for future references.

After walking back to the victim's body, he squatted down to get a closer look. On the ground, Eric Stanan's lifeless eyes were wide open, focused on the beyond, skyward. His designer suit was ruffled, the top half of the jacket stained with blood. In death he was still magnetic and attention grabbing in his garbs. He still had on his jewelry; two rose gold and canary diamond studs, a matching diamond studded rose gold choker chain, 'E' pinky ring and five time zone, iced-out, watch. His wallet was accounted for, and a wad of cash in his inner jacket pocket, which ruled out the possibility of robbery. This was a hit that had nothing to do with money and would probably go unsolved, Shaw thought to himself before turning away.

Chapter 9

It felt good to have my car back on a sun beaming Friday, even if there was nothing to do. Well nothing interesting that came to mind immediately, but there was always all sorts of activities going on in some part of L.A. on a Friday.

"What we gon get into tonight?" Will asked from the passenger seat, fumbling with his cell phone.

"I was just thinking about that," I admitted. "You wanna hit the Shaw or Broadway, later on?"

"Nah, that shit get old."

"I don't know then. We'll figure something out," I said, cutting back up the radio, tuned into K-day. The DJ, Julio G, was premiering some local artist named Noni Spitz new song.

I was driving west on Rosecrans, coming out of Gardena into Hawthorne, coasting with no particular destination in mind. I figured I'd roll until I reached Inglewood Ave and take that street all the way up until we were back in the city to see what the homies had going on.

The light turned red at Hawthorne Blvd. Even though I was in the turning lane I had no intention of turning, not until the bus rode by. I seen a familiar head of curly hair barely concealing soft features, seated in the rear of the bus. I didn't know for sure if it was her, but had nothing else to do so I decided to make a right after the bus.

I swung into the lane left of the bus and peered in over Will's big head.

"What you doing?" Will asked.

"Ay, that's o'girl from last time. I'm about to go get at her."

"Who?" Will asked, looking in as well. "Oh her," he said, sounding disappointed. "That Mexican girl don't like niggas. You better leave her alone before we have to kill one of her brothers."

"First off, all women like me. Plus, I think she Puerto Rican."

"Puerto Rican. Ha," Will snorted. "This ain't New York, ain't no Puerto Ricans in L.A., that girl Mexican."

"Yeah whatever." I waved off Will's silly remark. "I'm about to ride up a couple of bus stops so I can get on. You just follow behind and pick me up when I get off," I said, speeding ahead.

Right on time, I thought to myself as I entered the nearly empty bus, strolling towards the back.

Ronni's head was lowered, focused intently on a book in her lap. She didn't bother to look up when I took the side seat across from her. We were the only two people in the very back of the bus.

"Excuse me miss, do you have the time?" I asked, knowing this question would gain her attention.

"Three-forty," she answered, turning her wrist over to look at the digital watch she wore, the entire time keeping her head down, peering at the book.

"What you reading?"

"The Souls of Black Folks by W.E.B Dubois," she replied non-chalantly, still focused on the pages.

"What you reading that for?" I asked, sounding a little more brusque than I intended, but garnered her attention.

"Why you say it like that?" She asked just as brusque.

"I didn't mean it like that. I just meant ..." I spoke, trying to gather my thoughts. "What interest would you have in a black book?"

"You sound ignorant."

Silence. Considering what she said.

Sighing, Ronni said, "It look interesting, so I wanted to see what was inside of it. Sort of like your interest in me."

I must have looked baffled.

"You still trying to win that bet?" She

asked with a smirk.

"Bet ... what you talkin' bout?" I asked, clearly confused.

"Bet, what you talkin' bout," was Ronni's weak attempt at mocking me. "You know what I'm talking about. $20."

"Oh, you talkin' bout that shit with Will. I been won that."

"I know, you dog. Where's my cut?" She said, holding her hand out.

"Right here." I fished in my pocket, with no intention of pulling any bills out, "Bam," I said, giving her an empty hand slap.

"Get off my bus," she demanded, pointing toward the exit.

"I didn't know this was your bus. You need to let me borrow this," I remarked, looking around the interior appraisingly.

"Why're you following me?"

"Following you? Girl I'm riding the bus like everybody else."

"Then why is your friend following on the side?"

I looked out of the large side-window behind me, lo and behold, Will was in the next lane to the left, with one hand on the wheel, the other out the window gesturing to an occupant in a newer model, beige, Camry.

"That's your car, right?" She went on.

"What makes you think that?" I asked, pulling my gaze from Will.

"From the accident."

"The accident," I said, thoughtfully, "With the little boy ... you were there?"

She nodded, "Yeah, and at the hospital as well. I thought that was big of you to get out of the car and help that kid instead of just driving off."

"It was the right thing to do. So that's how you knew my name."

She nodded, "Kaeshon Anthony."

"I was wondering why you looked familiar to me. So what's your real name?"

"Veronica ... Tomez," she answered cautiously, as if it was secret information she didn't want to reveal.

"Thank you for being there for me at the hospital. I needed that."

"It was the right thing to do."

"Can I take you out one day?" I asked.

"Wow, you don't waste time."

I shrugged, flashing what I knew was a charming smile.

"No," she shot without hesitation.

"No ... Damn, just break my heart. I didn't say today, I said one day."

"I'm almost married," she said with a weak smile, lifting her hand to reveal a gold band with a small diamond protruding out of its center.

"Almost doesn't count."

Studying me before she answered, "you're

not going to win this bet," she said while pulling the overhead wire to signal her stop.

"This ain't a bet. I'm for real."

Like before, she got up to stand by the rear exit doors with me on her trail.

"At least let me give you my number," I said, handing her an already prepared piece of paper the size of a chewing gum wrapper.

"You already had it written down?" She asked, looking at me skeptically.

"Yeah, make sure you keep it. You never know when it might come in handy."

"What do you want from me?"

"Your company," I said, after which she rolled her eyes. "I'm not that bad a guy, you said it yourself."

The bus pulled to a stop, its doors sliding open.

"Every dog has his day," she retorted as she exited the bus. Leaving me standing there with the doors sealing off our worlds once again.

"What happened?" Will asked as I re-entered the car.

"I'm workin' on it."

"You wastin' ya time. Anyways, I got a party for us to go to tonight."

"What kind of party? It better not be a house party. And why the hell do you have on all the TVs in my car?" I asked, turning off the screens.

"Oh you know, I had to get my floss on a lil bit," Will said, popping his collar. "And it is a house party. But it's cool, it's a white people house party."

I thought about the last house party we went to; which of course was shot up. It was like a thumb rule with house parties in the hood nowadays; not having fun, shoot the place up. Even with a white house party it would be the same, because if we knew about the party I'm quite sure that people from other hoods knew about the party as well.

Now that I thought about it. "What the hell would I want to go to a white people house party for?" I asked seriously.

"What you think? So we can rob the place." Will said as if I should know.

"You mean burglarize."

"Yeah, that too."

"Where you hear about this party at?"

"Slip. I just seen him on the road with some snow-bunny he kicking it with. I guess it's her party she throwing in Lawndale."

"Lawndale ... That ain't no all white city. It's a lot of Blacks and Mexicans out there."

"Yeah, but it's supposed to be an all white party. We don't got nothing else to do anyway."

*   *   *

"We never hang out anymore. I hardly even see you. It's like you're too busy all of a sudden." Jessica said, plopping down on her bed, positioning herself behind Slip.

"We seen each other at school yester-day." Ronni replied to Jessica through her home phone, held to her ear by shoulder, as she stood washing dishes.

"Please, seeing you around campus does not count. All I'm asking you to do is come to my party tonight. As a friend."

"I can't. I have a family. Whose going to look after Melissa?"

"What about her father?"

"He's gone for the day. Thank God," Ronni breathed.

"Well, bring her with you. She can stay in my room and watch movies."

"How would you like to stay in a room and watch movies while everyone around you party like animals?"

"Ohh, how about her aunt's house? She doesn't live too far from me, right? We took her there before, remember?" Jessica suggested with slight enthusiasm.

"Uhh," Ronni sighed.

"Oh come on Ronni, it's my birthday," Jessica pleaded.

"Your birthday is in two days."

"Please, I promise it will be fun, please."

"Alright, you don't have to beg."

"Great. I'll pick you up in an hour," Jess said with finality.

"I see you got ya stuck-up ass girlfriend to

come," Slip commented, focused on the chronic blunt he was rolling in his lap.

"Yeah, she's cool," Jessica said, seated with her legs wrapped around him, tracing the large Old English tattoo with her finger that spelled 'Inglewood' at the top of his back.

Chapter 10

"It sure is a lot of white people out here," I remarked as I parked across the street from where the house party took place.

Outside of the house stood a mingling crowd of people holding plastic cups in an ill-attempt to conceal liquor. The majority of them were Black and Hispanic, male and female alike.

"I know, huh," Will replied to my obvious sarcasm. "They all look like squares anyway."

"Su-whoop," Slip echoed out as Will and I approached the house. Not only gaining our attention but everyone else out front as well.

Anyone familiar with LA gang culture knew that 'Su-whoop' was a bird call of sorts, commonly used by Bloods.

"Su-whoop," we echoed back in unison.

"Su-whoop," The driver of the beige Camry Slip was sitting in; who happened to be a white female, chimed in.

"Who're you?" I asked, leaning down in the passenger side window. Slip raised a hand, "This my girl Jessica," he said instead.

"This the homie Kay, and you already met Will," Slip went on, now addressing Jessica.

"How're you guys doing?" Jessica asked, focused on me as if trying to commit my face to memory.

"We good," I answered. "This your house?"

"Yeah, and my party. Let's go in," She said, exiting the car.

I watched as she switched ahead of us, placing one child size red and white Nike in front of the other. She had on tight white Capri pants that stretched nicely over her heart shaped ass, headed by a likewise, shoe matching, red top that looked small enough to be her little sister's. Her hair was streaked blonde and brown in two long Pocahontas-style ponytails that went several inches past her shoulders.

"This way," she continued, leading us through a wooden side gate where a heavyset man held a small tin deposit box.

"You charging people to get in?" Will asked.

"Yep, it was Slip's idea. Three dollars, but you guys don't have to pay," she said.

"We wasn't going to," I replied.

Beyond the side gate was a modest sized backyard where a variety of people, the majority of whom looked like college students, stood around drinking beer and conversing while a DJ spun records behind a digital turntable station alongside the yard.

"There's beer in the coolers on the side and-"

"Where's your bathroom?" I cut her off to ask.

"This way," she gestured, leading me through a glass door at the rear of the house.

The house, a modern two-story California home, was creatively decorated with pricey looking furniture and light artwork throughout the living room. There were a few more college types standing around the house repeating the same action as those outside.

"HEY, no smoking weed in here asshole. Go outside." Jessica yelled to a guy who looked like a punk rocker, as we passed him in the hall.

"Like that?" I said in regard to her sudden outburst.

"I mean come on, it's my parents house," she replied. "Here's the bathroom." She stopped short of a door in the hallway reaching in to cut on the light.

"Good lookin' out," I said before closing the door.

"Jessica, come on, let's go," Ronni demanded, clearly irritated, walking down the stairs with Melissa in tow.

"Okay, let me-"

"No, now. We were supposed to take Melissa an hour ago, before the party started." Ronni went on, still agitated.

"It's only nine o'clock, we'll ..." Jessica started to say but stopped short noticing the angry look her friend's face projected. "Okay, come on." She relented, starting back toward the front door with Melissa and Ronni already ahead of her.

"Excuse me, lil lady," I said as I stepped out of the bathroom and was almost ran over by the little girl who was clearly in a hurry to get somewhere.

"Sorry," she replied sheepishly.

"Melissa, slowdown, watch where you're going," Ronni said, stooping down to the child who was now facing her.

The girl didn't reply beyond a head nod.

"I'm sorry about-" Ronni began in my direction, before stopping.

My face lit up in surprise to see her standing in front of me.

"You again. What are you doing here?" She asked.

"I'm happy to see you too," I replied.

"Don't flatter yourself," she said, attempting to brush past me, but was stopped by my hand on her mid-section.

"Is this your daughter?" I asked, awaiting her response and noticed the little girl looking up at her as well, as if she was waiting on the answer as well.

"Yes, and we're in a rush," she answered,

aggressively pushing my hand away.

"Okay, I'll see you when you get back," I said as she walked past me.

"I'm not coming back," she replied, still in route to the door.

"Wait, how do you two know each other?" Jessica asked with arms out as if she was demanding an answer.

"This is bus-boy," Veronica said brusquely.

"Ohhh, so this is the cute stalker you were telling me about." Jessica said with a smile in my direction.

"Bus-boy, stalker? Hell naw. You ain't gotta come back," I said, more for theatrics than anything else, and walked off towards the yard.

"Why were you so mean back at the house?" Jessica asked, focused on the road in front of her.

"I'm sorry for seeming a little rude with you earlier. I just wanted to get Melissa out of there," Veronica responded.

"I wasn't talking about that," Jess said, to which Ronni remained silent. "He seems like a nice guy."

"So did what's-his-name when I first met him," Ronni said, referring to Ricky.

"And yet you're still there."

"The second house on the right," Ronni directed, ignoring Jessica's remark as they approached their destination.

They pulled into the driveway of a small yellow, weather worn, house with a well manicured lawn brightly lit by a halogen porch light.

"Veronica," An older Hispanic woman called out as she opened the screen door of the home.

"Aunt Marie," Ronni said with a warm smile as she approached the house with Melissa in hand.

They embraced, with Melissa's small frame hugged around her grandaunt's waist.

"Hello there hija," aunt Marie said, reaching down to hug Melissa separately.

"Hi auntie Marie," The girl responded in turn.

"Are you ready to spend the night with me?" Aunt Marie asked, to which Melissa nodded an enthused 'yes.'

"I'm sorry for bringing her so late," Ronni said sincerely.

"Don't worry about it. You two are welcome here anytime, you hear me?" Aunt Marie asked, searching Ronni's eyes.

Nodding her head, Ronni replied, "Thank you." And they embraced once more.

"Hey, if there is anything you want to talk about," aunt Marie spoke as they hugged, rubbing Ronni's back, "Or if you ever need a place to stay ... To stay," With emphasis, "Then you can come to me anytime," she said, pulling back, hands on Ronni's shoulders to look at her, to read her. "You're so beautiful Veronica, and you deserve to be treated as such."

Ronni flashed a weak smile, "Thank you tia ... Um, I have to go."

"Be careful hija."

"Damn dawg, it's a lot of Rips back here. Who invited them to the party?" I overheard Will ask Slip as I approached where they were standing with drinks in their hands.

"No tellin'. You know how it goes with these parties, anybody shows up," Slip replied carelessly.

"Yeah, well, they looking over here real hard," Will said, clearly irritated.

I looked in the direction of which they spoke, at a group of six men; a couple of whom looked no older than 17, the rest in their early or mid-twenties.

Going off of what Will and Slip were saying, it was definitely easy to tell they were Crips. One in particular whose entire outfit consisted of blue, from the shoes he wore to the Dodgers cap on his head. If that didn't boast his affiliation then the blue rag he wore hanging from his left pocket sure did.

Their clear point of focus was on Slip. The red Phillies cap turned backwards on his head, the tank top revealing toned arms which served as a canvas for various tattoos. More attention grabbing was the red Dickies he wore draping over Air Force 1's.

"I think they on ya flame Dickies." I pointed out the obvious to Slip.

"Yeah, well they can get shut down tonight if they want a problem. The homies on the way," Slip replied.

"Kay, let me get the car keys, I left my hammer in the glove box," Will said, walking off after I handed him the keys.

On the spacious ground that separated us from them were the few people who stood in the wide gap between us, dancing, laughing, smoking, drinking. Just flat out enjoying themselves, oblivious to the unspoken animosity to each side of them. The seeping tension forming in each corner of the yard was thick enough to swim in.

The song changed, 'How We Do,' a tune from The Game and 50 Cent blared from the speakers causing a wave of excitement throughout the entire house and backyard. The few between us who weren't dancing soon joined in. Even the once silent, mean mugging, Crips started bobbing their heads, the two younger ones more than the others. One of them strutted into the small crowd of people through the invisible line that made up the dance floor.

Holding on to his sagging belt buckle, he started to slide, turn, and stomp his feet in sync with the beat while throwing up his right hand to flash a series of gang signs. The crowd backed away slightly to observe him doing the C-walk, watching with clear admiration at the way he was spinning, twisting, and stomping his legs and feet. He was joined by the other young Crip who was the apparent showman of the two, mixing his walk with Krumping, taking off his hat, flipping and twirling it like a Harlem Globetrotter.

"One of um get too close Im'a sleep um." Slip stated, sitting down his drink, fist in hand.

"Don't trip, I got it." Came from the right of us. It was Chico, a pretty-boy gangsta from around our neighborhood, who had four other homies with him.

"What up Blood!" Slip said, greeting everyone else.

I did the same and watched as Chico hopped into the dance session to challenge the two dancers from the other side, with equally skilled movement if not better, which got the onlookers excited by this battle as more started flocking towards the backyard. But all of the clown dancing didn't impress me in particular.

"I'm about to grab a drink," I spoke in Slip's direction.

"A'ight, get me one too."

I made my way to the cooler, more for the females idling around it than for the drinks. Two of them I noticed as the dancers from the Strip-Joint, Mahogany and Barbie. The two of them, and others, were engrossed in a conversation I couldn't quite make out because of the music.

I picked up a bottled beer from the cooler, taking an emphasized slurp and "Aagh," Like it was the most refreshing drink in the world.

"Damn, is it that good?" Mahogany asked as I looked in her direction.

"Hell yeah," I smiled. "How you doing?"

"I'm fine. What your meretricious ass doing here?" Mahogany spoke with a smile in return.

"Oh now I'm the meretricious one?"

"What's up baby?" One of the Crip members said, coming up behind Mahogany, wrapping his arms around her and planting a kiss on her cheek. Evidently marking his territory.

"I'm good. I was just having a conversation with- I didn't catch your name." She said, looking genuinely puzzled on the latter.

"Don't trip," I said, focused on Mahogany. "Y'all enjoy y'allselves." I said to the group of them, turning to walk away. Beer bottle in hand.

"That's Kay," Barbie said to Mahogany. "You don't remember him from the club?" She asked.

"Where you from, Kay?" The thug that was Mahogany's man picked up the conversation.

I turned back to face him, slightly angered by the question because I knew his intentions.

"Where you From?" I asked the same question in return.

"Hey, you owe me a dance," Ronni said, appearing at my side grabbing my hand in what I knew was an attempt to steer me away from the commotion I was in the process of creating.

I looked down at her, understanding, and decided to take her up on the offer.

"Oh, it's like that cuz. You need yo bitch to step in for you?" The said thug continued to say.

In the background, Mahogany was pleading with him to leave it alone.

I spun back around, jerking Ronni, as she remained attached to my hand with a kung fu grip.

"No, come on." she said, trying to drag me back to no avail. The verbal damage was done.

"What was that?" I asked with false calmness.

"You heard me cuz. This Comp-" He said before his sentence was cut short when I swung the bottle with a viciousness that would have made any bar brawler take notice. Connecting with a sickening crack on the side of his face, breaking the bottle upon impact, sending him down on one knee cupping the side of his face.

I lifted the remaining half of the bottle over my head once more with my free hand holding off Ronni who still attempted with relentless effort to defuse the ill situation. Still infuriated, I swung downward with the bottle before hearing, "This Neighborhood Piru," yelled, followed by a *POP POP POP* session of gun shots.

The whole party thundered into instant

pandemonium, it's participants running for their lives, shoving each other through the outside gate and house. While others opted to just hop over the fence leading to neighboring backyards for an escape. I seen Ronni grabbing a mystified Jessica through the house as I made my way through the maze and out the front door where Will was already sitting behind the wheel of my vehicle, signaling for me to hurry up. I jumped in the passenger seat obligingly and we drove off casually passing a fleet of flashing beaker police cars on their way to investigate the shooting.

"Damn dawg, you somethin' else," I nodded in Will's direction.

"Nah you somethin' else, beating somebody over the head with a bottle. Somebody was bound to get shot anyway," he retorted at my remark.

"You hit anybody?" I asked.

"Nope, just shot in the air to scare everybody off."

"Yeah, you did a good job."

My cell phone rang and vibrated simultaneously on my hip. "Yeah," I answered to a number listed as private.

"Where are you at?" A female voice asked with clear irritation in its tone.

"On the west side. Who this?"

"Ronni," The voice revealed itself. "Where are you at? Can we meet? I want to talk to you."

71

Akil Victor

"A'ight, I'm on my way to Rogers Park, but we can-"

"Okay." She cut me off with finality.

Chapter 11

Will made a left on Eucalyptus, pulling into the back of Roger's park. A park on the northwestern side of Inglewood, which sat in the middle of a known gang neighborhood. But that didn't bring down the park's value at all. It was well kept, with a recreation center that orchestrated after school programs where a kid could hone the skills necessary to become the next championship boxer or the next Paul Pierce, whom was also a person who spent a lot of time playing basketball at this park growing up.

There were a few hooked-up cars in the back parking spaces, which did belong to a couple of affiliates we knew. Will parked alongside a green low-rider, cut off the engine, and handed me the keys. "I'm about to go post up," he said, closing the door, heading past a row of cars towards the back where a few knuckleheads were hanging out.

I got out of the car as well with the same plan in mind when my phone vibrated revealing what I was sure was the same private number.

"Yeah?"

"I'm here," Ronni's voice chimed in.

"Where you at?" I asked.

"In the little parking lot, in the front."

"Okay." I hung up, cutting through the park towards the front parking lot which held four cars. One of the cars had its interior lights on, a beige Camry I noticed as Jessica's ride, mainly because of the two female occupants inside. Ronni stepped out of the passenger side and walked to meet me halfway.

She approached with her arms crossed, hugging herself, head lowered watching her heeled step or contemplating the basis of the conversation we would have.

She had on a zebra stripe blouse and hip hugging black skirt that ended just above her calves, with matching black three-inch heels. She looked great. Better than someone just attending a house party. I hadn't paid close enough attention to her earlier with the bullshit I had taken part in. I let myself get completely sidetracked from even attempting to enjoy myself and her company, possibly.

"I meant to tell you how good you looked earlier," I said as we stepped in front of each other.

She looked into my eyes, sighed, then looked off to the side. "Why couldn't you have just danced with me?" She asked, looking back in my direction. "I mean ... Like what is your point of living? To just start trouble?"

I honestly didn't know how to respond. Any kind of justification for my actions would have sounded immature, regardless of excuse. However, her eyes stayed focused on mine awaiting a response. "Do you think that would have stopped the party from getting shot up?" Was all I could think of.

"Look, that was my friend's birthday party. But you and your homies didn't take that into consideration. What if my daughter would have still been in the house?" She looked at me questionably.

"You know what, I'm sorry. I apologize. I didn't even consider that."

"You guys run around with your guns and gang lifestyle like ignorant little kids. You're not in high school anymore, grow up," she said, raising her voice a decibel.

"You're right." I replied evenly.

"You're just a waste of time. Why don't you get a job or go to school, do something to better yourself." She went on.

"You know what, kick back," I said, getting tired of her rebuke. "You don't even know me like that. You don't know what I got going on in my life-"

"And I don't want to." She cut me off. "I just know what I see and what I see I don't want to know."

"I don't want to know you either. Kick rocks." I returned rudeness with rudeness.

"What?" She challenged.

"Get out of my face," I said, tired of the conversation turned dispute.

"Or what?" She asked, taking a step closer to me. "Or what?" She repeated with another step, until we were close enough to feel one another's body heat. "What you gonna do? Hit me like that guy earlier." She continued, tauntingly.

"I would never put my hands on you," I said seriously. Looking past her, I noticed Jessica sitting behind the wheel of her car staring at us intently with her mouth agape.

"Or I have a better idea." Ronni pressed on. "Why don't you do it with your car."

I stared at her disbelievingly, "You know what," I started to say, point my finger at her, but decided the discussion was over. I turned around and headed back to where my car was parked. Stealing a glance back, I noticed her standing in the same spot with her arms crossed watching me walk off. It was hard to tell but it seemed like her features had softened a bit.

BOOM BOOM BOOM BOOM was the sound emitted from my firearm as I held it skyward to release any pinned up frustration still bottled up from this night.

"What the," Will said, running up with about seven other people in company with guns drawn. "Was that you?" He asked.

"Yeah, my bad homie. I was just upset," I replied.

"Man, don't be doing that shit around here for no reason," said an older homie before turning around with the others to walk back towards the spot they were previously occupying.

Chapter 12

Ronni walked into her apartment, which was engulfed in the night's darkness. Her head was crowded with more thoughts now than when she had left earlier in the evening. Apologetic thoughts she intended to share with Kay for her harsh remarks. Particularly those that had made him storm off. She didn't know what had come over her. Why'd she care enough to confront him in the first place; because he was an idiot. Better yet, why even apologize?

She was trying to convince herself that he was just like every other guy she'd met, nothing but trouble. A waste of time that wouldn't make it any further in life than the point in which he stood. However, when she really put it in perspective, she had a difficult time believing herself. For some reason she had a gut feeling that he might be different. Or maybe it was because; like he said, she hardly even knew him.

Ricky sat at the corner of the couch watching her closely. She hadn't noticed him sitting in the darkened room until the light from his cigarette blazed like an evil eye when he took a pull. "Hi," She said, a bit startled, turning the kitchen light on. "How long have you been here?"

He stared at her a beat before asking, "How long have you been gone?"

"Not too long. It's just midnight, maybe four hours," she answered, looking for the tell-tell signs of intoxication, but found none. Which meant nothing. He'd still have violent mood swings with or without alcohol.

"What you get all dressed up for a birthday party for?" He asked, easing toward her.

"Umm," she had no immediate answer. "This isn't really dressed up," she said, looking herself over. "Just clothes to hangout with the girls in. Besides, you're dressed up yourself." She said more for diversion purposes than anything else, looking at him in the black slacks and white Ascot button-up she ironed for him earlier.

He stepped in front of her, his eyes glowing with mischief, and fingered the waistband of her skirt, making her uncomfortable.

"Umm, so how'd the seminar go?" She asked, lightly brushing his hand away while moving toward the sink.

"Just some pyramid scheme bullshit," he said, still advancing.

"So, you decided not to stay at Mario's?" She asked, referring to his initial plans to spend the night at his brothers house in the San Fernando Valley.

"I'm here aren't I. Melissa's gone," Ricky cooed, pressing up behind her as she stood at the base of the kitchen sink adjusting the hot and cold knobs for dishwater.

There were only two dishes in the sink. A cup and a saucer.

She felt his hard-on as he put his hands around her on the opposite sides of the sink pressing himself onto her butt. She lurched forward, hiding her disgust at not wanting to be touched by him in this manner.

"Your aunt Marie said hi," Ronni stammered, trying to slide around him to no avail.

He wrapped his arms around her like that of a python coiling around its prey, squeezing tight enough to make her sides ache. "What's wrong with you?" He asked seriously.

"I can't breathe, my stomach hurts." She exasperated, breathing heavily as he let her go. Cautiously, she moved around him and walked to the bedroom, hoping to use sleep as an escape.

Ricky banged his palms on the edge of the sink in frustration, nodding his head furiously with fire in his eyes as he looked towards the bedroom. Unbuckling his belt, he stormed into the room startling Ronni as he slammed the door thunderously behind himself.

Chapter 13

I woke up the next morning feeling re-newed, having slept off the previous night's altercations. Of course Ronni had crossed my mind. The things she said, her attitude, her whole demeanor last night at the park had sum-marized the other half of her personality. On one hand there was this extremely gorgeous, compassionate, caring woman who would go out of her way to help someone in need regard-less of circumstance or consequence. A person who was one-hundred percent for whatever was right.

On the other hand, there's a pessimistic, relentless, individual who refused to back down after a challenge has been presented. Even at the unnecessary expense of going overboard. Yet, with these revelations in mind, it didn't change her appearance in my eyes. She was still enig-matic, but her character became more refined.

I'd made plans to be at a spring BBQ func-tion that was already in progress, and by the inconvenience of unprepared function holders, I was sent on the task of purchasing more beer and potato chips.

I pulled into the tiny parking lot of a liquor store on Hawthorne and Manhattan Beach Blvd. As I walked into the store my phone rang, the caller ID flashing a number listed as 'private', the pet-peeve of all phone calls, "Yeah?" I answered anyway.

"Why do you answer your phone like that? It's rude." Ronni's words filled my ears.

It felt good to hear her voice, especially since I thought last night might've been the last time that I'd ever get the chance to do so.

"It's a habit. What can I do for you?" I asked, exiting the store, putting the case of beer in the trunk.

"You can turn around." She hung up, approaching the small parking lot twenty yards behind.

I obeyed, gauging her as we stood silently before each other, "We cool?" I asked after a moment.

"Yeah," Was her simple reply.

"You don't want to beat me up no more, do you?" I joked, which gave me the benefit of seeing her smile.

"No. Look, I'm sorry about my attitude last night, and a few of the things I said."

"It's all good. Don't worry about it. Where you coming from?"

"School. I finished up early today. Figured I'd go home and clean up."

"School?" I questioned.

"Yeah, El Camino," she answered, referring to the community college."

"Oh, okay. I always wondered why you carried around a backpack," I said. "Can I give you a ride?"

"No, thank you, but you can walk with me to the bus stop right here on the corner," she said, turning to walk in that direction.

I walked alongside her without a clue as to how to proceed with any conversation. She, being silent as well, I assume had the same sentiments.

"I heard gunshots last night as we were driving off. It's crazy over there," Ronni announced as an icebreaker.

"Yeah, it is sometime," I replied, not bothering to tell her that it was me who did the shooting.

"So that's where you're from, huh?"

"For the most part. Why? You heard of that area?"

"Yeah, my friend Jessica dates one of your homies, um, I think his name is Slip. She's all crazy about him, she thinks she's a gangsta girl now." Ronni went on to say.

"Ha, yeah, I tripped out on her last night when we first went to the party. The way she carried herself, I thought she was from the hood."

Akil Victor

"Yeah, she's a good actress," Ronni said, taking a seat on the bus stop bench. "So, what do you have planned for today?" She asked.

"Just a barbecue gathering at the park down the street. Besides that, nothing else," I said indifferently.

"What do you do for a living?" She prodded.

"Music. I'm a recording artist."

"That's original," she smirked, "You already got your rap name and bling-bling picked out, huh?"

"Yeah, it's K.A., and the album is called Hustle Mentality. I figured I'd get a big ol' iced-out money medallion and thick rope chain and a kangol hat." I answered, going along with her joke with false excitement.

She doubled over with laughter, "Yeah, don't for get the Adidas.

"You getting a kick out of this, aren't you?"

"Come on, everybody and their father is trying to be a rapper. What happens if you put all of your energy into it and don't make it? Realistically speaking, everyone that picks up a microphone doesn't have a guarantee to be the next big thing. Only a small percentage. There's got to be a fall back career. Besides, I haven't heard any of your songs on the radio, so you still have some work to do."

"You haven't heard my songs on the radio because you don't stay up late enough. Between

2:27 and 2:30 I got the airwaves on lock."

"Seriously, what do you do in the meantime for money? What do you plan on doing if this aspiration doesn't become a beneficial career?"

I sat back against the bench, fingers on my chin, contemplating. I'd never put any substantial amount of thought into the possibility of me not making it in the music industry. Beside financial gain through crime, there was no other option for me.

"Wow," she chimed in with emphasis.

"What?" I asked, averting my focus back to her.

"You really don't know, do you? You've never thought about it, have you?" She asked and answered her own question.

"I know what I will do, and one thing I will do is make it regardless of what anybody else thinks." I responded somewhat defensively.

"I admire your verbal determination, but I'm quite sure that's what they all say," she said in return.

"It don't matter what they all say, I know me. And I ain't trippin' on the meantime because I got bread and I stay with dough."

"Oh I know you have money, but the question is, how do you get it? Do you sell drugs? Because it doesn't seem like you have a job."

"What are you, the police?" I retorted. "Whatever I do, just know that my business is taken care of and I'm hardly ever broke."

"Okay, I get it, you're in pre-rapper mode where you're committing crimes for studio time. Still living the street life, keeping it gang-sta so you can have something authentic to rap about," Ronni said with a nod.

"Ha," I snorted. "You know me so well."

The bus was pulling to a stop in front of the curb.

"I'm starting to think so," she said, standing, waiting for the doors to open.

"And I'm starting to think that you're timing your final remarks with this bus," I pointed out.

She smiled, "Talk to you tomorrow," she said upon entrance.

And my day was made.

Chapter 14

Will sat nervously outside of the Radisson hotel, tapping his foot rapidly before dropping his third consecutive, still lit, cigarette butt on the ground and grounding it out with the toe of his shoe. He was having second thoughts about the confidential meeting he was scheduled to take part in. Knowing the potential consequences of his planned deed could place him or his partner in danger, life threatening.

Thirty-five minutes had passed. He looked down at the digital clock on his cell, counting the time. "If she not here in five more minutes, then I'm out." He promised himself, for the second time.

"Hello." An older white couple greeted as they walked past where he was seated, to the hotel's entrance.

The vast parking lot was filled bumper to bumper, side to side, with a large number of rental cars loaned to out-of-towners, who happened to fly in for business or pleasure by way of the LAX. Which was half a mile west of the

Radisson.

Will glanced at the time again, 9:12 p.m. Seven minutes had passed, two more than the planned five he proposed to stay. He got up and started in the direction of the parking area, prolonging his steps, slow dragging towards the 03 Land Rover he'd bought earlier that evening. Specifically to transport himself, if needed be, to private meetings, similar to the one he planned this particular night. It was too risky to have anyone meddle in his business, even Kay at this point.

He deactivated the alarm on his silver SUV. Looking at his phone once more, he decided to get in and head home. As he continued to stare at the screen, the phone vibrated, the caller ID flashing a private number. A number that didn't need to be revealed because he knew the calls owner. He breathed a sigh of relief before picking up, "Hello."

"Room 120," A female voice said seductively before hanging up.

Chapter 15

'The women and the caviar. You know who we are- cuz we pimpin' all over the world.' Was the Ludacris and Bobby Valentino ringtone on my phone, as it lit-up on the dresser.

"Hello." I answered the phone rubbing my eyes, groggily, still half asleep.

"So, you're not rude this morning," Ronni said, chipper, on the other end.

"Huh?" I replied, barely above a whisper, still trying to shake off my slumber.

"Were you sleeping?"

"Yeah, like you should be."

"Well, in the real world us normal people get up around this time and earlier. Besides, I was calling because I want you to meet me for breakfast," she said in a tone that indicated that she'd been awake for sometime now.

I turned over to look at the alarm-clock stationed on the cheap wood dresser of the motel room I'd spent the night in. "Woman, it's seven o'clock in the morning. I'll talk to you at nine." Expecting no objection in return, I snapped the phone shut and placed it back on the dresser.

"Who was that?" Havana asked from behind me, sounding just as sleepy as I had been a minute ago.

'Pimpin all over the world.' The phone's ringtone blared again. I put up a hand to silence Havana as I answered, "Yup."

"I'm going to excuse the fact that you just hung up on me." Ronni's voice came in once more, evenly. "You asked me if you can take me out before, right?"

"Yeah, but I didn't know it was going to be this early."

"It is. Are you going to meet me for breakfast right now or what?"

Sighing before I answered, "yeah, when and where?"

"There's a Denny's on Inglewood Avenue and Rosecrans. You know it?"

"Yeah."

"Okay, meet me there at eight o'clock."

"How about nine?"

"If you arrive at nine you'll be eating alone," she said and hung up on me in return.

"Damn woman," I mumbled to myself, sitting up to pull on my boxers. Havana placed a hand on my back as I sat on the side of the bed getting dressed. I peered over my shoulder at her. She looked at me sheepishly, resting on one elbow with the sheet wrapped around the contours of her body; the top half barely concealing her breast with her hair draped over to one side.

"Everything alright?" She asked

"Yeah, I gotta go take care of some business."

She looked sad as she responded, "Okay, well am I going to talk to or see you again?"

I'd been in contact with her since ES's death. Outside of myself, who kept my feelings inward, she seemed to be the only one affected by the murder that night. I guess because, like myself, ES had also provided for her at one point.

"Of course," I replied to her question, bending down to give her a peck on the forehead, to which she pulled me down to return on my lips.

The kiss was passionate, lasting only seconds before her tongue trailed down my chest and abs before eventually taking me in her mouth. I laid back, losing myself in the feeling, stiffening beyond recognition as her hand tightly gripped my shaft and her tongue lapped circles around my engorged tip. I'd definitely call her again, I thought, reaching over to pull her silky hair behind her shoulders so I could better see her beautiful face as her mouth worked into a rhythmic frenzy.

I parked my SS on the side of the Denny's at 8:17 a.m. I ended up spending an extra forty minutes with Havana burning off the calories I knew this breakfast would amass.

I stepped out, heading for the entrance, adjusting the bill of my Phillies cap to the back right-side. As I walked in, I spotted Ronni at a booth in the rear shared with a paraplegic, whose wheelchair was seated to the side of the table. In front of them was two orange juice glasses and a water alongside menus.

"Morning," I spoke as I slid in the booth across from her.

"You're late," she replied, looking down at her wrist watch.

"I see I'm not the only one who's rude."

"Where are my manners," she said, feigning a smile. "Good morning, you're late."

"Better than nine o'clock, right?"

"This is Tone, Tone this is Kay," she said, directing her attention to her original company, and then me."

I reached around and shook his hand, "Sup."

"Nice to meet you," he responded.

He was an older brother, either late thirties or early forties, with a goatee and baritone voice. He was well dressed in black slacks and a white dress-shirt like he was a Mormon or on a job interview.

He had been observing me closely from the moment I walked in and I wondered what was his reason for being present.

"Tone is a good friend of mine. I met him

a few years ago at a mission in downtown LA where we were volunteering during the holiday season."

"Oh yeah, back when she was a snot-nosed kid fresh from New York too eager to please." Tone said, to which they both shared a laugh.

"He's also a community activist and youth advisor who works with at risk kids," Ronni went on.

"Yeah, mainly I work with willing individuals to clean up the community and try to deter kids from getting involved with gangs and drugs. You know, provide incentives for them." Tone spoke directly to me.

"Yeah," I said, uninterested, and looked towards Ronni giving her an- I know where this is going look. She met my glare briefly before refocusing on the menu in front of her.

"You all ready to order?" A waitress asked as she appeared in front of our table.

"I'll have a grand slam," Ronni said, ordering first.

"I'll have the same," Tone spoke up.

"Grand slams all around," I finished, willing to play along with their little game.

The waitress nodded and walked off to fill in our orders.

"So, Kay, Ronni's been telling me a lot of interesting things about you," Tone said, with intentions of jumpstarting a conversation.

"Yeah, like what?" I asked skeptically.

"Well, for one, you're a good forgiving person, but might be a little confused."

"About," I inquired.

"Mainly direction. Specifically what you want out of life."

"What gave you that idea?" I asked Ronni with a bit of edge in my tone.

"Oh, I don't know," She said, looking toward the ceiling like she was searching hard for an answer. "Maybe the whole thug rapper thing."

"And what does that have to do with you?" I directed my attention back to Tone.

"I also told him that you were a mischievous trouble maker." Ronni blurted before Tone could answer.

"Ha. What is this, an intervention?" I wisecracked.

"No, this isn't an intervention," Tone said evenly, "Especially if your life doesn't need any intervening."

I didn't respond. The waitress arrived with our meals and placed the dishes in front of us.

"So, you a Phillies fan?" Tone asked after a few forkfuls of food.

"Yup," I said monotonously. This whole breakfast had suddenly grown awkward.

"Can you name three players on that team?" He prodded further.

"Nah," I nodded, continuing my breakfast. Ronni did the same.

"But you're a fan ... You know out here in LA it's kind of hard to be a diehard sports fan, you know the type that like to wear his team insignia plastered all over the place. Yeah, out here when you're a fan like that, especially a Black or Hispanic one, people might take your apparel devotion to your team to mean something else." He paused for a sip of orange juice, all the while his eyes stayed glued to mine.

"Yeah," I chimed in, blandly, knowing the basis of this conversation and continued to eat.

"Yeah." Tone echoed. "Take you for example. You have on a Phillies jacket with a big ass 'P' on the front, a matching Phillies cap, and to top off the ensemble, you got on red and white Air Force 1's. At least you fresh with it. When I was coming up we only wore All-Stars. I bet you holding up those baggy Dickies with a red belt."

I stopped eating, sat down my fork, and studied Tone closely. "Go on," I said, wanting to see where the OG's insight would lead.

"You know, I was a fan like you once. Except everything I wore was Dodger blue. And I couldn't name two players on the team and could care less if they won or lost. But I was part of my own LA team, and we played for blood money and bragging rights. It felt like a family and I thought my teammates loved me to death, that they would kill or die with or for me. I thought they would look out for me if I took a fall for them, like they said they would." He paused.

"One day I took a fall for one of my teammates," Tone continued. "I was 18 and off to the big house to do six years. It didn't matter to me, I was young and wanted the respect. The whole time I was down I didn't get a single letter, dollar, or visit from any of my teammates. Only my family. My moms and my girl. But, then, you want to know what else happened?" He stopped to ask.

"What?" I asked in return, a bit more interested than I thought I would be.

"A couple of my teammates raped my girl," Tone said to which I noticed that Ronni had shifted uneasily in her seat. "And then a couple of my teammates burglarized my mother's house. But when I got out I was still young and stupid. I still ran the streets, still wanted to bang. Then I got shot," he said absently, forming his fingers like that of a shooting gun for effect. "I was out fighting with this guy one day and I won. Beat him up pretty bad. Next thing I knew, he was back with a gun. I seen him coming, lift up his arm. I turned to run but he had the drop on me. Four shots in the back. One cut through my spine. But one flew by me, one flew by me and hit an innocent bystander. A 14 year old kid, cutting his life short." A brief pause. "I sat in the hospital and then rehab for months. At first upset that I'd gotten hit and the kid that got hit died in my place. Then I was upset because I was alive and would never walk, run, or dance with these again." He said, patting his legs.

"I was grateful," he went on. "Grateful to God for letting me live and thought back on all the wrong I'd done and all the wrong done against my family. All the hurt that I and my so-called homies had caused them and how I didn't really have any teammates or homies to begin with. There was only my family, God, and no one else. I thought about what I was representing and seen it for the bullshit it was," he concluded.

"Excuse me fellas, I have to go to the ladies room," Ronni said, sliding out of the booth.

"She likes you a whole lot," Tone said after a brief silence as Ronni walked toward the rest-room.

"I think it's the other way around," I responded, looking at her empty seat.

"It's mutual, because I wouldn't have met you if she didn't. But she can't go from one bad thing to another, Kay."

"I know," I said, rising out of the booth. "Good lookin' out, Tone, you gave me a lot to think about," I said, extending my hand for a final shake.

"I hope so, that's all I ask you to do, just think. Think, because life is too short and precious to be in the wrong lane."

I dug in my pocket and fished out a $100 bill and placed it on the table. "Breakfast is on me."

"Don't bother," Tone said, scooping up the bill, attempting to hand it back. "Keep it. When you're living off of street funds you never know when that money will come in handy."

Ronni emerged from the restroom as I made my way through the exit. "Hey," she called out for me to wait.

I stopped in front of my car.

"Hey, is everything alright, you're leaving?" She asked when she stood in front of me.

"Yeah, I promised my mom that I would look out for my little brother today. You know, take him to get a hair cut and all that."

"Oh, okay. Uh, that wasn't too uncomfortable for you, was it?"

"Extremely," I kidded, "But it was a'ight. Tone seems like a good dude and I still enjoyed your company."

She smiled and pulled me down to her level to plant a kiss on my cheek. "Think about what he said," she said and walked back into the restaurant.

"Damn, that look like Will," I said out loud to myself, looking into the cockpit of a Land Rover idling in the opposite intersection. The driver resembled Will, but there was also a female passenger who I couldn't make out from the distance. "Nah, that ain't him," I thought and shrugged it off. He didn't even have a ride.

Chapter 16

My mother lived in a gated community fifty minutes, give or take, outside of Los Angeles. In a suburb located near Rancho Cucamonga.

"Hey Kay," she said as I walked into the house. My little brother Corey and little sister Rayona followed suit, hugging me to add with their excitement.

"Hey ma, how y'all been?" I asked, taking a seat on the worn wool couch in her living room.

"You know everything's the same, just working all the time," she said, busily working her way around the kitchen looking for ingredients to prepare an early dinner with. "Oh yeah, your brother called yesterday. He asked about you," she said, referring to my younger brother of 17, who was currently serving time in a juve camp.

"Yeah," was my simple reply, uninterested.

"Move cuz!" My little brother Corey said, shoving Rayona away from him, halting her attempt to impede on his online computer time.

"What'd you say?" I asked him a little louder than I intended, gaining my mother's attention who peered at us over the counter.

"Huh," he replied, just knowing he said something that he shouldn't have.

"Huh-nothing, come here boy."

"I'm sorry."

"Corey, c'mere," I demanded more sternly this time.

He obliged, walking towards me with his head down and Rayona in tow like she was in trouble as well. They stuck together that way.

"Don't ever let me hear you say that- look at me- don't ever let me hear you say that again. That's a bad word, you hear me?" I told him firmly.

He nodded his head, then said, "Yea," when he noticed that my focus on him was unwavering.

I didn't bother to ask him where he got the idea to use that word. Hearing it was commonplace. I knew it was a mixture of certain rap songs and my younger brother, who was currently serving time and happened to be a crip sympathizer, who used the word 'cuz' every three words or so when speaking to his associates. Which is another story within itself.

"I know why you don't want him to say that word," my little sister Rayona spoke up timidly.

"Why?" I asked curiously, wondering what her child insight would reveal.

"You gon be mad at me." She stated, rather than ask, softly.

"No I'm not. Tell me."

"No. You promise you won't be mad at me?" She asked this time seriously.

My curiosity peaked. "I promise I won't be mad at you. Tell me."

"Okay, you don't want him to say that word because you a Blood and Bloods don't like that word," she said in her tiny voice, looking down, fidgeting with her fingers nervously.

I was taken aback by her comments. "Where'd you hear that at? Come here," I said, sitting her on the couch next to me. "Who told you that?" I asked, to which her only reply was to shrug her shoulders, still looking downward. "Rayona, look at me." I raised her chin, "No, I'm not. I'm not a gang banger, so I don't want you to go around thinking that because it's not true. I don't want to hear either one of y'all talking about or mentioning gangs, okay."

They both nodded, "Okay," And went back to the computer.

I sat there for a few moments in deep thought. My sister, being only seven years old, had completely stunned me with what she knew, appallingly. Kids are more aware of what goes on in the world than what people give them credit for. Sometimes silently watching from the sidelines, observing friends, relatives, and whatever is on TV. Picking up good and bad habits alike. The fact that she and Corey, who's ten, both knew about their older brothers affiliations was a sign that read things need to change. If not, it would be inevitable for our ways not to rub off on them.

First the breakfast meeting with Ronni and Tone, followed by the knowledge my little brother and sister sprung on me was a full plate of thoughts for me to digest. I also needed some fresh air and decided to cut this reunion short.

"A'ight mom, I'm out. I got some things to take care of," I said, walking over to give her a kiss on the cheek.

"Why? I'm about to cook. I thought you were going to stay with the kids and eat."

"I can't. I got something to take care of in the city."

She let out a sigh and focused back on the potatoes she had been chopping on a cutting board before asking, "Where ... In Inglewood?" Assumedly. "I hate it that you keep hanging out there, Kay. I really do. That's a bad city for young guys."

"Come on, mom, you know I'll be a'ight. It's my hood." I reminded her for assurance purposes. She, like other mothers, had the maternal instinct to warn her children of potential dangers.

"I know, Kaeshon, but can you at least

change?" She asked, focused on my upper articles of clothing.

"What's wrong with what I got on? It don't look good?" I asked a few seconds before realizing what she meant.

"Yeah, but Kaeshon, that's a dangerous color. I just don't want you to get hurt."

"I mean, come on mom, we go through this all the time. I'm grown. It's all good. I'll be a'ight." I said but couldn't help but notice her worried facial expression as she picked up the knife and continued chopping potatoes once more. "Okay, I'll take it off," I said, pulling off the jacket and hat, leaving them on a chair next to the table off to the side of the kitchen and living room before leaving.

Placing the knife on the counter, she walked over to the items that were on the chair and regarded them for a moment before picking them up. In her room was a stationary six-by-four wooden armoire that sat off to the right of the room. The cabinet was double doored and sealed off with a padlock. Whenever anyone would ask her of the cabinet's contents, her simple fib would be that it contained her grandmother's priceless china.

She unlocked the armoire looking for space among its contents. There was a hanger pole stationed through the top half, with a divider down the middle. On one side of the divider hung several shirts, sweaters, and hoodies of every shade of red available. There was a pair, each, of white and burgundy Chuck Taylor's, both with red laces crossing them. There were belts and bandanas that followed those same color patterns crammed in as well.

She hung the jacket and hat up within the sea of red and burgundy items. On the opposite side of the divider sat a blue belt, reeboks, and a blue rag, that belonged to Kay's older brother. Above the items was a framed picture of the two siblings in elementary school, innocent, dressed alike with their arms around each other wearing enormous smiles.

She had been collecting incriminating clothing items from Kay for six years now. Although, she had assumptions about his association two years before she took the first article of clothing. Before him it was his older brother Keith, who shared the picture with him.

I rode back in silence from my mother's house. All the windows up, no radio on. Just the sound of the air conditioner's low hum. Days like this were made strictly for reflection, and reflect is what I did. I became consciously aware of my misguided deeds up until this point. Each playing out in my mind with dazzling effect.

I was far from confused. I just have to cover up what I do better, which I knew was naive to think, but the things that Rayona said were ... baffling to the point where it stung a bit. I mean she's a kid, a child, my favorite sibling, precious in my eyes, innocent. I didn't want her to think of me as a villain. Even though, in her eyes my value as her big brother more than likely would never lessen, but what she knew describe a villain none the less. That's why I had to lie to her, to them, Corey and her both.

'Man I miss my dawgs,' The Lil Wayne ringtone chimed in shortening my thoughts, letting me know it was either Will or Slip.

I looked at the caller ID, it was Will. "Wood up?" I answered.

"K.A., where you at homie?" Will asked, sounding distracted by someone in the background. "Watch-out." He told someone in the distance.

"I'm in traffic, on my way back to the city right now; about 20 minutes away," I answered.

"Is that right? Where you coming from? Moms?"

"Yup."

"Damn, why you didn't tell me? I know she cooked. You bring me a plate?" Will inquired before his question was answered by a female voice in his background that playfully yelled, 'Nah he didn't bring you back no plate, punk.'

"Yeah, what she said. Who is that?"

"Aw shit, nobody, don't trip. But anyways B, you ready for tonight?" Will asked, reminding me of the lick we had planned to hit on this particular day. It had slipped my mind completely.

"You already know I'm ready," I replied, instinctively patting my pockets, knowing my spending money was shrinking by the day. "You get at Slip?"

He moaned before answering, "Yeah, he dropped the accessories off at the spot."

"What the hell, what you over there doing? Getting head?"

"Huh? Nah." He stumbled.

"Anyways, look, I'm about to be staying at the spot for a few days so I can get my shit together," I announced.

"Why, what's up?" He inquired with some concern.

"Nothing, I just need to collect my thoughts, you know."

"Okay, well a'ight. I'm about to take care of this business tonight," he said distantly as if the phone was being snatched out of his hands and hung up.

"I wonder what hood rat he with?" I shrugged to myself, looking at the disconnected phone.

"It's about time you got off that damn thing," Gina said, standing in front of Will as he sat on the edge of the king sized bed in the suite they occupied in the Radisson. "You being on the phone while you with me is a no-no." She spoke while unzipping herself and shimmying out of the form fitting designer black dress, letting it slide to the floor.

What she had on underneath the dress made Will stiffen at mere sight. She posed before him in red satin and lace see-thru Victoria Secret boy shorts and matching strapless bra, which left little secret as it hugged the contours of her curvaceous body. She softly bit her bottom lip seductively as she took two steps to; a near salivating, Will, placing one leg over his to straddle him.

Chapter 17

Sleep did not come easy to Ronni that night. In between tossing and turning, when she was able to fall asleep at last, her dreams would be far from pleasant. She had been awake for the past twenty minutes, lying on her back staring lazily at the ceiling, contemplating. Her thoughts, for the moment, swirled around Kay. In a way, she was weighing every detail she knew of him, what she of the pros and what she knew of the cons. Although, the balancing scale rested directly in the middle, he was becoming more attractive to her with each passing thought. Even with his little red hat on backwards, she reflected inaudibly, but she wouldn't tell him that because she didn't want to influence him any further. She agreed with each word that Tone had spoke to him and hoped that it would at least sink in.

Her train of thought was derailed when Ricky stirred about on his side of the bed, briefly ... A moment before continuing his slumber now faced in her direction. He slept curled in a ball like a kitten, without blankets, in nothing but briefs. Veronica cautiously observed him from the corner of her eye, hoping he would not wake up. Although, he had been asleep since four o'clock in the afternoon. It was a possibility that he would wake up at any moment, and judging from the small bulge in his drawers, he would want to wake her up as well.

She glanced back over at his face, his hair was slicked with sweat, as were beads on his brow. His chiseled face and clear olive skin would have been appealing to a large number of women who did not know the troubled person lurking within. In Ronni's opinion, he was a complete monster, and was no longer attractive to her in the least bit.

She felt under the blanket, which was just above her breast, for her engagement ring. She touched it absently before lifting it up to observe it in the moonlight that shone through the blinds streaking the room's darkness. Two years had passed since the day he'd given it to her. A time when she had actually romanticized the idea of getting married. He made her feel special, secure, wanted, and overall he made her feel loved. For that, she loved him back and had gratefully and emotionally accepted when he had unexpectedly proposed in front of his family at a dinner party in the valley. It seemed like such a long time ago. She couldn't envision things being as they were before. It was hard to entertain the thought of them sharing complete happiness again together. The notion itself seemed distant. Far-fetched even.

In the beginning she had thought it was because of complications with his work; him being in between two jobs. Then the verbal abuse came, followed by the physical. And that was before the binge drinking began. She knew that if he'd be like this during the bad times, and there would be a number of ups and downs, then he was not worth being with.

Without being aware of it, she had taken off the ring. She studied it closely in the scarce light. An odd wave of relief washed over her as she looked at her finger without the ring. It was almost as if a spell had been broken. She started to put it back on but stopped short. She had noticeably grown weary again. I'll put it back on in the morning, she thought, wanting to let her finger breathe a while longer, sitting it on the nightstand next to the alarm clock. It was 1:10 a.m.

She immediately began dreaming.

In her dream she saw Kay. He was being chased on foot by men with assault rifles, three of them. None of which she could make out. He ran through a mall, a department store, and hid in between racks of clothing not far from an escalator. His pursuers were close by, running frantically, yelling jibberish and pointing regarding his location.

They ran past his hiding spot, and he

emerged to run through a near by exit, spilling out into the blinding sunlight. He raised his arm to deflect the glare while continuing to run through the parking structure. 'HOOONNK,' A horn blared, quickly, he jumped out of the way to avoid being hit. The car screeched to a halt ten yards in front of him. A black '67 convertible Chevy Impala with its soft-top down. The driver, whose head remained facing forward, signaled for him to get in. He did so, hopping over the side. The driver in turn drove off at breakneck speed racing forward through the parking structure into a street completely void of traffic.

The driver was clad in all black. His hands were in leather gloves, and his face was covered with a ski mask. He turned onto an unfamiliar residential street and parked before producing a large handgun. Upon seeing this, Kay jumped out of the car and started running. His heart began pounding so hard and vividly under his shirt that it seemed as if it was going to burst right out of his chest. His legs were pumping for the life of him but couldn't gain any momentum. The harder he tried to run the slower he went. There was a loud smashing clamor as she witnessed the first shot explode into his back, followed by another, then another, all striking his upper back. The sound of his heart grew louder as he continued to run slower..slower ... slow.

"Uhhh," Ronni gasped as she jerked out of her sleep. "Kay," she called out before quickly covering her mouth, hoping Ricky hadn't heard her. She realized that the heart beating from the dream was hers, as it still thumped violently within her. She was now drenched in sweat, trying to rid it by running a hand against her slicked throat. Her mouth had gone dry. She peered over at Ricky, who was still asleep, and then over to the nightstand at the glowing 2:00 a.m. She had been asleep for fifty minutes.

She sat on the edge of the bed carefully, making minimal movement, not trying to wake Ricky. She reached over the alarm clock for her cell phone. She knew it shouldn't be on her mind, but she had an urge to call him. Even if it was two o'clock in the morning. Carefully, she slipped out of the room and into the bathroom in the hall.

All three of us were silent as I drove cautiously down the street-lit La Brea, making sure I obeyed every known traffic signal. I wasn't planning on giving any graveyard shift working patrolman a reason to creep out of his hiding spot and pull us over for any other reason than being three black males in a suped-up car.

I slowly rolled into the tiny parking area of our spot. Which was a small, seedy, motel a block past Arbor Vitae. I parked in between two other cars. One: a maroon Cadillac Deville that belonged to Slip, and the other was a newer model Land Rover, whose owner I wasn't sure of.

These two cars in addition to mine in front of this cheap, thirty dollars a night, motel would make anyone think that drug dealers were camped out here for some sort of transaction.

We got out of the car collectively and gave the area a quick scan before entering the small, but tidy, motel room. Each of us leaving boot indentations in the thin brown carpet as we crossed to the full sized bed and dumped on it the contents out of the small black duffle bags we'd been carrying. Will doubled back, checking to make sure the door was locked before rejoining us.

"Damn, damn, damn. That's a good job right there," Will said enthusiastically, clasping his hands together.

On the bed sat several cell phones, pieces of gold and platinum, diamond jewelry, a pair of collector's item, gold plated and screw, WW II .45 caliber Ruger pistols, loose cash and other accessories. Amongst it all was three large stacks, $50,000 each, $150,000 in all that was lifted from the floor safe in the Asian dope dealers house we had invaded.

"Yeah, now you can buy you some rims for that square ass truck of yours out there." Slip said to Will.

"Oh, that's yo whip parked out there. When you get that?" I asked.

"The other day. What you think?"

"It's active. No wonder you ain't holla at

me in a minute. You been sneaking around buying cars and shit," I replied.

"Fifty-thousand a piece," Slip cut in, separating the three piles of money. "I thought it was gon be more than that," he said, a hint of disappointment in his tone.

"It's all good. I'm about to go cut up this murda gear and burn it in the toilet," I said, collecting the ski masks and nylon gloves, headed towards the bathroom.

"Ay, ya phone vibrating," Slip said, holding up the pulsating mobile. "Here," he tossed it to me.

"Damn, dawg, watch how you throwing my shit around," I said after I missed the pitch.

"It's time for a new one anyway," Slip retorted.

1 missed call, the caller ID read. I sat the phone down on the bathroom sink and picked up the plunger to rid the toilet of all water before cutting up the items to place in the bowl. I reached up on the counter for the first mask and clumsily knocked the phone down. "Damn," I cursed and picked up the now open flip phone. The screen lit up showing the number of the missed call, (310) 568-. I stopped, not recognizing the number.

"Who is this calling me at 2-" I said to myself out loud, stopping to look at the time, "2:10 in the morning." Probably a booty call, I thought and decided to return the call to see who the mystery number belonged to.

Ronni sat on the toilet of her apartment's bathroom. She was kind of relieved, but slightly disappointed that he did not pick up. However, she only let the phone ring twice before snapping her own phone shut. "He's sleep," she declared, in a whisper to herself. Knowing that even if he hadn't been sleep she still didn't give him a chance to answer.

Her phone vibrated in her hand, startling her. She answered it before the ring would accompany the vibrated silence. "Hello," she whispered.

"Somebody just call Kay?" Was said on the other end. The deep voice filling her ear caused nervous butterflies to enter her stomach.

She lowered the phone and fanned herself. "What's wrong with you?" She asked herself. "Get it together."

"Hello," she heard through the lowered phone.

"Um, yeah," she said, placing the phone back to her ear while silently cursing herself for forgetting to block her number when she called.

"Who is this?" I asked, leaning against the sink.

"Veronica," Was answered in a hush tone.

"Veronica? I don't know no ..." I stopped with realization. "Ronni?" I said questioningly.

"Hi," she replied sheepishly.

I lowered the phone to study it. "Nah, nah." I shook my head before saying, "Ronni," Once more into the phone with disbelief.

"Yeah."

"It's two o'clock in the morning." I said, unable to contain the huge smile that spread across my face.

"I know, I'm sorry. Were you sleep?"

"Nah ... you alright, you need some help or something?" I prodded.

"No. I'm okay," she said, sounding like she enjoyed the concern.

"You want me to pick you up?"

"No, it's okay."

"You sure you don't want me to pick you up? You know it's after two-in-the-morning. You know what I'm saying?" I said, trying further.

"No- wait a minute. What are you implying?" She asked, catching the drift.

"I'm implying me picking you up, caressing your neck and letting whatever else happen fall in place," I said, sensuously.

"I'm not your booty call," she replied, still keeping her voice down.

"I know, I'm yours. I wish you were here right now so I could look at that gorgeous face, stare into those sexy brown eyes, feel those beautiful lips."

"Where is all this coming from?" She butted in.

"It's coming from my lips to your ears," I

continued, "What're you wearing right now?"

"Just a T-shirt," she answered unintentionally, looking down at Ricky's large shirt that was around her drawn up knees like a tint.

"Damn, I wish you were wearing my T-shirt right now." I said before hearing a loud thump in the phone's background.

"I have to go, I have to go. Please don't call me back." Ronni said, hastily ending the call.

I looked at the message that read, 'call ended,' on my Motorola screen. Her man probably came, I thought before placing the phone back on the sink counter.

The locked doorknob jiggled as Ronni got up and flushed the toilet to pretend like she had just used it. She could tell it was Ricky on the other end by how aggressively the door had been jerked at. She looked at the phone in hand and knew it would require an explanation she could not provide. Thinking of nothing else, she put the phone in her panties before opening the door.

Chapter 18

"Melissa, baby, are you finished eating your cereal yet?" Ronni asked from the bathroom, applying a light coat of make-up to her face.

"Yes, I'm finish," Melissa replied from the kitchen table, staring at the cartoons on television as if in a trance.

"Okay. Go put your bowl in the sink. I'm almost ready to go."

A commercial came on. Melissa slid out of the wooden-back chair before carrying it over to the sink. She went back to the table to retrieve her half-eaten, soggy, cheerios, stood on the chair and started washing her bowl.

Ronni stood in front of the bathroom mirror with her head down and hands braced on the sink. "Am I ready for this?" She sighed to herself. But she couldn't have been more ready. She looked up at her tinted reflection through the large sun glasses on her face. After taking another deep breath, she reached down for her shoulder bag, which was stuffed with clothing, hygiene products, and a few personal items that held special value to her.

"Melissa, come on lets-" She stopped short to look at Melissa who stood in the center of the room hypnotized by the television, before noticing the water overflowing from the sink. "You forgot to turn off the water," she said, snapping Melissa back to reality, walking over to shut off the faucet.

"Sorry," the little girl said as she stood in the kitchen next to Ronni as she used the dish towel to wipe water off the counter.

"It's okay. Grab your things," Ronni said, motioning to a Dora the explorer backpack that sat next to the couch.

Her digital watch read 7:30 a.m. Ricky left for a carpentry job with his brother an hour ago. She figured he would be gone until at least mid-evening, but she wanted to make sure she wouldn't be around when he returned. Last night had been the last straw. Regardless of future risk, she was getting her and Melissa out of there.

"Come here. Let me fix you up," she said, kneeling down in front of Melissa to straighten out her clothes.

Melissa looked over her curiously. She knew something was wrong by the suddenness in which Ronni moved. She reached up slowly and tried to remove the glasses from Veronica's face, but her progress was stopped by Ronni gently grabbing her little hands.

"No. Come on," Ronni said, deflecting her before she could take off the shades. Melissa reached around and gave her a strong hug, despite her size.

They made it to aunt Marie's house twenty minutes later by way of bus and foot. Aunt Marie, expecting their arrival, sat on her front porch, rising as they approached.

"Aunt Marie." Melissa broke first. Running to embrace her.

"Hi babies!" She said to them both, exchanging hugs.

"You're welcome to stay here as long as you want. You can live here." Aunt Marie said compassionately to Ronni as they sat on the daisy patterned couch in her living room.

"Thank you, aunt Marie, it will only be temporary," Ronni replied.

"Oh hush. I don't care how long you stay. It's none of my business, but I don't want you to go back there. He's my nephew, but he's no good," aunt Marie said with the faintest hint of a Spanish accent in her diction. "Now, I'm going to make you two a big meal," she announced, off into the kitchen.

"Okay, let me put my things away and then I'll help you." Ronni offered, walking into the guest bedroom.

She took a seat on the edge of the twin sized box spring bed letting thoughts freeze her progress. She was over taken by a wave of uncertainty, preparing herself for the drama this move would bring. She knew with Ricky would come confrontation, and what about Melissa? It was too much to process at this point. She pushed the negative thoughts from her mind. Sorting through her bag she realized that the heart shaped locket that held a picture of her with her mother was not present. After searching through her belongings a second time, it was clear that the pendant was not there. "Damn it," she cursed to herself, a breath away from frustration. It was the most precious thing she owned, the only picture she had of her mother. She had to go back to retrieve it.

"Aunt Marie, I'll be back soon," she said loud enough to be heard, walking out of the front door.

"Where are you going?" The older woman asked aloud in return through the screen door.

"I forgot something," Ronni shouted back, headed towards the bus stop.

A song from Squeak Ru and 211 roared and thundered from the speakers and subwoofers as we rode down the boulevard. The music so loud in Will's Land Rover that it was near deafening. This was evident by the disdainful looks and head nods being shot in our direction from the occupants of vehicles in opposing lanes.

"Man, turn that shit down." I yelled over the music.

"WHAT?" Will shouted back.

I hit the volume. "What the hell you got the music so loud for?"

"What the hell you touching my stereo for?" He said, turning back the volume just as loud.

I turned it back down, "Pull into this novelty shop up here on the right," I said, pointing in the direction of a mini-mall.

"A'ight," he said, turning the music back up, pulling in to park in front of the joke store I gestured to.

"What you tryna get out of here?" He asked as we entered the store.

I purchased a dreadlock wig and sunglasses with a large nose attached to it like Shock G as Humpty Hump.

"What's this for?" Will asked after we re-entered the car, even though monkey see monkey do, he bought two similar wigs for himself and I assume Slip. In case we wanted to use it as a disguise during a robbery.

"You'll see." I looked past him, "Ay, there go the bus, follow it. Speed up so I can see." I said.

"You got it bad," Will said while speeding up to be side by side with the large transportation vehicle.

Akil Victor

"There she go, I knew it was her." I nudged Will with excitement.

He chuckled, "You want to get on?"

"Yup."

Will parked a couple of stops ahead so that I could get on. I entered the bus wearing the wig and sunglasses, sliding by to sit directly next to Ronni, whose head was lowered giving the impression that she was praying. After a minute, I put my arm around her shoulder, to which she recoiled, craning her neck back to study me. Looking at the wig and shades with the large nose she half laughed, nodding her head before declaring, "You're crazy."

"You knew it was me?" I asked, pulling off the disguise.

"No, I thought it was some weird Jamaican." She replied sarcastically.

"Ha. Ha. I see you in diva mode today with ya Jackie O shades on."

"Yeah, diva mode." She replied tonelessly before directing her attention towards the front of the bus as if preoccupied, not bothering to look in my direction any longer.

I reached over and touched her hair expecting a verbal warning regarding my hand ... None came. I wanted to see the side of her face, which was covered by long flowing curls. I gently moved them aside, over her shoulder. To this, she shifted uneasily in her seat, brushing her hair back over her shoulder, silent still.

Something was off, I thought before asking, "What's wrong? Are you alright?"

"I'm okay," she answered with a nod.

I didn't believe her. When I moved her hair back I thought I spied something on her left shoulder and figured she was using her hair as a blanket to cover what her shirt could not.

I reached over and set aside her crop once more. This time she brushed my hand away, saying, "Keep your hands to yourself," Defensively.

I put both of my hands up in front of me, showing her my palms, a gesture of harmlessness. Slowly, I advanced my right hand towards her hair, unable to describe the look on her face in that moment with any other word than concerned. "Kay," she said, pleadingly, while attempting to stop my hand from progressing.

Gently, I took hold of her wrist to stop her from stopping me. I nodded 'no' and continued to slide her hair aside. On her shoulder was the top half of a jaggedly shaped bruise. To get a better look, I moved down the collar of her midnight-blue, form fitting, shirt. The contusion was fresh, couldn't have been any older than a day. I sat back contemplatively before asking, "How'd you get that?"

She provided no answer, just sat silently looking off into the distance at the passing traffic beyond the bus. "Ronni," I said, my voice lowered, scooting closer. "Did he put his hands on you?"

She turned to face me, to look into my eyes, still withholding words because that question did not require an answer. I returned her stare, searchingly. ... And slowly reached for her glasses, but stopped short. I didn't need to take them off. I could see the dark outline under her left eye behind the shaded lens.

In some cases you make up your mind without knowing the full story. She didn't have to say that he hit her, that he put his hands on her several times in the past. That he forced himself on her, over and over, when she wouldn't submit. No, at that moment, she didn't tell me that. She could've told me that she had slipped stepping out of the shower. Or, that she banged herself by accident opening the door. Although neither scenario would have mattered because I had already drawn my conclusion the moment I saw her.

I sat back on the bus bench with her, sharing silence, despite the clamor around us. The tension inside of me was building up, the anger rising volcanically, making its way to the top from the thought of what had been done to her. There was also so much compassion inside of me as well in that moment, to the point of me not being able to express it. I stared down at my hands blankly, just becoming aware of the fact that they were clenched into fist with my fingers pressed so tightly into my palms that the veins on top of my hands were bulging abnormally.

It hurt me to discover that she had been hurt in this fashion. I always figured there was something under the surface, and now that something had emerged. I peered over at her, watching her wipe a single tear at its base before it could escape down her face. Her stop was coming up and I stood with her. My mind made up.

Chapter 19

"Where are you going?" Ronni asked, suddenly walking ahead before turning into my path so that she could stand in front of me.

"Come on, let's go." I demanded, providing no explanation as I walked around her.

She sidestepped and hopped back in front of my path. "Let's go where? Where are you going?"

"You know where I'm going." I said, strolling around her once more.

"Kay, what's up?" Will asked, driving beside us.

I didn't answer.

"Will, get your friend." Ronni raised her voice, pointing at my trailing off back.

"Kay," Will called again to no answer.

"You don't know where I live," Ronni yelled.

"Yes I do." I countered, which was a lie, figuring she would lead the way.

She strode behind me. "How? What'd you do, follow me home before?" She asked.

"Yup." I lied again.

"You followed me home?" She reiterated, not receiving an answer. "Well it doesn't matter, he's not there."

"Good, then you don't have a problem with me walking you home." I stated, continuing my trek, keeping pace with her now.

"Yes I do. Look I'm not going to stay there, I'm just going to grab something I forgot."

"Okay, let's go get it and then I'll give you a ride back." I said quickly.

"No." She stopped and grabbed my arm. "If you follow me, I'll never speak to you again." She said; I knew, trying to read the blank expression on my face. I flexed the muscles in my arm she had hold of, jerking her forward, breaking her grip.

"Okay, come on." I said, walking forward.

"No. If you go to my house … I'll call the police and tell them you're stalking me," she announced with a look that said she regretted those words as soon as they escaped her mouth.

"You'll what?" I asked incredulously. "Did you call the police on his ass when he put his hands on you? Huh, did you Ronni?" I said with disbelief, raising my voice.

With an odd look of confusion and hurt, she brushed past me, taking three steps before stopping in her tracks abruptly.

Ricky and his brother stood in front of a light blue apartment building engrossed in conversation.

Ronni spun heel, standing directly in front of me. Staring at her, I could easily tell that something was wrong by the way she paused. I looked beyond her to the opposite side of the street where two Hispanic men in their late twenties or early thirties stood in debate.

"Kay," Ronni said, shaken, as I flew past her powerfully, crossing the street diagonally towards where the men were standing.

"No. No. Please, no." She continued, lowering her voice, trying to divert me.

Didn't matter. I wasn't having it. I was too strong, moving her out of the way easily with every attempt.

Ricky turned around, startled at first to see Veronica tugging on another man's shirt, headed in his direction. Then he became angry at the sight of Veronica tugging on another man's shirt who headed towards him.

"What the-. What's up fool?" He challenged, walking to the edge of the sidewalk.

"You." I answered, breaking free of Ronni at the curb, throwing a train wreck right-cross as hard as I could at the man's chin. Landing square, dropping him like a large sack before jumping on top of him to pound on his face like a meat cleaver on ground beef.

"Get back, before I put a hole in yo ass." Will yelled from the driver seat of the Land

Rover with his arm sticking out of the window gripping a black .44 Desert Eagle. Which was trained on Ricky's brother. Halting his movement. Forcing him to look between the triangle orifice of the firearm and his brother being beaten without mercy.

"Hey. Hey. STOP. STOP IT. GET OFF OF HIM," Ronni yelled, returning to tug at my shirt. "STOP IT, THAT'S ENOUGH."

"Kay, come on dawg. Somebody gon call the squad." Will added, referring to the police, after noticing the gathering crowd.

Hearing Will's warning, I backed off of Ronni's man, who was sprawled on the ground a swollen, bloody, mess breathing raggedly. I booted him one last time, my foot meeting an agonizing groan before grabbing hold of Ronni's wrist as she stood there in shock.

"Come on. Get in the car," I said, throwing open the rear door for her, which she readily hurried in.

I relaxed back in the leather passenger seat letting heavy breath escape, unclenching my fist, easing out of fight mode.

"Where are we going?" Will asked after observing me out of the corner of his eye.

I gave him a wave of dismissal, not feeling like being bothered and continued to stare out of the window. I knew that Will would take us to the spot regardless.

Chapter 20

We were idling around the motel room in silence before Will said, "If y'all don't need anything, Kay, I got some business to take care of," From the corner of the room. He looked from me to Ronni, who stood in the opposite corner near the small table.

I peered at Ronni, who remained expressionless, before saying to Will, "Nah, we good. I'll take care of it."

"A'ight then B," he said, exiting the room.

"You don't have to stand over there like a statue, you can sit down." I said while inspecting the bruise forming on my knuckles.

"You don't expect me to stay here do you?" Ronni stated, still standing.

I turned my focus to her. "No, I don't ... You ready to go?" I asked, suddenly feeling weary.

"That your bathroom back there?" She asked instead.

Ronni stood in the cramped bathroom

with her back against the door as thoughts of anger and confusion swirled throughout her mind. She was angry beyond relief at Ricky for the way things had turned out. She was confused, yet upset with Kay for his getting involved. Most of all, she was worried about Melissa. What would happen to Melissa during all of this? As much as she loved her, not being with Ricky, ultimately, meant not being with Melissa. Melissa was not her daughter biologically, so she couldn't just run off with her, no matter how bad she desired to. She loved her and aunt Marie wholeheartedly but her stay with them could only be temporary. They're Ricky's family and she knew he would not stay away and who knows what he'll try to do after today.

And what about Kay? As much as the idea of his positive qualities and personality toward her seemed appeasing, it would not work. From what she knew, guys like Kay never made it past the point in life in which they stood. Not without a proper wake up call. He was too street oriented. It was evident in the way he carried himself and the company he kept. From what she gathered, he refused to let anyone cross him or anyone he cared about ... Anyone he care about. She repeated the thought, without physical consequences.

She decided to call aunt Marie, to fill her in on what had happened.

Twenty minutes later she walked out of

the bathroom.

"I thought you climbed out the bathroom window or somethin'," I said, staring blankly at the television tuned in to Jerry Springer.

"Why would I do that?" She asked, sitting next to me so closely that our sides touched.

I shrugged, "You were gone a long time."

"Is your hand okay?" She asked, lifting it up to examine the odd shaped knuckle in the middle.

"It's been through that a hundred times. It'll bounce back." I said, observing my large hand held by her two smaller ones. "I see you're not wearing your ring anymore."

She placed my hand back on my lap, as if suddenly aware, looking at her left hand to observe her ring finger, which had a pale mark wrapped around it. Evidence of the ring's absence.

"So, this is where you live?" She changed the subject, looking towards the duffle bags and other items placed orderly within the room.

"Nah. This is where I come when I need to clear my head. Actually, the room next door is where I clear my head when I really don't want to be bothered by anyone. Will included. They'll spend days wondering where I'm at, never thinking I'll be somewhere as simple as next door."

"What about your car being outside? Doesn't that give you away?" She asked, resting her head on my shoulder.

"If I don't want to be bothered it won't be outside. There's a commercial parking garage two blocks west of here. I just pay to leave it in there."

"You have it all figured out, don't you?" She said lazily, lifting my arm over her shoulder before wrapping her arms around my waist, nuzzling our bodies closer.

"Almost," I replied, withholding the comment I had in mind. It was too soon.

I laid back on the mattress with Ronni still wrapped around me. I could tell she had grown tired, and maybe after the recent turn of events needed a little comforting. Deciding to help her out, I reached over to take off her glasses. "Don't," she said as I touched them. Clutching them back to her face.

"You don't wanna take um off, put um on the table?"

"No," she said, pulling herself closer still.

I watched as she dozed off, her body peacefully rising up and down with each inhale, exhale. Her frame was still pressed and partially wrapped around mine, her breast against my side, her arm across my chest and her leg over my leg. The day had progressed well into the night. I peered at her as the light from the silent TV illuminated our bodies. I couldn't help but to think again about how beautiful she was through and through and wondered how she ended up with a guy that abused her. No woman should have to go through a man putting his hands on her to prove a point. Even if I had just met her today on the bus, I probably would have done the same thing. But the fact that I knew her and possessed strong feelings for her pushed me even further.

Regardless if it wasn't my business to get involved or not. I made it my business, and maybe that coward would think twice before he put his paws on another woman.

Chapter 21

Big Reck lay motionless on the large circular mattress in his spacious bedroom, focused on giving the impression of him being asleep. Next to the bed was a small glass table which housed a fifth of bourbon circled within several glasses. Thirty minutes prior to his pretending, he consumed four, one cup glasses, back to back in his wife's presence. His plan was to make her believe that he was drunk and passed out. Falling into a liquor induced slumber, which carried the myth that a drunk could sleep through a natural disaster or marching band outside of his door and not stir. That's what he wanted her to think. He even passed on sex with her before then just so he wouldn't deter her from the sneaking around he figured she would do before the night was over.

Gina crept into the bedroom and looked over the large frame of her husband lying on his stomach with his arms sprawled out in different directions like a wildman, apparently sleep.

"Baby," she called. "Baby," loudly, once

more. Looking for any signs of him being awake.

He remained unresponsive. She closed the door softly and entered the adjacent his and hers bathroom and hung the purple cashmere robe she wore on the hook behind the door. She stood in front of the mirror that lined the entire wall behind the dual sink, in black suede, open toe, stilettos, skin tight denim jeans that complimented her hips and ass to perfection. Wrapped around her torso was a black bustier-esqe top made to be zipped in front that lifted and insinuated her bust.

She viewed her reflection. Playing with several poses before looking at the small, diamond encrusted, Cartier watch on her wrist, gauging the time she'd have for her so-thought liberation, before leaving the house.

Big Reck sat up immediately after hearing the front door close and rushed into the living room to steal a look out of the curtains.

"Slip," he said into his phone, glimpsing the tail lights of Gina's Lexus as she sped off, "she rounding the corner right now."

Chapter 22

"Kay," Ronni gasped, waking up suddenly. She reached out for him, but he was not there, felt around for him but he was no longer on the bed. "Kay," she called out a second time, her eyes adjusting to the room's darkness. She had the same nightmare she dreamt involving him the night before last.

She saw light spill out of the bathroom as the door opened.

"Yeah," I answered, exiting the bathroom after hearing Ronni call my name. "I'm right here," I said, noting her slightly disheveled appearance. "You a'ight?"

She sighed heavily and nodded a quick yes. She was warm. I could feel the heat radiate from her body as I sat next to her. Her skin was also slick with perspiration. "You sure you okay?" I asked, rubbing a comforting hand across her back. "You seem a lil hot, you need me to get you somethin'?" I asked, rising up from the bed in case she said yes.

"No. Stay here," she said quickly, pulling me back down by the arm.

"Okay ... what's wrong?"

"Nothing. I just had a bad dream," she said and leaned on me for support.

"It's all good." I brushed her hair out of the way to give her a kiss on the forehead; and then, as if automatic, another.

She looked up at me, about to say something but was hesitant before I met her lips with mine, indulgently, taking in their fullness before parting our mouths once more. I reached for the glasses that were still in place on her face, sensing her reluctance as she began to turn away from me, I said, "Ronni, I don't care about that," and softly turned her chin back toward me, slowly slipping them from her face. She kept her eyes closed the entire time as I observed her. The small bruise under her eye was insignificant. It did nothing to take away from her beauty, I assured her as I kissed her again.

Chapter 23

Slip parked his Deville on the opposite side of the street from the Waterfront Cafe. Camouflaging in the small parking lot between other cars in a spot that provided a perfect view of the cafe/nightclub's entrance. The cafe was given its water front name because it was only 100 yards from the shore. The sand and water could be seen from the cafe's patio and parking lot where Slip was stationed.

Five minutes ago, he watched as Gina entered the locale alone. He had been enlisted by Big Reck to follow an alleged cheating Gina around. This being the first night after Gina was said to have snuck out of the house on three occasions the previous week. He hoped that she wasn't cheating at all, that she just wanted a little time away from Reck. That she was just going out to clear her head, maybe have a drink or two. Alone. He could understand a situation like that. Hell, he could even agree with her. Big Reck seemed like he could be a powerfully annoying individual at times. He was also demanding, bossy, stubborn, and ultimately ... unforgiving.

If she was cheating, she couldn't have made a more fatal mistake. And whoever she was cheating with ... well, more than likely their name will be applied to a death certificate. Even if it was an unsuspecting fool.

He got out of the car and casually strolled to the entrance. He was halted by the bouncer- "Hey man, what's up?" The bouncer said, using his body to block the entrance. He was a tall overly muscular man with a buzz cut and bad tan.

"What you mean what's up? Can I get in?" Slip said, looking over the man's shoulder to see if he could spot Gina before returning his focus back to the bouncer's eyes.

"Not like that you can't," Buzz cut said, giving Slip the 'once over.'

"Like what?" Slip asked, staring at him icily.

"You know, your sneakers. You can't wear them in here." The bouncer returned his glare, but without malice. Although he outweighed him by at least twenty pounds, he could tell the guy was no pushover and probably a gang member. One thing bouncers were taught was not to push around the wrong kind of guys. Gang members were at the top of that list, as they were known to come back and shoot up the place. "That's all, you just gotta change your shoes," he said.

Slip held out a hundred-dollar bill.

"Aww-man, I can't take that. I wish I could, but can't," buzz cut said convincingly.

"I just need to use your restroom," Slip countered, still holding the bill, looking over the bouncer's shoulder a second time.

He spotted Gina on the dance floor. Moving with her back to a partner Slip couldn't make out because of her position as she twirled her ass and hips into him rhythmically with the music. She bent over and twerked her ass like that of a skilled stripper. The guy she was dancing with was doing his best to keep up. Slip squinted his eyes to make out the man's features in the flashing lights.

"I can't," he heard the bouncer say.

"What? Neva mind. Don't trip, keep it." He shoved the bill into the bouncer's palm and jogged back to his car, cell phone in hand.

'Man I miss my dawgs,' My ringtone chimed and phone vibrated in my pocket, waking me out of a brief sleep as I sat in the chair of the motel room over looking a now awake Ronni.

"Slip, wood up?

"Where you at?" Slip asked with haste.

"The spot. Why what's up?"

"I'm coming to pick you up. I got somethin' to show you," He said, hanging up before I could answer.

"What's wrong?" Ronni asked, sitting up.

"Nothing. I gotta take a ride real quick. I'll be right back."

"A ride where? I'll go with you," she said, getting out of bed.

"No. I'm not driving. I'll be right back. I'll bring you something to eat." I opened the door at the same time Slip's Cadillac pulled into the parking lot.

"What's up?" I asked as we drove down the street.

"Reck think his wife cheating on him right. So he get at me like, 'I want you to follow her around.' So I say it's no problem, right. So ol' girl sneak out of the house like clockwork. Looking all good, dressed up and shit. So I follow her to this Waterfront club in Manhattan Beach." Slip paused to round the corner headed towards the beach.

"I get to the door and can't get in because of some dress code bullshit." He continued. "But I don't need to get in though because I can see her on the middle of the dance floor getting her dry hump on." Slip cut his words short to look over at me.

At the mention of Big Reck and his wife, my suspicion had been roused. Gina cheating and Reck sending Slip out seemed like deja vu.

"So what, we about to go put hands on whoever it is? Let him know he can't dance with her no more?" I said, feeling like he was expecting me to say something.

"Yeah. You ready to put hands on the homie?"

"What homie?" I asked, not knowing if that was a question or statement.

He didn't answer as we slowed in front of the Waterfront Cafe, with its patrons staggering out towards the parking lot alongside the building.

Slip nodded his head towards Gina who walked out of the club arm in arm with … Will.

"Damn," escaped my mouth. Although Will was not the last person I expected to see with her, he was the last person I hoped to see with her. "What's this fool doing?" I started to open my door to retrieve him for reprieve but was stopped by Slip reaching for my arm.

"Nah, come on. He drove up here by himself, that's how we'll get at him. I don't want to alert her to the fact that we on to her."

"Don't matter. She's going to find out after tonight."

We sat parked in the opposite parking lot for 10 minutes, watching them act like two high school kids crushing on each other. Hugged up one minute, horse playing the next, energetic gestures in one instant and kissing in the next.

"Damn, Will, what you doing?" I asked myself out loud.

Slip nodded his head. "Man, she tryna get

my boy caught up."

I didn't feel like sitting on an all night stakeout. With no sign of their departure being near, I decided to call Will to break up tonight's infidelity.

"What you doing?" Slip asked as I held the phone to my ear.

"What you think I'm doing? Stopping Will from diggin' himself into a deeper hole."

"The proof in the puddin' homie. That hole already deep," slip said. Speaking words that rung true.

I dialed Will's number three times back to back. Each time, he looked at the caller ID and chose to ignore my call instead of answering or turning off his phone. So I decided to bombard him with calls. If I knew Will, which I did, then if I kept calling he would pick up thinking something was wrong. "Pick up. Pick up. Pick up." I chanted to myself as if my words would have a magic sway over him.

"What you gon say if he answer the phone?" Slip asked.

"I don't know yet. I'll figure it out by that time."

"Who is that blowin' up your phone?" Gina asked will as they stood hugged up against his Land Rover.

"Kay."

"Ugh. What does he want- I know you

ain't going to answer that." Gina broke their embraced comfort, crossing her arms to study him with the phone.

"He might be in trouble," Will replied, looking from her to the phone.

"Ain't he a gangsta? He can handle it."

Will ignored her as he answered, "Kay, what's brackin wit it homie?"

"I know you didn't-" Gina started to say but was silenced by Will holding out his hand.

"What? I'm on my way." He hung up, moving for his car door.

"What happened?" Gina asked with minor concern.

"A shoot out, huh?" Slip said of the false emergency I fed Will.

"It was the first thing that came to mind," I replied.

I told Will that I was holed-up in the motel exchanging shots with a couple of cholos. One being the guy that I got into it with over Ronni. I knew saying this would cause him to drop whatever he was doing with haste. Nothing like being the one to blame for not being there when something bad happened.

Ronni open the motel room door, closing it behind her as she stepped out into the lazy breeze of the late spring night. It was 2:20 in the morning. The sky was blue-black with faint traces of stars visible in its veil. Around her, traffic was almost nonexistent. There was blackness within the interior of closed establishments, but that of a well lit 7-eleven on the opposite corner diagonally from where she stood.

Two cars rested in the parking lot before her, an '88, busted exterior, brown box Caprice. And one space over, Kay's black Impala. She looked it over with the eye of an appraiser, running fingertips along its sleek black paint before reaching its tail and leaning against the trunk.

Her reason for being out there was to wait for Jessica, whom she called to pick her up twenty minutes prior. On the phone, Jessica said that she would be right there, she was leaving the house as they spoke. Ronni knew she was asleep when she first called, although Jess claimed otherwise. Ronni could tell by the feminine baritone voice in which she answered the phone. She estimated the time it would take her to arrive. She; Jessica, lived fifteen minutes away. She drove ten miles above the speed limit. It would take her ten minutes to gather herself before leaving, although she said she was leaving the moment they spoke. So that would be twenty-five minutes, but Ronni decided to add an extra five for good measure. Jessica made it there in thirty-seven.

"So, you practically spent the night with him." Jessica remarked after Ronni filled her in on the entire day's events, as they cruised down the street.

"After everything I tell you, that's the first thing you say?" Ronni said.

"Well, I'm sorry. But everything you told me up until the point where you two made out was ... tragic. And I don't respond well to bad things happening to my friends. I always thought there was something going on, but I wasn't sure. Maybe I should have asked more. I'm sorry," Jessica said sincerely.

"Don't be. It's alright."

"I'm just glad that Kay was there for you today. Because if he wasn't, who knows what would have happened."

"Yeah, who knows." Ronni said, almost to herself.

"So, you practically spent the night with him, huh?" Jessica reiterated, jokingly, this time as a question.

"No, I didn't sleep with him. If that's what you're asking."

"Why not? After all the things you two have been through, it seemed like the perfect moment."

"After all the crap I've been through, I don't want to be with anyone for a long time."

"You sure you don't want to go back to the hotel and wait for the guys?" Jessica joked.

"No, you pain-in-the-ass. Just take me to your house so I can get some sleep."

Jessica laughed. "Your wish is my command."

"Damn, he drivin' fast as hell. Speed up," I said as we zoomed down the street after Will.

"I got this," Slip said, wheeling the Deville around a Honda that was driving the speed limit.

"Pull up. I'm about to throw this at his car to get his attention." I said, holding a large paper cup half full of coke from McDonald's.

Slip sped up, almost bumper to bumper with the Land Rover. I launched the soda cup at the rear window.

"What the fuck!" Will said as something splashed on the back of his car, partially blurring the rear window. He stuck his head out of his side window to look back at who might've thrown something out of the trailing car before pulling over to see what it was.

Will marched back from his whip to meet us alongside the quiet road.

"What they hell y'all throwing shit at my car for?" He asked as he stepped in front of us.

"A better question is why you sneaking around with Big Reck's wife?" Slip countered.

"What?" Will looked at us both. "I don't know what you talkin' 'bout'" he said without hitch. "Anyways, Kay, what's up with that situation on the phone?"

"It looks like the real situation right here,"

I said, studying him closely.

He returned my glare. "What's this about?" Arms spread.

"You know what this about. Answer the question. What you doin' with Reck's wife?" Slip said, jabbing a finger in the air towards Will.

"None of yo business. Get ya hand out of my face," Will demanded testily, slapping it out of the way, to which Slip grabbed him by the collar. Will responded likewise with equal aggression in return.

"What the fuck wrong with you?" Slip asked while forcing his weight forward, shoving Will into the SUV's hatch door.

"What's wrong with you?" Will said defensively, countering, spinning Slip quickly, slamming his back into the same spot his own back left.

What ensued next was a wrestling match between the two, grappling each other, going at it like two walruses for kingship of the clan.

"You better take ya hands off me," Will threatened through his teeth.

"Or what?" Slip retorted.

"Ay," I said, noticing it was growing a bit too serious, stepping in to break it up. "Both of y'all need to knock this shit off." I held them apart. "Will, you wrong homie. Messing with her gon get you chipped," I warned.

"What?" He said, breaking free. "Man, fuck both of y'all," He declared before hopping into his car.

"You know he the homie. We gotta cover this up for him. I know you mad but what you gon tell Reck when he ask you about Gina's night?" I inquired as we rode back to the spot.

He exhaled heavily before answering, "I don't know. I mean damn." He tightened his grip on the steering wheel. "I'll think of sumthin, she was in the club by herself as far as I'm concerned."

"Yeah, hopefully that'll fly ... Ay, pull into this Jack in the Box drive-thru," I said as we reached Hawthorne Blvd and Marine.

"Hey, I got you some-" I said, cutting my sentence short. The room was draped in darkness when I entered. The TV screen, pitch black. No light shone under the bathroom door. No silhouette on the bed. I placed the food on the table stationed to the right of the door and took a seat in one of its thrifty wood and cushion chairs.

I checked my phone to make sure that I didn't miss any calls or messages. I hadn't. No one called in the time I was gone. I knew she wasn't wandering around out there and the bus didn't run this late. Someone picked her up.

She could have at least had the decency to call me and let me know she was leaving, I thought while dialing her number to tell her the same. It went straight to voicemail, meaning she had turned off her phone. I hung up, tired again, receiving the same result. This time I decided to leave a message.

Chapter 24

Ronni sat up in the guest bed, in the lone room that sat in the corner opposite Jessica's room, upstairs. The sun shone brilliantly through the crack in the window's oatmeal tone curtains. The watch on her wrist displayed 7:20 a.m. exactly. She felt rested, relieved even, waking up in a bed that didn't house Ricky's smell or indentation of his body. The feeling lasted a minute as she exited the room to enter the guest bathroom. She heard the cackling of grease and smelled bacon before closing off the smell with the door.

The guest bathroom was hospitably filled with spare toothbrushes, face towels and other cosmetics that Ronni dabbled in freely before marching downstairs into the kitchen. She rounded the corner expecting to see Jessica and her mother Cynthia (the home's only other permanent occupant) enjoying breakfast. Instead, the first person she viewed was a tank top and boxer clad Slip, sitting at the dinning table reading the times.

"Good morning." She spoke to him, entering the kitchen to find Jessica handling a spatula over a skillet.

"Morning," Slip replied in his deep, near raspy, voice as he raised an eyebrow in her direction before focusing back on the newspaper.

"Good morning," Jessica said chipperly. "Have a seat. I'm almost finished making us breakfast," she said, working with the experience of a line cook. Standing over the stove with the same underwear on as Slip, tank top and boxers that were rolled over the top to keep them from falling. On her head was a burgundy bandana tied down like a pirate over her loosely hanging locks.

Ronni took a seat across from Slip, who sat the paper down as Jessica placed a saucer portioned with bacon, scrambled eggs and toast in front of them.

"Hey babe, you remember my friend Ronni, right?"

"Yeah, somewhat," Slip said, looking at Ronni lazily again.

Ronni avoided eye contact with him, focusing on the plate of food instead. Something about him just didn't sit well with her. Maybe her nerves were on edge, but he gave her a bad vibe.

"She's Kay's girlfriend," Jessica continued.

"Jess," Ronni started.

"Is that right?" Slip asked with a smile that

seemed warm beside himself.

Seeing this made Ronni ease up a bit. He had a nice smile and was handsome in a rugged street thug sort of way. Initially it had been the tattoos and his seemingly self-assured gangsta demeanor that had made her uncomfortable. "No. Jess is just talking out of the side of her mouth," she said.

Ignoring her, Slip tilted his head and focused on her face, "He didn't put that little mark around your eye, did he?"

"No, no, he didn't." Ronni stammered, uncomfortable once more.

"No, on the contrary," Jessica cut in. "He's the reason she doesn't have to worry about that happening anymore-"

"Jessica." Ronni raised her voice this time.

"I'm sorry," Jessica blurted, unconvincingly.

Silence.

"Hey, you gon be all good," Slip assured Ronni. "Kay's a decent homie. You in good hands if you with him."

"I know. Um, will you guys excuse me?" Ronni said, making her way back upstairs to the guest room.

"Hey babe, I'm going to go put myself together. She's going to be ready to leave in a minute," Jessica said, excusing herself from the table as well.

Chapter 25

Last night, I sat up in deep thought until about 5 a.m., thinking about all the BS that had taken place before falling asleep. I was awakened by a loud rap on the door after getting a mere three hours of rest. I answered the door to Will, who stepped in looking like he stayed up for the majority of the night as well.

"Unc asked about you this morning," Will said, settling in one of the chairs. "Asked where you been at. You ain't been to the house in a minute. He thought you was in jail."

"Ha! Not yet," I replied.

"You know you cried wolf last nite. Had me thinkin' you were over here getting shot at."

"Yeah, well I knew it would get you away from o'girl so we could holla at you."

"About that. I don't like how Slip got at me last nite." He shifted uneasily in his seat.

"Think about it like this, if he didn't care about you or have love for you, then he wouldn't have gotten at you like that."

"How long y'all been following me?"

"We," I said with emphasis, "ain't been following you long. And I ain't been following you at all. It's just that Slip called me last night, telling me about how he been following Gina around for Big Reck to see who she been creeping with. Last night was his first night playing P.I. and he happened to see you with her and gave me a call so I could see it too."

"Damn, so Big Reck know?"

"As far as I know, nah. He just know that Gina been sneakin' out. But he don't know who with." I concluded, noticing the worried expression on Will's face, I added, "You know Slip not gon say nothing about you, so you all to the good."

"Yeah." He replied absently.

"What was you thinkin' from the gate dawg? You know you weren't supposed to go there with her."

"I know, but damn Kay, you seen her." Will said as if in a trance. "I mean that face, that body, her attitude. Honey just had me mesmerized."

"Just like Jezebel. I mean, was it good though?" I asked, knowing I shouldn't have.

"Was it?" He said, as if I should know the answer. "Dawg, not only that, it's pretty. Always waxed, perfectly tight, always wet. The way she get up there and just be ... real aggressive, rockin', bouncin', twistin'. Biting her lower lip, running her fingers roughly through her own hair. The way she bend over, it just spreads like a butterfly. A pretty brown butterfly, and I don't even gotta talk about the head. Blood, she had me stuck." Will said, nodding, coming out of the trance.

"Yeah," I replied, thinking I wouldn't mind trying that myself, under different circumstances.

"Yeah. So what's up with you and that proper lil Spanish broad? I know you got that. What's that like?"

I shrugged.

"Aw man, don't be acting brand new, tryna hide the details." Will said, regarding my gesture.

"I'm not. I didn't get it. It's not about that."

"It's not about that? What, you tryna take it to another level then?"

"Nah, but I like her."

"Oh, I meant to tell you yesterday. You had a straight 'S' on ya chest with a superman cape," Will grinned.

"What?" I said, knowing exactly what he was getting at.

"Dawg, you was on some straight captain save-a-hoe shit." Will stood up to do a salute and put his fists on his sides and stuck out his chest like superman.

We both started laughing wholeheartedly.

"You know you my boy. I just want you to be all good out there, not getting caught up in nothin'," I said, more seriously now.

"Yeah, me too," Will replied. "I don't want you getting caught up in nothin' either, tryin' to knock everybody out."

"You got it. As long as you don't get caught creepin' no more."

"Agreed," Will said as we stood to give each other a handshake, half hug.

Chapter 26

"You sure you don't just want to get your things and come stay with me?" Jessica asked Ronni as they pulled in front of aunt Marie's house.

"No, it's alright. I'm welcome here, plus I have Melissa with me."

"She can come too. You both can stay. It's no problem." Jess countered.

"No, but thanks Jess. We're going to be okay here." Ronni reached over the seat to give Jessica a hug before getting out of the car.

"Okay, but call me if you guys need anything. And when you're settled in."

"Okay," Ronni closed the Camry door with finality.

"Aunt Marie," Ronni called out as she opened the, oddly unlocked, door and entered the house.

Aunt Marie emerged from the first room in the hall. Her hands were clasped together nervously as she walked to hug Ronni firmly.

"Hey I-" Ronni started, but was silenced by the older woman's hands on her arms.

"He's here." Aunt Marie stated frightfully.

"Wha-what?" Ronni stammered.

Her 'what' was answered when Ricky appeared out of the same room guiding Melissa with his hands rested lightly on her shoulders.

"Ronni," Melissa gasped with joy, attempting to run to her but was halted by her father's hands. She looked up at him over her shoulders.

"Hey, go in the room with your tia. I'm going to talk to Ronni, alright," Ricky said, looking down at Melissa.

"No," Aunt Marie blurted out at his mention of 'tia', "What are you going to do?" Marie said, walking over to retrieve Melissa's hand. "We're staying right here." She spoke, taking a seat with Melissa on the couch.

"I don't have anything to say to you." Ronni said, breaking her silence.

"You have some guy come to my house and sucker punch me and you don't want to talk." Ricky stated rather than ask.

"First off, I had no one go to our house. Anyone could see your handiwork," she said, pointing to the fading bruise under her eye. "He just followed me off the bus, and you happened to be outside. He wouldn't have known who you were if you didn't come up like you wanted to fight him."

"What you expect me to do? I see some

fool walking with my wife down the street and you tugging on his shirt like you sleep with him or something." Ricky said, easing his way toward her.

"I'm not your wife- STAY BACK," Ronni warned, raising her voice as he moved closer.

Without obliging, Ricky continued to advance toward her, "Come on. We're going home," he reached out for her.

"Stay back," Ronni repeated sternly, swaying his reaching hand.

He lunged at her and was met with two quick punches, a right jab and left cross, startling him before he could grab her wrist to halt the assault. He tightened his grip on her as he tasted traces of coppery blood in his mouth.

"Ricardo," Aunt Marie yelled from the couch behind them. "Don't."

There was fire in Veronica's eyes that Ricky never knew existed before this day. A combination of fury and disdain. A look that revealed the end of whatever kind of relationship they had. He dropped his hold on her and broke their brief glare to look at her naked ring finger. The ring he'd found earlier and placed in his pocket before leaving for this trip.

"You throw away your ring and you run off with my daughter."

"She's my daughter too," Ronni barked back.

"This is my daughter. My daughter," he

said, walking to pick Melissa up and head towards the door.

Ronni blocked his way, "You're not taking her," she protested.

"Move," Ricky said. She didn't budge. "Move." This time with a forceful shove past her.

"No," Melissa wailed. "No. I want to stay with mommy. Please daddy." She cried as he continued to walk towards the white Ford pick-up parked in the driveway. "I want to stay with mommy," she reached out to Ronni to no avail as her father jerked away, opening the car door.

"She doesn't want to go with you." Ronni clawed at him, reaching around for Melissa as he sat her in the car.

"Move," Ricky said with less steam this time. "This is my daughter," he spoke, pulling away from Veronica as she tugged on his shirt, pushing her hand away to shut the door as he climbed in the truck. Inside, Melissa was still crying for mommy between racking sobs. The ignition hummed as Ricky backed out of the driveway. He almost ran over Ronni's foot as she pulled at the locked door handle and banged on the side of the truck, yelling words Ricky numbly tuned out as he drove away.

Ronni collapsed at the edge of the driveway and cried uncontrollably as aunt Marie lifted her up to guide her back inside of the house, shedding tears of her own. "It's alright, it's okay," she comforted. "We're going to get her

back," she said, but couldn't fully believe the
words herself, she's his daughter.

Chapter 27

"Let me get this straight," Big Reck said, pausing to weigh his question. "You followed her to a club by the beach where she sat inside for two hours, by herself, and nothing else?"

"Pretty much. The only thing I saw her do is dance with one guy, only once. Then she walked back to the bar by herself and bought like two drinks and just watched everybody else do they thing," Slip explained, "A few guys approached her within that time but she just turned them all away." Slip continued working his lie together. He knew it wasn't the best lie, but it wasn't far-fetched and would hopefully suffice.

"Hmm." Big Reck tapped his chin, leaning back in the soft beige leather of the Hummer's seat. They were in the Hollywood Park Casino's rear parking lot, for the second time. The eventide sunlight glared off of the windows and glossy paint of the numerous cars around them. "What about the bartender?" Big Reck asked. "Was she talking to the bartender a lot?"

"The bartender was a broad. But nah, she wasn't talkin' to her a lot."

"Was she checking her phone a lot?" She probably got stood up. Did she look like she was searching for somebody in the club?" Big Reck continued questioning.

"No, I didn't really see her check her phone. And she didn't look like she was searching for anybody out of the ordinary. One guy pushed up on her and she lifted her hand to show him the wedding ring."

"How could you tell?"

"How could I tell? That diamond on her finger the size of a quarter. Anybody within a mile can tell," Slip answered.

Big Reck smirked, "Yeah, but still, something's not adding up right. I'll see how she act in the next few days and give you a call."

Chapter 28

Three days had passed, and I hadn't seen or heard from Ronni. I was tripping after the first day, concerned after the second, and honestly worried during the third. She wasn't returning my calls, any of my messages, since her phone was never on when I attempted to call her. And embarrassingly, I left at least seven messages between the days. But I couldn't help it. I needed to know something. I needed to at least know she was okay.

I had been driving up and down La Brea and Hawthorne boulevard the past two days during certain times within the hour, particularly when the bus ran. Hoping I would spot her aboard, but each day turned up nothing. I didn't go down the street she stayed on because I was sure she wouldn't be there.

After racking my brain for the last hour, the night of the incident at Jessica's house came to mind. Jessica's house, Slip's girl. Maybe he would be there. I hadn't heard from him in the past two days either. I dialed his number as I drove toward the street I knew her house was on. Six rings, no answer. I made a left on Manhattan Beach Blvd. and cruised a quarter mile before stopping at a house I thought to be Jessica's. I got out and walked up the stone pathway to knock on the door. My knock was answered by scrapping and barking behind the door by what sounded like a large dog. My speculation was confirmed at the large pane window to the left of the door as it hoisted itself up to stick its large wolf-like head through the curtain and continued barking at me.

I didn't remember her having a dog, maybe it was in one of the room's upstairs. No, squash that. A dog slash half beast that big would've made its presence known behind whatever door in the house, especially with all of the commotion going on during the party. Maybe I was at the wrong place.

I took a few steps back to survey the row of houses on the busy street. Two cribs down, a beige Camry was parked in a driveway. I headed towards it, not wanting to get too close and it not be her car and have someone call the police and report a suspicious Black guy creeping around houses and cars. However, I slow dragged by the vehicle to steal a look inside, sure enough, there was a red bandana hanging from the base of the rearview mirror. It had to be her car. I walked up and rang the doorbell, waiting a minute before it was answered.

"Kay!" Jessica said as she opened the door and gave me a hug like we were old friends. "You caught me right before I was about to walk out," she said, pulling her long blonde and brunette streaked hair into a ponytail held by a red scrunchie.

"Yeah, where you about to go?" I asked, not really caring unless it had something to do with Veronica.

"The gym," she said, brimming with pride.

"The gym." I stepped back to check her out. I didn't really pay attention to her before, but she had a nice body, in great shape. The tight black spandex left no room to second guess and her face looked like it belonged on some sort of crest add coupled with her smile. She had a universal appeal.

"Like that?" I went on to ask, regarding her entire outfit. Above the tights, she had on a bright red sports top, and below the tights, on her feet, were red hi-top Chuck's with the sides folded down as well as the tongue with the laces tied over it. New-age gangsta style turned fad.

"Like what?" She asked.

"You flamed up and got on Chucks going to the gym."

"What? They're still athletic shoes," she countered. "And I'm going to the Balley's gym off of Century in Inglewood. So I'll blend in, right?"

"Blend in? I don't know. I'm sure a few white people workout there. But I don't know if you'll completely blend in."

"Okay, I was talking about me blending in by wearing red." She said with a 'duh' tone to it as if I should know.

"Oh, yeah, I guess you'll blend in then," I said indifferently. "But that's not why I came over here though."

"I know," she said, taking a step forward to sit down on the stoop stationed in front of her home's front door, and signaled for me to do the same. "It's about Ronni, huh?"

"Yeah. Where is she?"

"She's with family, and she's okay. She hasn't gone back to Ricky."

Silence. I didn't know what to say or ask next. What Jessica said was brief, to the point, and made it seem as if I didn't have any conclusion in her sentence.

"Kay, she really likes you a lot, but she's also been through a lot. She's having trust issues right now." She looked at me for some sort of reaction, as I sat beside her looking at the passing traffic on the boulevard.

"Did she tell you that I've been trying to call her?" I asked.

She shook her head sympathetically, "You have to understand all she's been through with Ricky, and then he just took Melissa from her the other day."

"He took their daughter away from her?" I asked, now facing her.

"Well, actually it's just his daughter. Melissa's real mom died in a car accident when Melissa was three. But Ronni loves that little girl with all of her heart. So, you can see how it hurts her."

"Jessica, I need to see her. I need to talk to her." I stood up and grabbed her hand to help her up as well.

"Tomorrow, we go back to school. She said she will be there. I don't know if she will, but our course lets out at eleven-thirty."

The living room of Big Reck's palatial home would be referred to as 'laid'. Which is another term for hooked-up or extravagant. Sorrel colored, plush, carpet swept each end of the room's 1500 square feet. Three white couches upholstered in Italian silk formed a semi-circle around a life sized golden lion base and crystal-top table. All of which was stationed on top of an authentic West African woven rug. A 60 inch HD flat screen and entertainment center lined the wall in view from the couches, next to a 100 gallon, exotic housed, fish tank. In the opposite corner sat a small club-sized, mirror backed bar, filled with various spirits and vintage wine.

Gina was seated on the middle couch with her legs drawn to her body, leaning on the arm rest, reading about a failing relationship in a Terry McMillan novel. The room was dimly lit by the two candle stick lamps in separate corners from the door. That and the open window curtains exposing a street light assisted night sky.

Big Reck entered the living room carrying a medium sized suitcase. He placed it alongside the couch as Gina stood to help him straighten out the collar of his shirt and the lapels of his suit jacket.

"How long are you going to be gone again?" Gina asked, trying her best to sound disappointed because he was leaving.

"Three days. I'll be back Sunday afternoon, the latest." Reck answered.

"Well, why can't I go with you then?" Gina pouted this time.

"Don't ask stupid questions. I'll be back in three days."

A horn blared in front of the house. Reck and Gina both knew it was Slip idling outside, awaiting Reck to walk out so they could make the short drive to LAX.

"I gotta go. I'll leave you a message tonight or call you first thing in the morning," Reck said, giving Gina a peck before heading out the door.

Three days, Gina thought with her back against the door listening to the car hum off into the distance. She knew three days only meant two. One for Reck's business and one for Reck's pleasure. The extra day was falsely added to throw her off; as if she would get caught cheating in the house.

She walked over to the bar to retrieve the cordless phone and dialed Will's number. It had been days since she'd seen him. Ever-since that day she was followed by Slip, Big Reck's new little errand boy. Although she wanted to be more careful in her rendezvousing with Will, he wanted to cease their affair completely. Her affair. He was just the insignificant decision maker of the party. What she said went, and if otherwise, she could use his fear of Reck against him.

Initially, she had decided to stay home and lay low for a while. She knew that Will's friend hadn't told Reck about them being caught together, because he wouldn't have kept it a secret. Her staying home the past few days had brought back some of his trust. And she needed his trust in order to keep her secret relationship afloat.

"Hey," Gina said into the receiver after Will finally answered his phone, "Reck and Slip just flew to New York for two days."

Chapter 29

I parked in the only vacant space available in the El Camino college's front parking lot. Which faced administration buildings, class rooms, or whatever else was inside the rectangle and square buildings in view.

The time on my cell read 11:21 a.m. I sat back and watched as a number of attractive faces passed my line of vision. Mature adults mixed in with young adults in their late-teens to early twenties. A diverse bunch of Whites, Blacks, Hispanics, Asians, others. Squares, jocks, punk rockers, hip hoppers, geeks, and everyone else in between pursuing higher education for their own benefit.

Every time I was around an environment such as this, it made me wonder where I would be heading in life had I stayed on the right path. In my family, the only person that ever graduated from college was my mother's sister Rosa. And that had been five years ago when she was 35. She had decided to go back to school after her daughter became an adult and moved out.

Leaving her with a lot of free time on her hands.

Besides my aunt, the only other person I knew that graduated from college was an old friend of mine named Tim, who graduated from UC Santa Barbara last year in 2003. I'd known Tim a few months over ten years now, since we were 12 and 13 years old. In the beginning he was my best friend, at a time when I considered myself to have friends. We were like Siamese twins. We did everything together, from fighting to girls, from sports to recording music.

We were big on talking about our future, always daydreaming about being these big time rappers with tons of money and women and cars. But as the years drifted by I realized that our dreams were no longer the same. Even though we grew up in the same neighborhood, we were from two different worlds, separated by two different blocks. Mines housed gang members and dope dealers; his, working class and senior citizens. He grew up in a home with two hard working parents who taught him the meaning of hard work and responsibility. I grew up in a home with a mother who dated low-life's and drug dealers who got our house raided for drugs every three months.

There came a time when we had to make a decision regarding our so-called future career. We needed money to record a professional quality demo before presenting it to a show sponsored by Death Row Records. Neither one of our families would give us the $600 needed for the project, so I came up with an illegal proposal, which he readily agreed upon. When it came down to carrying out the plan of action, he flaked on me. I ended up completing the task alone, getting us the money needed for the demo, which we recorded successfully. But when it came down to perform our work in front of record execs, I stood alone yet again. Tim had a job interview at a movie theater he refused to skip. Our music career together was over after that. He continued to work and go to school. I pursued illegal opportunities for money, went to juvenile hall, before eventually dropping out of high school.

When Tim got accepted into UCSB I attended a couple of the parties and loved them so much that I thought maybe college life would work for me as well. But it never panned out. I got shot and stabbed while trying to convince myself that I was robbing and selling drugs to save for tuition. The truth was, I was living for the now not the later.

My attention was brought back to the present as I seen Jessica emerge from the row of buildings. Her arms were full of books as she strolled scanning the parking lot for what I assumed to be me. A few people behind her, I saw Ronni walking with some big linebacker looking white guy in his early twenties. I got out of the car and beelined in their direction.

"Su-whoop," Jessica chanted as she spotted me approaching and flashed what would be mistaken for an 'A-Ok' hand sign, but what I knew to be her throwing up a 'b'. I almost laughed at her attempt to be down as she almost lost balance of the four thick books she was carrying.

"What's up Jessica?" I stopped in front of her.

"Why didn't you say it back?" She asked, handing me her books.

"Why didn't I say what back?"

"You know ... The call," she said with that 'duh' tone again.

"I didn't know you got put on," I retorted with a mixture of nonchalance and sarcasm. "Excuse me." I moved past her and stepped in front of Ronni, who looked good in a white blouse, black Capri pants, and solid white Nike tennis shoes. Her hair was pulled into a long braided ponytail, her face was without glasses, the bruise completely vanished.

"How you been?" I asked as we made eye contact.

"I've been fine, just living life, you know." She replied, breaking eye contact.

"I been tryna get at you these last few days, but ya phone been off. Did you get any of my messages?"

She nodded her head, "I've been real busy, and I'm kind of in a rush. I'll talk to you later," she said, walking around me.

"Ay," I said, reaching around to grab her hand before she could fully walk away.

"Hey. Is there a problem here?" The linebacker she was with said, stepping between us.

We faced off, eye to eye, for a couple of seconds before Ronni stepped back between us.

"No Brett, there is no problem. It's not that type of situation." Ronni spoke to him. In the background Jessica said, "Yeah Brett, you don't want that problem."

"Are you sure?" Brett asked Ronni.

"Yes, I'm sure. I'll catch up with you next week," she said, to which Brett hesitated a moment before strolling off.

She looked back at me without saying anything, turned around and continued walking towards the parking area. Jessica signaled for me to follow. I did so, accompanying them one step behind to Jessica's car. She opened the trunk so I could put the text books in there. Ronni waited, hand on the handle of the passenger side door for Jessica to unlock the car.

"Ronni," I said, holding the door closed as she tried to pull it open after Jessica popped the lock. She looked at me with a face that was part impatient, part frustrated, part weary. "Look, I know you've been through a lot this past week, and I'm sorry to hear about that situation with you daughter," I said, to which she shot Jessica an icy glare. "But I mean you no harm and I want to

179

be here for you in this time of need. As a friend, if nothing else." I concluded.

"Okay, I'll talk to you later," she said and tried the handle again.

"No, you won't."

"What do you want from me, huh? What do you want from me, Kay? Answer me that?" She demanded.

I regarded her a moment before taking my hand off of the door, "You should already know the answer to that by now."

She opened the door and got in, slamming it shut, without any further words.

Ronni entered the house and walked straight into her new room and closed the door behind her. Bypassing aunt Marie, who sat at the kitchen table drinking tea, without a greeting. Inside her room, she flopped down on the twin sized bed and stared blankly at the white of the ceiling.

The room was militantly neat. Everything was in its proper place. To the right of her bed was a nightstand and lamp; to the left, past the door, was a closet filled with her neatly set clothing and numerous shoes. Against the wall directly in front of the bed was a book case with five shelves filled to capacity. Books on history, social studies, life skills, and other educational text along with self-help books and classical novels. To each side of the book case stood twin dressers, one housed a laptop; the other, nothing. The room did not contain a television, which was by choice. She felt that TV was an unnecessary distraction.

There was a rap on the door. "Veronica, may I come in please?" Aunt Marie asked from the other side.

"Yes ma'am," Ronni said, sitting up as the door opened. "I apologize for not speaking when I came in. I just had so much on my mind that I was sidetracked when I walked through the door."

"It's okay," aunt Marie said with a reassuring smile and patted her on the knee. "Who is he?" She asked after careful consideration.

"Oh, it's nothing. I just had a bad morning."

"Veronica, I too am a woman, and have been young once. I will not be turned away that easily."

Ronni let out an uneasy chuckle.

"It's okay, you can talk to me." Aunt Marie reassured.

"Okay, well, his name is Kaeshon. But it's not what you think."

"What do I think?" Aunt Marie asked quizzically.

"Well, I'm not with him or anything. I haven't even been away from Ricky for like a week."

"Officially, but we both know that things have not been right between you and Ricardo for some time now."

"Yeah, but-"

"But, what about this new guy?" Aunt Marie said, cutting her protest short.

"He just will not give up. Every time I try to push him away, he just comes back. I can be mean to him but he's never mean in return and the next time I see him, he's just ... cool. Not to mention forgiving, like it never happened. Then on the other hand he wants to be my protector. If another guy says anything disrespectful or ..." She paused briefly, thinking of the incident at Jessica's party as well as the incident with Ricky. "It's like he thinks I'm helpless," she concluded knowing further details were not needed.

"Is that why you're mad at him?"

"No. I'm not mad at him at all. I'm mad at myself for being confused. For the way things have turned out in my life lately."

"Is that the reason you're holding yourself back?" Aunt Marie asked, the former guidance counselor side of her emerging in her inquiries.

"Holding myself back?" Ronni repeated to herself.

"Veronica, you have to live your life. You can not let one bad experience stop you from pursuing happiness. Life can be hard sometime, and the people we care about can make it harder. You can't sit around waiting, hoping Ricardo will come to his senses and change his ways just because you want to be with Melissa."

Silence. Ronni could do nothing but think.

"This is the same man Ricardo spoke of?" Marie asked, to which Ronni confirmed by nodding her head. "There aren't too many men out there who barely know you and will fight for you and keep coming back offering you help until your problems are gone. Not too many of them want to deal with the headache. It takes someone special. Or someone with a lot of tolerance." she said, nudging Ronni playfully.

"Thank you for coming to talk to me, aunt Marie."

"I have an idea," The older woman smiled. "Why don't we invite him over for dinner?"

"Tonight?" Ronni asked, unsure if it was a good idea.

"Yes, tonight. I want to cook for someone else besides you." Aunt Marie smiled at the notion.

"Well, okay, I guess I'll go ask him."

"You don't have his number?"

"I do, but I need some fresh air as well."

Chapter 30

"Yeah," I answered my cell, after the caller Id displayed Will's number.

"What you got going on?" Will asked.

"Just about to leave the spot to take this X-Box to little dude I got him for his b-day," I said, packing up the Best Buy bag containing the game console.

"You seen Slip?"

"Not for a minute, why, what's up?"

"Nothin'. I was just tryna get in contact with him," Will said, sounding like he was fishing for info.

"Now that I think about it, I think him and Reck OT," I added.

"Is that right? Okay, I'll get at you later."

I was surprised to see Ronni approaching as I closed the motel room door behind me and walked the four steps to my car.

"Where you coming from?" I asked when she was within earshot.

"Home, I just got off the bus."

"Home?"

"My new home." She answered, I guess figuring I was asking about the place with her ex.

"Well you're just in time. Two minutes later I would have been gone." I walked around to the passenger side, "Get in."

"Where are we going?" She asked, buckling her seat belt as I got in on my side.

"Remember the little kid from my accident?"

"Yeah."

"His name's Mario. Today is his 7th birthday. I got him this X-Box and a couple of games." I spoke while pulling into traffic then immediately into the left turning lane.

"Pretty expensive gift. Where does he live?"

"Right around this corner," I said, making a left on Arbor Vitae and then another left on Flower.

We parked two houses from the corner in front of a little three unit section 8 duplex.

"Right here?" Ronni asked skeptically.

"Yup."

"You're kidding right?"

"Nope."

"We could have walked over here."

"We could've walked." I mocked with a chuckle, getting out of the car, signaling for her to do the same.

"Yeah, what's so funny about that? It's not

even a full block from where you stay."

"That's not the point. Certain streets you just don't walk down."

"This is one of them?" She asked, visually scanning up and down the block, which was predominately apartment buildings. "It doesn't look that bad. It doesn't look great, but it doesn't look that bad, either. I've seen a lot worse."

"That's because you're looking at the buildings on the block and not the people that stay in them. The people in any environment are the one who determine if it's good or bad."

"You're right." Ronni agreed.

"Check out those guys down the street," I said, referring to a group of five a few apartments down on the same sidewalk as we were.

"What about them?"

"Where are they from?"

"How should I know?" She replied, stumped.

"I don't know either. But I have an assumption, just like they have an assumption about me. And I'm sure that we came to the same conclusion. We're not from the same side."

"How can you tell? They just have on white and black t-shirts. Their not wearing any red or blue or anything that would state an affiliation."

"Can you tell with me? Do I look affiliated?"

"Well, not the last couple of times I've seen you. You've been wearing a lot of like, nice jeans and boots. But I don't know, I guess you could be like a casually dressed gangster," she said, looking me up and down.

"Well, the same goes for them. Their clothing doesn't matter, it's their demeanor. The way they're standing around. If you notice, they've been looking over here a lot. They checked you out, probably thought, 'damn, she look good, she got ass.' But their main focus has been on me. And we both know that you're the better looking one out of us."

"Maybe to you I am, but who knows what they think," she joked.

"I do. They're thinking about where I'm from, what I'm doing over here, who'd I come to see."

"Well, come on before they come say something to us." Ronni said, looping her arm in mine.

"It don't matter," I said as we started to stroll. "As soon as we come out they'll be standing closer to my car."

Mona, Mario's mother, answered the door immediately after I knocked.

"Hello, Kay." The short Hispanic woman greeted in heavily accented English, leaning around the door.

"How you doing, Mona? I got something

187

for Mario," I said, extending my free arm to give her a hug.

"Thank you. Is this tu girlfriend?" She asked, referring to Ronni.

"This is Ronni," I introduced.

"Hi, I Mona. Nice to meet you."

"Tengo mucho gusto en conocerle." Veronica replied in Spanish as we entered the house.

The place was small but tidy. Full of life but cozy. We sat on a brown wool couch facing a 19 inch television that was tuned in to afternoon cartoons. Along the same wall as the TV, in the corner, was a large cardboard box full of toys. Evidence of a young family. Mona shared the place with not only her son, but her older brother Juan, the mechanic, as well.

Mona was a single parent, for what reason I didn't ask. There were a few pictures around the house of her, Mario, and some tough looking cholo type who was bald with a tear drop under his right eye. Who I assumed was in prison if not worse. Mona, who was 25 but looker closer to 30, had a tight curvaceous body that she kept in small boy-like shirts, form fitting jeans, and slightly worn tennis shoes. She had auburn hair that was always in a ponytail that reached the middle of her back. Although she looked older than her age, she had an attractive face with brown mini-kiwi shaped eyes and full lips that often revealed a beautiful smile.

This was my fourth visit to their home since the accident. I had initially visited to offer my apologies and some money to help them out. Which she thankfully accepted. The last two visits, Mona had hit on me and even stole a kiss, but I made sure that it didn't go any further. Under different circumstances I would've hit, but I figured she was only doing it because she was grateful and wanted to pay me back somehow. I let her know that it wasn't about that, sensing that they were a struggling family, I was looking out for them out of the kindness of my heart. I didn't want anything in return.

"Kay!" Mario said excitedly, hobbling out of the bedroom on small wooden crutches, holding out his cast leg.

"Mario, what up lil man?" I stood to give him a low five, while holding on to his shoulder so he wouldn't lose his balance. "Look what I got for you, birthday boy." I showed him the X-Box, extra controller and three video games I'd bought him.

"Aww man, aww man," he said, dropping the crutches and diving for the game. "Ma, look what he got me."

"Thank you," Mona said, smiling, her eyes growing watery.

"Thank you, Kay" Mario said, cheerfully throwing a death grip hug around my neck as I kneeled beside him.

"A'ight lil man, lets hook it up so we can

play," I said to which he looked at his mother for permission, who nodded her head positively as I started to plug the audio and video jax into the TV.

"Let's play the boxing game first," Mario said, holding the case out to me.

"A'ight, if you wanna lose," I said, putting it on.

"Yeah right!"

Ronni and Mona sat closely on the couch watching us play in between conversing in Spanish. After a few quick matches with Mario in Fight Night, I looked over my shoulder to see what they were doing. Just as I thought, they were staring in my direction and talking. I cocked my head at them and asked, "What y'all talkin' bout?"

"No es nada concerniente a usted," Ronni said, with Mona smiling beside her.

"In English, por favor," I replied.

"It isn't anything about you," she responded.

"You ready to do it moving?" I asked, knowing it was unnecessary to ask her was she ready to leave.

"Whenever you are."

"Awww man," Mario whined as I got up to leave.

"Awww man," I mocked, "I'ma be back soon man."

"You promise?"

"All the time." I shook his little hand and hugged his mother before walking out.

The group of five guys I spoke about earlier where standing one house away from my car, as I predicted. They stood talking louder than normal and showing out for our benefit.

"You were right about those guys," Ronni said, as we approached the car.

"Told you."

"Ay, what's brackin wit it homie?" One of the guys in the pack said. He was the apparent alpha male of the bunch, no older than 25, but he was taller, heavier, and older than the rest.

"What's up blood?" Another one asked, which was an attempt to throw me off.

I nodded my head, "Sup," I said, closing the door for Ronni, then walking around to get in myself, with all eyes on me.

"What's brackin?" Ronni said, confused, as I started the ignition.

"Same thing as 'what's crackin,' except with a 'B' instead of a 'C.'" I responded, pulling off.

"Oh, so those guys are Bloods?" Her inquiry continued.

"Nope, but they think I am and wanted me to say it back so they could catch me slippin'."

"Catch you slipping and do what?"

I didn't respond to that question, but shot her a look that read she should already know the answer to that question.

"What would you have done?" She went on to ask.

"I would have shot um," I said, making the right on Arbor Vitae, immediately getting into the turning lane to make the left back into the motel parking lot.

"Just like that? You would have shot them?" She asked with a bit of edge.

Silence. I didn't reiterate the answer I knew she wouldn't want to hear.

"Do you have a gun on you right now?"

"No." I parked.

"Kay, seriously, do you?" She asked again, staring at me.

"I told you, no."

She got out of the car, closed the door behind herself and started walking towards the bus stop on the corner.

"Where are you going?" I shouted.

"I'm going home because you're not being real with me," she paused to say.

"I am being real with you, come here."

"I don't want to be around you when you're carrying guns and shit like that."

"You always are," I said, half jokingly, to which she turned around and tried to walk off again. I jogged a few steps and grabbed her arm, "I'm just playin', stop trippin'."

"For real, Kay. Go put the gun up before we go anywhere else," she said, facing me, arms crossed.

I lifted up my shirt and spun around to show her I wasn't packing, physically. "I told you I don't have one."

"Lift up your pants leg," she said, unsatisfied with what I showed her.

"Come on, this ain't the movies. I'm not a cop with a revolver by my ankle."

"In New York, a lot of guys carry small pistols in their Timbs, and you have on Timbs," she argued.

"Well, in L.A. if it ain't on our waist, it ain't on us." I said, to which she just stared at me impassively. "Okay, look," I said, pulling up my pants' cuffs to show her there was no piece down there.

"Okay, then it's in your trunk."

"Ain't nothing in my trunk but $3500 dollars worth of beat."

"Okay then, in your glove box, under the seat."

"Come on, I was just in the house with a kid. I wouldn't have a gun on me while I'm around him," I said, which didn't ease the stare she continued to give me. "Damn, you just don't give up," I sighed and walked to the car, followed by her, opened the door and popped the hood. After propping up the hood, I dug around the front left side before pulling out the .380 I had stashed there wrapped in cloth.

"You happy?" I said, lifting the top half of

the cloth to show her the pistol, before walking into the room to stuff it in my suitcase.

"Yes. Thank you." She answered, smiling.

That was my Trojan Horse pistol. I kept another one stashed inside a secret compartment of my driver door panel.

"You don't have anymore in there, right?" She asked.

"Who do you think I am? Rambo," I retorted. "Damn, you difficult."

"I'm not the only one. Do you want to go to dinner with me?" She said, adding the latter quickly.

"Where?"

When we arrived at our destination, the sky was a combination of burnt orange and lavender as the sun slowly descended. I parked in the driveway of aunt Marie's home before following Ronni past a little wooden bench stationed next to the screen door of the house. The inner wooden door was open and a mixture of wonderful smells met our noses as we entered the foyer.

"Aunt Marie, I'm here, with company." Ronni called out as we stood in the living room.

To the right of the room was the dining area. It's center piece, a medium sized six seat maple table. On top, in the center of place mats topped with china and silverware, were several covered dishes.

"Hello, you two," Aunt Marie said, emerging from the rear of the kitchen.

"Hello, Mrs. Marquez," I extended my hand, "My name is Kaeshon," I said, my introduction pre-rehearsed in my mind.

"Oh, please, call me aunt Marie. Everyone else does," she said, bypassing my hand to give me a hug instead.

"Okay," I said, returning the hug.

"Veronica never told me you were so handsome," she said, backing away to observe me. "And tall."

I couldn't help but blush. "Thank you ma'am," I replied in return to her compliments. Although, I wouldn't completely agree with the tall part. I was barely six feet, but seeing as how she was petite and only about five feet even herself, I could understand why she considered me tall. "You have a lovely home, and the food smells great," I complimented.

"Thank you, and you're just in time. Come on, have a seat," she said, directing us to the dining room table. "I hope you like Spanish food." She pulled back the foil and lids from the glass dishes on the table to reveal a small feast that made my mouth water.

"I love it."

"Then you'll enjoy this." She spoke, filling my plate with two large chicken enchiladas, Spanish rice and beans, corn, guacamole, sour cream, shredded beef and tortillas. With apple cinnamon empanadas for desert.

"Wow, thank you," I said, wasting no time with the meal in front of me. "This is great."

"So, Kaeshon, what do you do with the majority of your time?" Aunt Marie asked in between small bites of food.

"Music. I'm a recording artist. I spend a lot of time trying to perfect my craft, to have it ready for the world."

"Sounds interesting. So you have music on CD already?"

"About two albums worth," I nodded my head.

"I would love to hear some of it one day."

"Okay, but I have to pre-warn you, it's rap."

"You make it sound bad," Aunt Marie said with a warm smile. "I've heard my share of rap and some of it I liked."

"You've actually sat down and listened to some?" I asked, thinking the thought of her listening to rap seemed far-fetched.

"In passing. I've heard the little bit that my students played around school, and I've stopped on the music channel more than once."

"So you're a teacher?"

"I'm a retiree. I was a guidance counselor for Saint Mary's Catholic school and Washington high school."

"Washington? My brother went there for about two years." I spoke my thought.

"About how long ago? I've only been retired four years."

"The last time he attended that school was eight years ago." I said, noticing how aunt Marie had been staring at me closely since I mentioned my brother attended that school.

"You look just like him," She stated absently.

"Yeah, I've heard that before," I said, unsure if the awkwardness I felt was evident.

"So, you know his brother?" Ronni asked, speaking for the first time since we sat down to eat dinner.

"Yes, I knew him. He was a remarkable young man with a large amount of potential," Aunt Marie said evenly.

"Excuse me ma'am, may I use your restroom?" I asked in order to relive myself in two ways, one being that conversation.

"Of course. It's the last door down the hall," She answered, to which I got up and headed in that direction.

"You spoke in the past ense. Did his brother die?" Ronni asked as they sat alone at the table.

"Yes, eight years ago. He was seventeen," Aunt Marie said tonelessly, rising from her seat to gather the dishes.

Ronni did the same, deciding not to ask further questions.

"Can I help?" I asked after returning from the restroom.

"No, you may not. You're a guest. You're welcome to relax and watch cable."

"But it's not a problem. I don't mind helping clean up."

"And I like being a good hostess," Aunt Marie said, smiling her warm infectious smile, which caused me to do the same.

"Okay you win."

"Veronica will keep you company. I also put some food together for you, for later."

"Thank you," I said as Ronni handed me a wrapped plate of food.

"Come on, I'll grab my sweater," she said, walking towards a room I assumed was hers.

"So, this is where you lay ya head at huh?" I said, standing in the doorway. "You live a very solitary life."

"And you don't? Living in that motel room of yours," she replied, searching for her sweater in the closet.

"I only live there part time."

"Yeah, the part when you're not there," she retorted.

I entered the room to look at the collection of CD's stacked neatly in three rows of ten on the dresser, left of the bookcase. She had an indiscriminate collection of alternative rock, country, pop, R&B, jazz, and hip hop. From

Kenny G to B.I.G., Sheryl Crow to Miles Davis, Shania Twain to Staind, and of course several Madonna CD's.

"You have a schizo CD collection."

"Explain," she said from the closet.

"Usually people buy like one or two music types. But you have like every music genre that exist."

"I'm open minded," she replied blandly.

"Where's your TV at?"

"Don't need one. What's better than books and music?"

"Uh, MTV, BET, HBO."

I walked around to the nightstand next to her bed; which housed a small lamp. Next to the lamp was a 5x7 inch brown cased diary. I picked it up, examining it. There was a little golden key slot on top.

"Do I go around your motel room picking up things that don't belong to me?" Ronni said, staring at me from the other side of the bed.

"Don't worry, I didn't violate the no diary reading rule."

"Come on."

"Aunt Marie," I called out before we got to the front door.

"Yes?" She answered, coming out of the kitchen.

"Thank you for the wonderful meal and the extra food you put together for me."

"Oh, you're welcome. It was my pleasure,"

she said, her face glowing. "I'll see you again soon, right?"

"Most definitely."

"Aunt Marie, I'll just be out front," Ronni said, closing the door behind us.

I started walking towards my car when Ronni pulled me down on the wooden porch bench beside her.

"Were you just going to dine and dash?"

"Nah, I thought you was ready for me to go," I said.

"It's beautiful out here," she commented, looking up at the midnight-blue sky flaked with stars.

"It is," I agreed.

"What makes it beautiful?" She asked, her eyes resting on me skeptically.

"Just … everything." I answered with a sweeping gesture to show what I meant.

She smirked. "When you've lived somewhere all of your life, it's harder to appreciate that place's beauty like someone from out-of-town. Because you're use to it."

"New York seem like an alright place, so what made you move out west?"

Sighing, she said, "I fell in love with this guy originally from L.A. and California seemed like a great place to go at a time when I was following my heart."

"In love and adventurous," I commented.

"I was, but only to a certain extent. I

wasn't adventurous to the point where I would hop on a boxcar and travel America. At the time I was 19, in love, and curious about what life elsewhere was like."

"That's understandable, I guess."

"You guess ... So I take it your not one for adventure?" She asked.

"My life's full of adventure."

"I'm quite sure it is, Pistol Pete. But what about an adventure that involves you uprooting your life for the ambitions of someone you love?"

"Sounds like a compromise to me," I answered dully.

"So, if there was someone you thought was the one-" she began, before I chuckled, causing her to cut her sentence short.

"What?" She asked, her brow wrinkled.

"Okay, look, if I was in love with someone. I mean really in love, and that person had a golden opportunity at life elsewhere and wanted me to go, then maybe, maybe," I repeated with emphasis. "I would go."

"Maybe."

"Only maybe."

"Yeah, sometimes things don't go as planned, right?" She said, her eyes drifting to the sky's blackness once more.

"If you don't mind me asking, what did your family think about you moving out of state like that?"

She sat silently for a moment, as if weighing the question before answering, "I didn't have anyone to consult, well anyone whose opinion mattered ... My father, I never knew. And my mother died from heart complications when I was five." She paused briefly, a distant look on her face. "I grew up in a series of ... not so great foster homes. One after the other until I was about 17. When I was 17 I found out that my mother had a half-sister named Valencia, who's married to some real estate mogul, out in Miami. She flew out for my birthday that year and gave me a huge financial gift and for the most part I've been taking care of myself."

"Sorry to hear about your parents," I said, not sure of what else to say.

Silence.

"What did your aunt say when you told her you were moving out this way?"

"She told me that decisions are to be made only after careful consideration," Ronni said, taking the plate of food out of my hand to place it on the other side of her and my arm around her shoulder. "Whichever route you choose will prove to be a bad or good idea in due time," she concluded.

"Sounds like a smart lady," I replied. "Are you still in contact with her?"

"Once a month," she nodded.

"So which part of the family aunt Marie belongs to?"

"Ricky's."

I grunted, "And how often does he come over?"

"He doesn't. They're not close."

"Okay, I guess."

"You don't have to, I told you." She leaned against me.

"About Ricky, so I figure he was the guy you came to LA with, right?"

She nodded.

"So how'd you two meet?"

"Umm ... Well, he was grieving when I met him," she began slowly. "I was 18 and waiting tables at a diner in the Lower East Side. He had family out there and when I first saw him ... Here was this great looking guy who was so sad. I later found out that his ex, Melissa's mother, was in a fatal car accident like three months prior. He had been staying out there unable to leave the city for the memory of her. He came to the diner often and over the course of a year, we got to know each other pretty well.

His brother was big in construction out here and had been trying to convince Ricky to return the entire time he was out there." She trailed off. "Everything was going so well and I wanted to be with him where ever he was." She went on to say.

"I understand," I said, my chin resting on top of her soft bed of hair.

"Can I ask you a question?" She asked.

"Shoot."

"Why did you confront Ricky that day?"

"When I was about four years old ..." I said, taking my time to answer. "I remember my dad staggering into the house late, from where I assume was the bar. My mother had been up all night worried something had happened to him. So she questioned his whereabouts when he came in. Why he'd gotten so upset about this, I don't know. I remember hiding in the closet when all the commotion started, eventually falling asleep. I'll never forget the bruises on my mother's body and face when I seen her that following morning.

As time went on, so did the beating. Sometimes he would disappear for a year or two at a time, whether he went to jail or hell, I don't know. But he always came back begging for forgiveness, protesting he was a changed man, a better man. All lies. The same thing would happen. Sometimes in as little as a week. He'd use fist, belts, brooms or whatever he could get his hands on or take from her if she used it as a weapon to defend herself with. When I was 12 and my brother Keith 15, we had seen enough and decided to take matters into our own hands. We fought him, the cops came, and he eventually got sentenced to a few years in prison. I haven't seen him since." I paused momentarily to reflect. Ronni pressed her soft lips against my cheek. "You know, I think any man that puts his hands on a woman is a piece of shit. I like and respect you a whole lot Ronni, and when I seen that had happened to you ... I just lost it."

"Thank you," she replied softly.

A light smile formed across my face. I gave her a kiss on the forehead. "I gotta go." I rose, walking towards my car with her in tow. Before I could turn around, she wrapped her arms around my torso and rested her head on my back. Spreading a feeling of comfort and warmth throughout my entire body.

"What are you doing tomorrow?" She asked.

"I gotta go to the studio at nine in the morning," I said, turning around to hug her.

"Can I go?" She asked quickly, looking up at me from our embrace.

"I'll pick you up at 8:30."

Chapter 31

It was a gloomy spring morning full of breeze that required the use of a black and grey leather Sean John, letterman, jacket that I wore over a long white T-shirt as I left the spot to pick up Ronni.

The studio sat in a small shopping center around the corner from a ran-down part of town. Behind which was an alley where drug dealers, crack heads, and vagrants wandered freely looking for customers and handouts.

The inside of the studio was finely furnished with expensive recording and producing equipment wrapped in woodgrain. It reminded me of an old saying about inner beauty because it looked like it belonged in a totally different world from the one beyond its door. We sat outside of the booth behind the 64 track digital board listening to DJ Seismo, the in house producer, fine-tune a guitar and drum laden beat for my album. I noticed Ronni lightly tapping her feet to the tangy riffs of the guitar and boom boom baps of the 808 drums instrumental that flooded through the large overhead speakers.

"What you think? It sound like a hit?" I asked, rolling my chair closer to hers.

"Yeah, it sounds good," she nodded her head. "You're not about to rap about bitches and hoes, right?"

I responded by laughing, "You somethin' else."

"K.A. you ready to get in there and put it down?" Seismo paused the beat to ask.

"No doubt," I responded, getting up to walk into the glass booth facing them, adjusting the mic and headphones in place.

"Here we go," Seismo said through the intercom, holding up a finger before starting the beat.

I let the beat drift, its drums thundering in my ears, the guitar riffs taking me on a melodic journey before ...

I take off, in a whip that's fine-tuned/In a city where scars and big nutts define a goon/And out here-it's some blue, but mainly red and maroon/On brown and black backs-that'll prolly lay in a casket soon/But until then, we try to get rich and be where the pretty girls loom/That's harder to dig out than a prisoner in a tunnel with a spoon/Uh-posted up looking for opportunities at braggin rights/Fitted caps- White T's and belts holding a magnum tight/This is the city of champions, A"IGHT/Where thugs blast with no mask just to higher their rank/And every pretty shank tryna be the next Tyra Banks ...

I bopped, spitting the lyrics with bite and stern emotion, letting the beat bang before the hook came in.

"Okay, it was alright. You have a little bit of skill." Ronni admitted as we walked out of the studio.

"A lil," I said, holding up my fingers as such. "We both know I'm the next best thing-"

"Excuse me, young blood." Said an older homeless man, beside us. "I don't mean to bother y'all, but I need some help out here man." The vagrant pleaded.

I regarded him a moment before answering. He was an older Black man with holed and oil stained jeans, extremely worn tennis shoes, and a T-shirt too small for his bony upper body. His beard was a matted mess, the majority of his teeth absent, the remaining were rotten. His eyes were wide, the pupils brown with a gray glaze around them and the outside traffic light yellow where it should've been white. I knew him, had seen him around for years on and off.

"What you need, old-school?" I asked.

"Everything, man. It's cold, I'm hungry." He paused for a violent cough. "I-I just need help. I'll clean your car or somethin'. Man I need help."

"Here you go," Ronni said, holding out a ten dollar bill. I took it from her hand before he could grab it. "Kay," she said as I placed the bill in my coat pocket.

"When the last time you had a drink?" I asked the homeless man, putting my hand up so Ronni wouldn't interfere.

He looked at Ronni pleadingly before focusing on me to answer, "I don't know. It's been a while," nodding his head.

"When the last time you smoked some dope, The last time you got high?" I continued to grill him.

"Kay," Ronni said again, empathetically, but was ignored.

"I can't afford no dope, man. I'm just hungry and real cold, that's it that's all. I ain't tryna get high, man, I swear," he whined, hugging himself.

"Okay, this what I'ma do, I'll go over there and get you some chicken since you hungry. But I'm not giving you no money," I said, pointing at the Popeye's Chicken restaurant corner.

"Thank you, youngsta," he said, glowing. "But can we go to this corner store," he spoke, referring to the liquor store at the edge of the shopping center. "They sell bread and packs of bologna. It last me longer."

"You know what, I'll do this instead," I said, satisfied with his answer, taking off my jacket. "Since it's cold out here, you can have this jacket and the ten dollars my girl was going to give you."

"Man, I can't take this jacket, it's real leather, man. It probably cost you a lot of money."

"Don't worry about it. Just don't let me find out you sold it for some bullshit or I'ma do something to you. Now go in there and buy some bologna. I'm going to be waiting right here to see if you did." I said, sitting on the hood of my car.

"Okay," He replied, walking towards the store with the large jacket hanging off of his back like a second set of heavy skin. Emerging a moment later holding up a loaf of bread, two packs of bologna, and a triumphant snagga-tooth smile.

"What?" I asked, looking over at Ronni who was staring at me as I drove her home.

"You just gave a homeless man your jacket," she said like she was still trying to process what had just taken place.

"It's nothing," I said, nonchalantly.

"Like a 500 dollar jacket," she continued.

"I got it on sale," I shrugged.

"At first I thought you weren't going to give him anything. Just patronize him."

"He wasn't going to get anything had he been drunk or high, or if I figured that was what he was about to do. Ain't no point in supporting a bums addiction. But he was sincere in the kind of help he needed," I said, to which she just continued to stare at me.

"That was nice of you," she responded before directing her focus to a brown '72 Monte

Carlo low-rider, occupied by four shaved head, heavily tattooed, ese's in the next lane glaring at us. "What's their problem?" She asked, rolling up the tinted window.

"You already know," I said, figuring she did.

In LA, the relationship between Blacks and Hispanics was dire and at times always a step away from war. Both racial groups-although their plight has little difference- found reasons to be envious of the other. What started out as a dispute over drugs, turned into a gang rivalry. What became of that gang rivalry was, in some cities, a racial war. Leaving innocent bystanders from each group sometimes purposely caught in the crossfire. The theory was, 'if I can't get to the person I want, then I'll get to them through their family or people in their neighborhood'.

"You seen my phone?" I asked, watching the cholos make a right on Manchester.

"No, do you want me to call it?"

"Nah, I don't remember bringing it with me to the studio. I'ma stop and get it before I drop you off."

"I'll be right back," I said, getting out of the car after parking in front of the motel.

"I'm not in a rush," she said, climbing out as well.

"Su-Whoop," Slip called out from a black

Expedition as we were entering the room. "Let me get at you real quick," he signaled.

"I'll be there in a minute," I turned to say to Ronni before walking to the SUV.

"What up wit' it?" I asked, leaning in the passenger window.

"The homies just got into it with these Mexicans. They came through bussin', nobody got hit, but you already know what's up."

I peered over my shoulder before answering. Ronni was observing us through the window without being discreet. "Nobody got hit. I'll have to catch it on the rebound."

"Don't trip," Slip said abruptly, peering around at Ronni before saying, "Just slide me two of those thangs for somebody who wit' it."

"Where are you going?" Veronica asked when I entered to grab an empty sports bag from the closet.

"Nowhere," I answered, moving to the bathroom. I removed the toilet bowl to retrieve a Ziploc bag containing a chrome .45, dropping it in the duffle bag, then to my suitcase to grab the .380 I placed in there the previous day.

"Does nowhere involve guns?"

"Nah, nowhere involves me being here with you," I responded, headed for the door.

"Don't bother. You're going to be here by yourself," she said in pursuit.

"What?"

"If you're going to give him the guns to go kill someone, then you might as well go with him yourself because what you're doing is no better."

"Yeah, whatever." I waved her off, handing Slip the bag through the window.

"What's up with yo girl, dawg?" Slip asked, looking over the seat at her as she walked to the bus stop.

"She on some goody-two-shoes shit, always trippin' when she think I'm about to put in some work."

"Why she getting on the bus?" He asked, head still over his shoulder.

"I'll get at you later," I said, jogging over, trying to reach her before she could enter the bus. "Ronni," I shouted, which was a waste of breath that didn't stop her from getting on.

"Damn, that broad sumthin else." I cursed to myself.

"Ha, ha, ha. You might as well roll with me now." Slip laughed.

"Man, get cha ass outta here," I barked, walking back to the room.

"You need to get rid of that bitch because she got you on some straight bullshit," Slip said before pulling off.

Ignoring Slip, I thought about Ronni. I wasn't going after her. The cat and mouse game between us was growing old fast. I was tired anyway.

I flopped down on the bed, scanning around the miserable room I was in. Both of our cell phones were on the table. She forgot to grab her's before storming out. "That's what she get for being so worked up. I'm not taking it to her," I said to myself before falling asleep.

"You know I miss you right?" Gina said into her cell phone. "We have to set something up so we won't have to sneak around." She was stationed in her room on the large circular bed watching the closed door knowing Big Reck could enter at any moment. "What?" She giggled at the comment Will made. "You crazy-ohh, I gotta go." She snapped the phone shut.

"Who were you talking to?" Big Reck asked, standing in the doorway.

"My mother, she sick. We need to fly out there and spend some time with her. She sounds really bad." Gina answered quickly.

"Fly out there when?"

"Like right now, tomorrow, this week. She's sick right now, Derreck, life is short, I need to be with her in case anything happens." Gina said, keeping up the theatrics.

Big Reck sighed, "I'm not trying to be out in no hot humid-ass New Orleans with yo crazy ass Creole family. But I will get you a ticket and have one of my peoples fly out there with you for a couple of days."

"Look, if you not trying to go, I don't need

you to send one of your goons as a replacement. I'll be alright by myself."

"Okay, I'll have Slip get the ticket and take you to the airport tomorrow."

"Thank you, baby," Gina said, rising to give him a hug, grinning over his shoulder. Her spur of the moment plan had worked out perfectly.

Chapter 32

Veronica entered the motel room and took a seat at the table stationed a couple of feet from the bed on which Kay slept. She watched as his body slowly rose and fell with each breath. She came back for her cell phone after waiting impatiently for him to bring it to her for three hours. When he didn't bring it, like she hoped he would, she decided to go to him instead, knowing he'd be at the motel and possibly sleep. Her assumption was confirmed as she sat there not bothering to wake him, but the ringing of her phone 20 seconds later would.

"Hello … Hello," She repeated into the silent phone. "Hello," A third time before hanging up on the private number.

That was the fourth time in two days someone had called without saying anything. She figured it was Ricky, who prior to the silent call she had told not to call her anymore. Simply put, it was over, she found someone else. He just couldn't get over it but had nothing else to say. She didn't think it was Melissa, although the girl had called her several times since the incident. On each occasion they spoke briefly, but spoke.

"How long have you been here?" I asked after opening my eyes and noticing Ronni sitting in a chair staring at her phone.

"Ten minutes, you left the door unlocked. Which is surprising seeing how many enemies you have."

"What enemies?" I sat up.

"Umm, other gang members, maybe those Mexicans you guys were going to shoot," she retorted.

"There you go with that BS again," I said, walking to the bathroom to piss. "I don't have anything to hide. If I tell you I'm not going to do something, I'm not. If I tell you that I am, then I am," I said from the bathroom, washing my hands.

"Okay, then tell me you're going to grow up," she said, making her way to the bathroom's doorway. "Tell me that you're going to start acting like the man you're supposed to be instead of some thug playing street games."

"You somethin' else," I said, trying to walk by her before she sidestepped in front of me so I wouldn't exit the bathroom.

"Seriously Kaeshon, because I don't want to be with you or around you if you're going to keep acting like this," she said, her eyes holding mine intently.

"So you came back to give me an ultimatum?" I asked, knowing she was serious but decided to yank her chain a little bit. "Okay then, goodbye." I craned down to give her a kiss, to which she turned her head and I planted it on her cheek.

She looked back at me, her eyes beginning to moisten. "You're stupid." She turned in a hurry for the door.

So much for playing with her. "Veronica, Ronni," I said, catching up and wrapping my arms around her before she could reach the door. "Hey, it's all good. I was just fuckin with you."

"Let me go," she demanded as I held her from behind.

"No. I don't want you to leave," I replied. I could tell she didn't want to leave because of her lack of struggle.

"I'm serious, Kay. Don't you care about your life? Because I do?"

"Yeah, I care about-"

"One minute you're helping a little kid and his mother out. You'll give a homeless man you don't even know the shirt off your back. You're here for me no matter the circumstance," She continued, I let her go and took two steps back to sit on the bed. "In the next instance, you're an impulsive gangster with guns all over the place willing to prove an idiotic point to other men for no reason. It's like you don't care if you live or die or go to prison," She said, before taking a breath.

"I care." I stated simply.

"I keep having these nightmares about you getting shot by some guy in a car you know and I don't understand it. I don't want it to happen," She went on intensely.

"Nothing's going to happen-"

"Your brother was only 17 when he died, right?"

"Yeah, but-"

"Your barely in your twenties, that isn't much more of a life." She said before taking a seat in the corner next to the door, burying her head in her lap.

I watched her as her head rested on her arms across her drawn up knees. The last time she had challenged me on my lifestyle had been at the park and it had been out of frustration and anger. This time it had been out of love. Although she didn't use as strong a word, her whole attitude and delivery conveyed it.

I walked over to her, standing there a moment. Whether she was aware of my being there before I looped my arm under her leg and the other around her back to lift her up, I don't know. She kept her head buried in my chest as I walked her back to the bed not bothering to look up at me until she was laid down.

Words couldn't express the way I felt about her in that moment as I looked down at her. So, I didn't use any as I kissed her cheek, her lips, and her neck, while gently helping her out of her clothes. Her milky brown complexion blended perfectly with my chocolate. Her mounds well portioned, her curves generous as I slowly slid in her labia, which was as moist as the tears that washed her cheeks ... This time she didn't stop me, but simply wrapped her arms around me and whispered, "I just don't want you to hurt me."

There comes a time in every man's life when he has to make a decision, whether White or Black, rich or poor, from the hood or from the burbs. That decision is to be or not to be. As Shakespearian as it may sound, it couldn't have been said better in other words.

When it comes down to it, we all have a choice, and it always involves a good or bad decision. Either one having life altering affects. I think about Slip, who is among the most intelligent people I've met, street-wise or scholastically. I remember watching him play football, observing his strength, speed, and cat-like agility as a running back. He was a brilliant player, one of the best I've ever seen. I thought for sure he was going to be in the NFL one day, and I knew him. But somewhere along the line he made his decision, and now he stood as a convicted felon. His only stats are a former state number and penal codes. The only M.V.P he'll receive from here on out is Most Valuable Piru.

The same goes for Will. He had actually

made it to the college of his dreams, a step farther than practically anyone I knew. He had his foot in the door. But having immediate money was more appealing than struggling like the average college student and having it pay off in the end. Having money now, for Will, was more important than his education and a possible beneficial career, and for that, the result was being expelled and ineligible. I was no different, but now I found myself with a different decision to make.

I was swimming in thought while laying in bed, hands under my head, gazing towards the ceiling. Ronni was pressed against my side with half of her blanket covered, nude body, wrapped around mine like a garden snake. She had been sleep for some time now. I on the other hand could not. I kept revisiting her earlier arguments and the intensity in which she delivered them. I thought about how our situation evolved, from the first time we spoke, until now. I remembered the way she looked at me the day I spent time playing video games with Mario, and on the day, after the exchange, with the vagrant. It was in those moments that she had made up her mind about me.

I peered down at her, she looked so beautiful and at peace resting next to me. I brushed the loose strands of her silky hair away from her face so I could get a better look at her soft features. She was truly a gem and deserved everything that she desired. I knew it from the second I first laid eyes on her, which was probably the reason I didn't just try to have sex with her and keep going about my business like she didn't exist anymore. The last thing she said to me was, "I just don't want you to hurt me." Even though she said it in an intimate moment, she didn't mean sexually, she meant in general. I didn't want to hurt a woman who had experienced a lifetime of hurt, but the question was, could I change?

My phone began to spasm on the table, letting me know I had a new text message. I slid from under Veronica to retrieve it without waking her.

U at da spot?: The message read, which was from Will.

Yup: I sent my reply.

B there N 2min: He replied quickly.

I threw on my beige jeans and Air Force's, not bothering with a shirt and stepped outside. Will's Land Rover pulled in and parked as I closed the door behind me.

"K.A." Will said, extending his hand for our usual greeting. "What, you got company in there?" He asked, I assume regarding my missing shirt and the fact we were standing out side.

"Yeah, What's up?"

"Who?" He asked curiously.

"Don't worry about it. What's up?"

"I know who," He declared with a devilish grin. "Anyways, I got a lick for us. Six figures, guaranteed"

"Yeah, I'm good. I'll leave that to you and Slip," I said, uninterested; at least for right now.

"You good? What you mean you good? You didn't hear what I just said, six figures. I'm talkin' 250 stacks," he said with emphasis.

"Hmm, 250 thousand dollars?" I said skeptically.

"Real talk."

"Nah, I'm good, N. I don't need it. I'll leave that to you and Slip."

"Me and Slip." Will repeated, sounding a bit upset. "I'm talkin' me and you, straight across the board and you talkin' 'bout you good. You must mean ya money still good, what you sitting on a mountain? Let me hold sumthin."

"What you need?" I asked.

He sucked his teeth before saying, "125 thousand. My cut of the lick I thought me and my best homeboy was supposed to pull off."

"Hold on, let me get that for you," I replied jokingly, walking back to the door.

"Whatever. I'm outta here," Will said sourly, hopping in his vehicle, leaving as quickly as he came.

Ronni was sitting on the newly made up bed when I walked in. She had her hair up in a ponytail and was wearing my long black T-shirt, which almost looked like a nightgown on her because of its length reaching her knees. "So, you're good, huh?" She asked as I took a seat next to her.

I laid my upper half back while keeping my feet on the ground. "Do you always ease drop on conversations that have nothing to do with you?" I asked instead.

"If it was meant to be private I'm sure you wouldn't have been talking in front of an ajar window," she replied before laying sideways so she could stare at me.

"Mmph," I grunted. "You ready for me to take you home?"

"Yeah, so I can grab a few of my things."

"Grab a few of your things," I repeated. "What you plan on moving in?"

"here? Yeah right. I just need a few things for when I'm around."

Chapter 33

"You don't have to wait with me, I'm a big girl I know how to get on the plane by myself." Gina told Slip, who sat next to her in a sun-filled LAX terminal reading an article in Smooth magazine.

"You are going to get on the plane by yourself. I'm just waiting until you do," Slip said, not bothering to look up from the magazine. What he neglected to tell her was that five seats down, Black, one of his associates had been enlisted to fly out to New Orleans as well to keep an eye on her from a distance.

Damn, how can I get rid of him? Gina asked herself before saying, "So, this is one of ya job descriptions, huh? You might as well be on blunt rolling and car washing detail. You got a straight loser job. Why don't you go get you some or something. Instead of being by a bitch that don't want you by her."

"Well, you can scoot ya ass over then if you don't want me by you," Slip said, his focus never leaving the mag.

"Aah!" Gina sighed out loud. "Okay, look, I'll give you a G if you just leave. I'm saying, I wanna be by myself right now. I got a headache, that's how much I want to be left alone." She looked at Slip, noticing his unwavering focus on the pages in front of him. She put her hand down over the magazine, forcing it to his lap. "Look, Slip, right? I know you a ryder and all that, otherwise you wouldn't be here. But look, it's a lot of people around here and ain't nothing going to happen to me without nobody seeing it. So, I'm safe. I don't need protection."

"Okay," Slip replied carelessly.

"Plus, you a criminal. So if I start screaming and cause a scene, that'll make the police escort you out of here. I hope you ain't got no warrants or nothing because that wouldn't be a good look," Gina said, slyly.

Grinning, Slip replied, "okay, I'm out," shooting a knowing glance in Black's direction before rising to walk away.

"Hey, keep it gangsta, boo. This conversation was just between me and you," Gina called out with a winning smile.

Watching him off into the distance, she immediately pulled out her cell and walked towards an opposite exit.

"Tell Black don't let her leave his sight, and you come pick me up right now." Big Reck's demanding voice boomed through Slip's phone.

"I'm on my way," Slip said with finality.

Chapter 34

"Where are we going?" Ronni asked, looking out of the window at neighboring traffic and sights passed as we traveled east on the 10 freeway.

"Rancho, this lil spot I know, where we can get somethin' good to eat," I responded.

"It must be good if it's this far."

"Ay moms, I'm here." I called out as we entered her home.

"Kay!" My little sister said, running towards me from her room. "Ohh, hi," she halted to say to Ronni.

"Hi little lady, I'm Ronni. What's your name."

"Rayona, nice to meet you," she said before running off to fetch our mother. "Mom, Kaeshon brought a lady with him," she yelled on the way.

"She is so cute," Ronni said after her.

My mother emerged from the room with my little brother and sister in tow. "Hey Kay," she said, giving me a hug.

"Mom, this is Veronica, but everyone calls her Ronni. Ronni this is my mother Cheryl," I introduced.

"Hi, nice to meet you." They said simultaneously.

"Ronni you are very pretty." My mother complimented her, still smiling. She always enjoyed new company.

"Thank you, and so is your home and children."

"And polite," She turned to me, "Kay, I'm proud of you."

"Mom, you somethin' else." I had to smile, nodding my head. "What up with you cooking dinner?" I changed the subject.

"That reminds me, I have some heavy bags in the car, laundry detergent and flour to cook your food with," She said, with emphasis on flour, trying to be sarcastic and funny. "So grab it. Ronni you can have a seat."

"Come on Corey," I called for my little brother before walking out.

"So Ronni, you're from LA, right?"

"No, I'm from New York originally. I've been out here for a few years."

"Compared to New York, how do you like it?"

"Umm, the most I can say is that the weather's great," Ronni said, to which they both shared a brief laugh.

Akil Victor

"Yeah, I hear you. I had to leave LA myself, too much going on. My next move is out of California altogether. I'm getting tired of it. I'm thinking Texas or someplace else in the south, baby."

"Texas is nice. I was thinking of relocating myself, hopefully Miami if I get accepted into the university," Ronni said.

"Miami," Cheryl repeated to herself, "You know, I've been trying to get Kay to move away from terrible Inglewood for sometime now, but he will not leave. No matter how much trouble he get in. You need to take him with you."

"T-To Miami?" Ronni asked hesitantly.

Cheryl tilted her head, as if reassessing her thought. "Yeah. That doesn't sound bad. If you two are together like that. I mean, he has never brought a girl home before, never ever. So you must mean a lot to him for you to be here."

"You think so?"

"Baby, trust me, I know so." Cheryl assured her.

"Well, I never talked to him about it. I don't know if he would want to go," Ronni said, adding the latter more for herself than anyone else.

"You don't know if he would want to go where?" I asked, walking in, catching the tail end of my mother and Ronni's conversation.

"Did you get all the groceries," My mother

230

asked, focused on the bags in our hands.

"Yeah, speaking of which, you left all the groceries in the car on purpose because you knew I was coming over here, huh?"

"I sure did," She said, retrieving a bag of canned goods out of my hand.

"What if I wouldn't have come, then you would have had all that food in the car for nothing."

"Oh you would have came, so tell that to somebody who don't know how you eat."

We sat down to a mouth watering meal consisting of fried chicken, rice, cornbread, four cheese macaroni, collared greens and a marshmallow-cinnamon-swirled pumpkin pie. Soul food.

"Mm, Cheryl, the food is great," Ronni said, finishing a bite.

Smiling gleefully, my mother responded, "Thank you sweetheart." And then to me, "I'm glad somebody appreciates it."

"Mm, mom, the food's great," I said, in an attempt at mocking Ronni, which caused my little bro and sis to giggle.

"Shut up," My mother said, throwing a crumpled napkin at me. "You see what I have to deal with Ronni? Ain't he something else?"

Ronni shot a wanna be evil glare in my direction, "He sure is."

"Ronni, my best friend Dolores is Mexican." My little sister Rayona blurted out, forever the outspoken one.

"Rayona." Mother said with a look that let her know she was out of line.

"It's okay," Ronni said with an easy smile. "Rayona, I'm not Mexican, I'm Puerto Rican. Do you know what that is?"

Rayona nodded her head enthusiastically.

"Like J-Lo," Corey chimed in before Rayona could answer.

"Corey, she didn't ask you, she asked me, dang." She pouted.

"Stop acting like a baby," Corey said.

"You a baby," She retorted.

"Hey, both of y'all go put up your dishes and go to your rooms."

"Aww, mom," They whined simultaneously, obliging.

"See Corey, this is your fault." Rayona could be heard saying as they stormed off.

"Now they somethin' else," I said with a chuckle.

Chapter 35

The suite was well lit with a series of jasmine scented candles placed seductively throughout the room. Romantically simple, just how Gina liked it. It was her who insisted on them occupying the same suite they had first coupled in. That, and the fact that it was close to home excited her. Will, initially, of course knowing the circumstances of their encounter, had protested. He would have rather been on a whole other island with her or a cruise for that matter. Which he suggested. Anywhere far away from Big Reck and his henchmen. But Gina being Gina had shot down any idea Will had. "Stop bitchin," She told him. "You sound like a coward. Nobody's going to know we're here. For one, Reck trust me, and two, I'm in New Orleans, remember?"

"Yeah, but come on, we right between Inglewood and the airport," Will countered.

"And, what that mean? It's not like we're going to be cruising between the cities." She said, unzipping his pants and taking him in her hands, squeezing and lightly stroking until he became erect.

Moments later, she laid in the rose petal filled bed covered in silk sheets from the waist down. "Damn, baby," She moaned, cupping the top of Will's head.

Her phone rang on the nightstand next to the bed, for the forth time consecutively.

Big Reck sat back in the passenger seat of Slip's Expedition "That damn bitch," he said, fuming, squeezing his flip phone until its plastic case began to crack. "Y'all sure she went into that hotel?" He asked Slip, referring to him and Black, who was idling in his vehicle at the opposite end of the parking lot.

"Yeah, this is where Black said he followed her to. She got out of the taxi and went up in there." Slip answered for the third time within the last hour. That question annoyed him because he was already paranoid at what the outcome would be if Reck found out that it was Will with Gina in that hotel. Something he hoped against hope wouldn't happen, but he had a feeling otherwise.

"Hold on, Will stop," Gina crooned. "This reck, I gotta answer this," She said, which caused Will to pause. "Hello."

"So, now you wanna pick up the phone. Where the hell you been at?" Big Reck barked into the receiver.

"Well hi baby to you too." Gina tried to make light of the situation.

"Don't play with me."

"I'm not, my phone was still tucked away in my luggage. I'm just barely getting around to checking my messages. I had to catch up with my family."

"Catch up with ya family, huh? Okay, let me talk to yo momma."

"Now Derreck, you know she don't want to talk to you. She was already mad, talking shit about you because you didn't fly down here with me," Gina said, starting to press buttons.

"Yeah, she always-" Big Reck began to agree with her, "What's that noise?" He stopped to say.

"Oh baby, my phone-" Gina said, pressing buttons and breaking off her voice. "Battery ... about to ..." She hung up and turned off her phone.

Turning to Will, "Let me use your phone so I can call my mom," she said.

Big Reck stared at his phone a moment longer, "Phone battery ... I know that bitch didn't just hang up on me," He said to himself before redialing her number, which went straight to voicemail.

"I'ma call her momma," Reck continued talking to himself, dialing the number, figuring he would expose the lie. "Hello, Mrs. La Salle … Yeah, this is Derreck … What you mean what I want? I want to talk to yo daughter … Look I don't got time to play games. Is she there?"

In the background, Slip could hear a woman answer, "Yeah, she here," Through the phone.

"Okay, how long she been there?" Reck continued the phone conversation, "What … Yeah I know this ain't her phone … Her battery died, I know … What you mean don't call there? Well, itchy, itchy, ay ya to you too." He slammed his phone shut.

"Her momma said she been there for the last two hours." Big Reck turned to Slip.

Slip hesitated a moment before answering, "I doubt she can be in two places at once."

"Okay, well, do this. Have Black go into the hotel lobby and pay somebody to find out what room she staying in. Drop me off and you come back, because y'all two gon be on cop duty," Reck said.

Slip knew he was in for a long night.

Chapter 36

24 hours later ...

Aunt Marie looked lovely in the white and emerald green, swirl patterned, dress she wore. Her smile was radiant as the three of us conversed while sitting in her living room. I could see that she had been a very beautiful woman in her youth, a beauty that traveled well with her as she aged.

"So, did Veronica tell you that she got into NYU?" Aunt Marie asked, glowing.

"NYU, that's what's up. Congratulations. So we ready to hit the Big Apple again?" I asked.

"Well, not quite. It's just an option. I wanted to see if I could get in. I'm waiting on the University of Miami to return a response. If I don't get accepted, then it's back to the Big Apple," Ronni said.

"What do you mean if you don't get accepted? Kaeshon, this woman is a genius when it comes to history. Whether it's American, African American, Hispanic, world history. She knows it all." Aunt Marie said matter-of-factly.

"Is that right? So we're sitting next to the future history professor of the year?" I said.

"We're years off, but hopefully," Ronni said with a smile.

"Nothing to hope about dear, soon you will be," Aunt Marie said before turning to me, "So, where are you two headed tonight?"

"Yeah, where are we going?" Ronni asked as well.

"What you get all dressed up for?" Will asked Gina as she walked out of the bathroom in body strangling clothes. She sauntered around like she was ready to be the center of attention in one of LA's most scantly clad filled nightclubs.

"The same reason you about to get dressed for, so you can take me out."

"Take you out? Where?"

"I don't know. Be creative," Gina said, hands on hips.

"It was ya idea to get this suite and stay in for the couple of days we got together."

"Okay, and now it's my idea to go out."

Will nodded his head, "You on some other shit. You playin' with fire."

"No, you on some other shit, and you started playing with fire the first day I met you. So if you was really scared of Der-reck so much, then you wouldn't have been getting at his wife so tuff and making her fall in love with you," Gina said, taking a seat on his boxered lap.

"So, you in love with me?" Will asked, wrapping his arms around her.

"No, we in love with you," Gina said, taking his right hand and placing it on her belly.

"We," Will said, not getting it at first. "We," He repeated again, rubbing her belly, to which she nodded an enthusiastic yes. "We ... Naw, you bullshittin'." Will said giddily.

Gina continued her enthusiastic nod, "Yeah, we pregnant."

Malibu Castle was a combination of a water park during the day, batting cages, miniature golf and a large arcadium well into the night. With it being dark, and the mini amusement park being well lit, I thought it was a great time for us to brush up on our miniature golf skills.

"This place is awesome," Ronni said after the windmill prop deflected her putt.

"Yeah, but not your game. Come on, let me show you how a pro do this," I said, wrapping my arms around her to assist with the next shot.

"Oh, so you're Tiger Woods now," She said, pressing her back further onto me.

"More like Tiger Hood, but ya know. See what you wanna do is line up the stick perfectly with the ball and tap it just right so that it rolls smoothly into the hole," I said, assisting her light swing which ended up being deflected as well.

"Ha ha," Ronni laughed at the missed shot. "Maybe I should stand behind you while you swing, tyro."

"It happens to the best of 'em."

"And the worst," she countered.

"Yeah, yeah. Come on, let's go get something to drink," I said, leading us back inside through the arcades to where the snack and beverage stand was located.

"So, did you spend a lot of time at this place in your less mature days?" Ronni asked as we stood waiting on nachos and soda.

"Less mature days," I said with a brief laugh. "As a matter-of-fact, I did. From time to time, me and my boys used to come here back in the day to jack the more privileged kids from Redondo."

"You came here to jack?"

"Yeah, skateboards, bikes, shoes, pocket change, whatever interested us." I answered nonchalantly.

"Ay dios mio, was there ever hope for you?" She asked playfully.

"There is now," I said, giving her the once-over, making her blush.

"Don't try to flatter me, just get my nachos and soda," she joked, looking around me at the concession stand.

I paid and thanked the cashier before we walked off.

"You know, that woman over there has

been checking you out the entire time we've been in the arcade," Ronni said as we traveled back toward the golf course.

"Who?"

"Her sitting in the spaceship game making out with that guy," She nodded in the direction of a spacecraft video game console, that was without doors, partially concealing the French kissing couple.

"I don't know her, she's with her man anyways. Maybe she just cross-eyed and wasn't looking at me in the first place," I replied.

"Maybe," Ronni shrugged it off.

"Or maybe not," I said, backing up to get a better look at the two. Gina, I thought before saying, "Gina?"

She didn't look happy to see me, slightly upset even. She rolled her eyes before saying, "Kay, how have you been cutie?" In a voice as sweet as honey.

I ignored her, keeping my eyes on her companion who faced the opposite direction, refusing to look at me. "Wassup Will?" I said, emphasizing the words, which was more like saying 'you're busted again.'

"Kay," Will said, scooting from under Gina, walking around to face me, "Come on, let's go out and talk real quick," He said, leading the way out of the castle's front entrance, with me on his tail:

"So, are you Kay's ex or something?" Ronni asked Gina, trying to make small talk after they were left standing alone.

"Kay, please," Gina said before checking herself, "No offense."

"None taken," Ronni replied.

"It's just Will for me. But y'all two make a good couple."

I was as mad as a starved pit-bull by the time we descended the entrance-exit steps. Angry at the fact that Will was an idiot playing Russian Roulette with a six-shot pistol only missing one bullet. And this was his second turn to pull the trigger.

"Before you say anything-" Will started.

"Before you say anything," I let loose, "You a dumbass. You stupid as fuck."

"Yeah, what else is new."

"I guess nothing because you still creepin' around, and in public with this bitch," I spat.

Anger flashed across Will's face, "You betta kick back and watch who girl you calling a bitch."

"Girl?" I said, incredulously, "Girl," A second time.

Gina and Ronni walked out of the castle.

"You ready to go?" I asked, looking up at Ronni. She nodded a silent yes.

"Kay," Will called, reaching out.

I slapped his hand away and walked off to my car.

"You got all that?" Black asked Slip, pointing his Motorola video phone at Gina and Will as they stood watching Kay and Ronni get into the Impala and speed off.

"If I didn't, then you did, right?" Slip stated rather than ask, while he himself held up a small video camera. Which wasn't turned on.

"Yeah, I got the part that matters," Black answered.

They were parked in between a row of cars in the back watching the whole situation transpire. With Black present, Slip knew for sure that Big Reck would soon know of Gina and Will's romantic involvement.

"I apologize for cutting our night short. I should've thought about the fact that we were spending time together instead of letting Will get to me," I said to Ronni in an attempt to eradicate the silence we were riding in.

"It's okay," she answered, pausing for a beat, "I know you had your reasons, whatever they were." She said in a way that sounded like a statement and a question at the same time.

"Yeah." My simple answer, choosing to leave it as a statement and not answer a question.

"Why were you upset with him?" She

243

asked, clearly not satisfied with my simple reply.

"Will's my dawg, but he's been doing some things to put himself in harm's way lately with serious person, people." I corrected. "I don't want to see him doing anything that'll get him smashed on."

"Does it have anything to do with his girl?"

"His girl, ha," I snorted. "That happens to be the G-homie's wife."

"Whoa, I see. And the big coincidence is that we were all at the same place at the same time," Ronni said, before adding, "You know, you two are a lot alike."

"Alike how?"

"Well, let's see," She paused like she was about to state the obvious. "How ironic was it, like I said a minute ago, that we all ended up here on the same night?"

"Just a coincidence, like you said a minute ago."

She nodded her head, 'no.' "Doubtful, it proves you two think alike. You guys carry yourselves in the same manner and probably have the same goals in mind."

"Doubtful," I said, this time.

"Okay," she continued, "not to mention the fact that he's out with someone else's wife."

"What does that have to do with us being alike?"

"Come on, like you didn't see the ring on

my finger when we first met."

"You were engaged, almost married doesn't count. But her, Gina, she's married, and to the G-homie at that. A boss. I wouldn't go there. So that makes us not alike."

"How do you know Ricky wasn't a boss?"

"Because every time I seen her," I said, pointing to her, "She rode the bus, and a boss wouldn't let his woman ride the bus. It goes against one of the boss laws."

"The boss laws," she repeated with a chuckle. "What is a Boss? someone who's in charge or rich or something like that?"

"Yeah, all that. In charge, rich, the man. All that makes a boss."

"So, because I rode the bus from time to time, that eliminates Ricky from being a boss."

"Bingo."

"That's bull. There are people who live in New York who are rich and in charge who prefer to ride in taxi's or take the subway. A lot of them don't even own a car, by choice."

"Well, that may be true but this ain't New York. In LA we use cars if we have the choice. Public transportation is a dangerous inconvenience ... Do you know how to drive?" I asked after the thought came to mind.

"I choose not to drive," she answered.

"Why?"

"Because, I have you as a chauffeur now." She responded playfully.

"You don't know how to drive, huh?" I prodded further. "You don't know how to drive, do you?"

"I don't drive, but's what's so complicated about it?" She said before asking, "Why are you stopping?"

"Because," I threw the car in park on a residential street two blocks from where she lived, "You're about to drive the rest of the way home." I said after getting out to open her door.

"Yeah right, stop playing."

"I'm not. Get behind the wheel."

"No Kay, I don't want to drive."

"That's because you don't know how. I'ma show you, come on." I held my hand out.

"Un un," she pouted, crossing her arms.

"Girl, you 23 going on 38. Now get ya mature ass behind the wheel so I can show you how to drive."

She punched me in the arm before obliging. "If I dent your car it's your fault," she said, buckling up.

"Okay, your gas is on the right and your brake is on the left. You have to put your foot on the brake before you can put the car back in gear," I instructed.

"I wasn't born yesterday."

"Okay, but you have to adjust the mirrors before you start driving, to cover your blind spots."

"Okay," she said, doing so nervously.

"Okay," Putting the car in drive. "Okay," she breathed and drove up about three yards before braking, two more yards, brake, four yards, brake. The car jerking back and fourth with each brake pump.

"Hey. Okay. Ay," I said, one hand bracing the dashboard, the other towards her. "Newborn, you're not supposed to drive with both feet on the pedals."

She looked at me, hands turned over as if to ask, 'how?'

"Okay, it might be easier to use only your right foot on the brake. When you're ready to drive, switch it to the gas, easily."

"Okay." She did so, driving forward once more, smoothly this time.

"Okay, you have to keep the car in the middle of the lane. You don't want to veer off and hit someone's parked car."

"Okay, okay." She breathed, straightening out the wheel.

"It's not like riding go-carts at the Coney Island boardwalk, is it?" I joked, to which we both shared a laugh.

I felt somewhat better when I returned to the motel room, until I noticed Will's SUV parked at the far end of the lot. I know he didn't like the way things ended with us earlier, so he probably was waiting on me to explain his position. Which didn't matter because he didn't keep his original word to me about ceasing his relationship with Gina.

When I opened the door, Gina was sitting on the bed, legs crossed, watching an 11:30 p.m. news program.

"What you doing here?" I asked upon eye contact.

"I need to talk to you," Gina responded.

"Where Will at?" I asked, noticing the room was dark but for the TV's glare. I cut on the table lamp, filling the room with its dull yellow light.

"Back at our room, sleep. He don't know I'm here."

"Bullshit, because you wouldn't have known where this spot was, let alone have the key to get in," I responded to her lie.

She stood up and took the couple of steps to stand in front of me. "Look, Kay, I know you don't like me, right ..." She began talking but I tuned her out to look at her person instead. She had on expensive looking, Fendi, dark brown open toed four inch suede stilettos. A small, thorned, red rose was tattooed above her right ankle, which was the only mark on her caramel complexion legs. Her black skirt was silk and at least five inches above her knees, exposing toned thigh muscles. Surprisingly, the dark brown top she wore reached the waistband of her skirt, but the cross-top for cleavage left nothing but the nipples to the imagination. She looked like a high priced call girl.

"Kay, Will needs you, as his friend to be supportive of him and his decisions," Gina went on.

"And what decision is that? What y'all gon do, run away together?"

She lowered her head, her long press and curled hair brushing past her shoulders. "If we have to," She said, and I knew she was serious.

Why it came to mind, immediately I don't know, but, "You were kicking it with ES before Reck got out of the FEDS?" I asked, which was more like an accusation.

She made eye contact with me, "ES … No, I barely knew ES." She broke eye contact. "I never kicked it with him."

I didn't believe her. "Why'd you marry Big Reck?" I asked.

"Money."

"Well, Will ain't got it like that."

"I know, it's not about that," she said defensively.

"I think you need to put more thought into the situation you put my homie in. As far as I know, you probably being followed."

"No, as far as they know, I'm out of state," she countered.

"Yeah, okay," I said, stepping back to hold the door open.

"You know the difference between Big Reck and Will?" She asked, stopping in front of me on her way out. "I don't love Big Reck, I never have, but I love Will and I want to be with him. Money or not." She put one foot through the open door before stopping again, "Look, Will needs you just like I need him. He told me you one of the only people he trust, and if you his homie like you say you is, then you'll ride for him. You all he got, because Slip is a snake." She stepped out.

I did a peripheral scan before slinking back in to watch her take off in Will's ride through the cracked curtains until the tail lights had completely vanished. I was sure no one was following her.

I was awakened by a combination of my phone's loud ringtone and someone banging on the door. The alarm clock on the stand displayed 10:01 a.m. I reached for my cell, which had stopped ringing by the time I got grip of it. There were 4 missed calls, 2 from Slip, 2 from Ronni.

I opened the door, "What the hell you bangin' on the door like a madman for?" I asked when I found Will standing there.

"What the hell you still sleeping like an old man for?" He replied, walking in.

"What you want?"

"To whoop yo ass, but that's a different story."

"You wanna whoop my ass, you better had packed a lunch," I yawned. "I should whoop yo ass for sending Gina here last night."

He looked baffled, "She came over here?"

"Don't play stupid."

"I'm not. What she tell you?"

"Before or after I hit it from the back?"

Silence. Will sat there looking at me seriously.

"I don't know, she told me some bullshit about Slip being a snake. Uh, she love you, and um, that y'all gon run away together."

"That's it?"

"That's it? What you mean that's it? That's all I need to know. Y'all gon run away together?"

"I came here to talk to you about that lick," Will said, instead of answering the question.

Without hesitation, I nodded 'no'.

"This is a minimum of $250,000 I'm talkin' about, and you turning this down?"

"Yeah, a quarter mil sound good, but that's the kind of money that people put their life on the line for."

"And we done put our lives on the line for less," Will countered.

"Understandable, but somebody might get laid down chasing this lick. Whether it be us or them. Mo money, mo problems."

"No money all problems," Will retorted.

"I'm kick back for a while."

"Is that you or what's her name talkin'?"

Silence.

"What's up with you, Kay? You use to be all for this type of shit," Will continued. "Remember what we use to say …"

"All we need is one good lick," I answered, which Will repeated with me.

"That's all we need, and this is it. Think about it Kay, yo album, all them songs you made, hot. We was always talkin' about starting our own label. Putting it out ourselves, making them come to us. You know what I'm sayin'? It's me and you, Hustle Official Entertainment."

A smile crossed my face thinking of the label we had thought up some years ago. "Yeah, I came across some new beats from Dae-One and the Trendsettas. Yeah, that shit been bangin' lately."

"See that's what I'm saying, it's always been bangin'. You got the website, all we need is to press up a hundred-thousand CDs, get the shirts, chains, and we in the game," Will said.

"Sounds good, but I don't know."

"What's not to know?"

I sighed, "It's gotta be a better way."

"A better way?" He questioned.

"Look, I recommend that you don't do it at all, but if you do, get at Slip. We both know he wit' it."

"Nah, I need you on this."

"I'm not-" I started to say before …

"She pregnant," he cut me off.

"What?"

"She pregnant," he repeated.

"Gina? ... Hell nah, dawg. Are you serious? Tell me you playin', right?"

"This is as real as it gets," he responded.

"Damn it, Will. What the fuck was you thinkin'? Damn!" I said, hardly able to believe this predicament.

"I know, but it's mine. I gotta get my paper straight, put it into somethin' productive. So I can have a future and be able to take care of my responsibility," Will said before pausing a beat. "Ay, if you help me with this, on everything, this the last time and we ain't gotta worry about no more penitentiary chances."

My phone rang, the screen displaying Ronni's number. Sighing, I looked up at Will, "A'ight, when and where?" I asked and listened before returning her call.

Chapter 37

"So, the letter just came and guess what?" Ronni asked Jessica and Slip, who faced her in their booth at a sparsely filled Denny's.

"What? You got in?" Jessica asked excitedly.

Ronni nodded, equally excited. "I got in."

"Aaah," Jessica shrieked excitedly, sliding past Slip to grab Ronni and jump for joy.

"Congratulations Ronni, where'd you get into?" Slip inquired.

"She got into the University of Miami," Jessica answered before she could.

"That's what's up. Lunch and drinks on me," He said before pausing, "Where Kay at?"

"He should be on his way," Ronni answered.

"There he goes right there," Jessica said, watching the Impala pull into the restaurant's parking lot.

"Sup, sup," I said, exchanging greetings, sliding in the booth beside Ronni; giving her a big kiss on the cheek. "Y'all look hella pleasant today," I commented on their bouncy behavior.

"That's because we're all about to go on vacation," Jessica said.

"Where?"

Slip said, "Jess, this isn't your moment to give away," before Jessica could speak.

"Tell him Ronni," Jessica said instead.

"Tell me Ronni."

"Miami, I got accepted," Ronni said with a light shrug.

"No shit?" I asked.

"Yeah," she agreed.

"That's what I'm talkin' about," I said, wrapping my arm around her, giving her a kiss on the forehead above her enormous smile.

"And we are all going out there to spend a week with her before the summer is over," Jessica said, matter-of-factly.

"Yeah," I said, looking from Jessica to Slip.

"Yeah." Slip agreed.

I nodded, "Sounds like a plan." I signaled for Slip, "Let me get at you real brief," I said, sliding out of the booth.

"What's up Kay?" Slip asked as soon as we made it outside, before lighting up a black&mild cigarillo.

"You, my nig. I haven't seen you around lately, what's up with that?"

"Shit, you know, been working lately, getting down with Reck. Keepin' my pockets chunky," Slip replied, taking another pull on the cigar.

"I'm good." I waved off his offer of the cigar, "What you got going on in the next couple of days?"

"Not too much. Nothin' today. I'm pickin' up Gina from the airport tomorrow."

"Where she coming from?"

Another pull and exhale. "New Orleans," Slip answered, which lead me to believe that he didn't know about Will and Gina this second time.

"What's up with the G-homie?" I asked, fishing further.

"Who? Big Reck? You know the big homie just livin' up. As a matter-of-fact, he asked about you and Will. You know, why y'all don't come holla at him. Shit like that."

"Yeah, I'll have to stop by, hopefully I can get on and start ballin' like you," I joked.

"Cut that out. You Scrooge McDuck, you stay savin'. Shit, this car the only thing you ever put money into. A Chevy at that. Like you ain't got Benz money. I know yo bank account stay fat."

"I wish," I said, looking inside the restaurant to see Jessica and Veronica approaching. "You feel like going somewhere better to celebrate?"

Chapter 38

"I like Jessica and Slip as a couple, as odd as the two of them together may seem, they're cool people. I had a great time with them, and you." Ronni said, pressing her body closer to mine, lying with her head directly under my chin, on my chest. Which I knew she was doing to listen to the sound of my heartbeat.

"Why're Jessica and Slip an odd couple?" I asked, my focus on the ceiling above. We were in Ronni's room in aunt Marie's house; fully clothed of course.

"Well, it's Slip mainly. Like his whole style, the way he walks, talks, the tattoos, the way he's always serious," Ronni said.

"Gangsta," I said, breaking her description down to one word.

"Yeah, but like, volcanic. It's like he has the patience of a person who has done a lot of years in prison, and the low tolerance level of a person who has done a lot of years in prison."

"Yeah."

"And compare that to Jessica who's like ..."

"White," I said, providing another one word description.

Ronni chuckled, "Yeah, white, but adorable and so much different from what I would imagine Slip being with or her with him, for that matter."

"You sure have been checking into Slip's gangsta a whole lot lately. What's up with that?"

"Huh?"

"Huh," I mocked. "Too many long Island iced teas, huh? You tipsy?"

"Shut up, it's not like that. I'm not checking into anybody's gangsta. Just pointing out the obvious."

"Okay, since you're pointing out the obvious, what about my gangsta?"

"What?" She tilted her head back to observe me.

"Yeah, you like the Boriqua equivalent to Jessica when it comes to me and this gangstaness."

She laughed. "You're cute," she said before kissing me on the chin.

"I'm serious, fa real."

She studied me a moment before saying, "You are so much more than that."

"If you only knew."

"I do." She placed her head back on my chest.

"Hey, so I'm glad you enjoyed yourself today," I said, deciding to change the subject.

"Not just today, lately. I've been enjoying myself lately. Every time I go somewhere with you I enjoy myself."

"That's good to know. So, if I could take you anywhere in the world, where would you want to go?"

"The beach."

"The beach?"

"Yeah, the beach is great, especially late at night. I love the atmosphere."

"Of all the places in the world you would want me to take you to, you want to go to the beach?"

"Yeah, the beach, and … when it's time to go, I want you to take me to Miami," Ronni said.

"Okay, so the beach at night, and when it's time to go, you want me to fly with you out to Miami, right?"

"Yeah, the beach and then with me to Miami … to stay."

Chapter 39

Flight 714 from New Orleans to LAX was scheduled to arrive at 3:45 p.m. Gina had called Reck the previous night and informed him of the estimated landing time. Predictably, he insured her that Slip would be waiting on her when she walked through the gate.

The current time was 3:27 p.m., her scheduled flight hadn't arrived yet, and neither had Slip. She was praying that he wouldn't arrive until the last minute, hopefully by that time the plane would have, so that she and her lone carry-on bag could blend in with the rest of the passengers.

She sat in the back of the terminal lobby, between several people, with a sun hat on and large block-style D&G shades. This morning her and Will had went over their plans for the future. Before catching a taxi to the airport, she withdrew all of her savings, $79,000, in a single cashiers check. $79,000, she thought to herself. What she had been able to save over the years from the allowance Big Reck gave her. She should've had ten-times as much being married to a multi-millionaire. But Reck was stringent and liked to keep people dependent him. Want some new shoes, new clothes, ask big daddy, satisfy his ego. No joint bank account like a traditional married couple, no, the only thing they shared was a bed. Which could hardly be said, thanks to his constant 'business' absences. He didn't want her anymore, ever since the rumor spread about her being with ES while he was in prison. But, he felt he owned her, that she was his to keep for life.

At 3:40 p.m., her thoughts drifted to Will. Will appreciated her, showered her with compliments and praise, always put her first sexually, and treated her like the queen she felt she was. He was strong and wasn't afraid to go after what he wanted. She had developed strong feelings for him and the new life she carried within only added fuel to her emotions. Today it would all come down to them. However their robbery of Reck's connect would go, their success would determine how good a start her and Will would have. She was glad that they could convince Kay to go along with it. Seeing as how it wasn't a one man mission, maybe not even two, but according to the stories Will shared about their previous stick-ups, she knew that the two of them could get the job done.

At 3:52, the New Orleans flight had arrived. Gina called Slip's phone to discover that he'd been waiting in the airport's entrance/exit lobby for the past 20 minutes. She met him at his car in front of the airport express way.

"How was ya trip?" He asked when she approached.

"Fine, thank you." She replied, holding her Burberry luggage bag towards him.

"What I look like? You betta put that shit in the back yourself," he said, walking around to get in the car.

Chapter 40

"How're we supposed to do this again?" I asked Will from the passenger seat of the tinted window, '96, midnight blue, Honda Civic we idled in. We were in an alley sandwiched between four empty cars at the edge of Downtown LA, not far from Chinatown.

"As soon as they make the drop, we roll up and ambush um. Simple as that," He replied easily.

Looking at my cell, it was 6:10 in the evening. The sun was still beaming bright but was shadowed by the building lengths between the alley. "And they ain't got nobody watchin' they back from a distance?" I prodded further.

"I sat at every angle around this area for the last month watching them make the money and dope switch. Which they do every second Tuesday. I ain't never seen nobody but the Mexican dude and woman. As far as I know, it's just them two and whatever weapons they got. Now the people they switch with is always the same Samoan dude and a Black dude, in business suits.

They get out, give them the cash in a brief case, get they dope and leave."

"Let me see the binoculars." I reached for them, scanning the rooftops in view.

Will scrunched up his face. "What you lookin' for? Snipers? Man ain't no snipers on the roof."

"Never can tell dealing with you. You say they wear suits, they might be the FEDS."

"They ain't no FEDS."

"How you know?"

"Because they damu. I followed them to they hood in Carson, and the Mexican couple I followed up into Pico Rivera before turning back when I realized they were going to East LA."

"So they meet here, sorta like a middle ground?"

"Exactly, but our target is the Mexican couple, because they end up with the money. So we gotta move quickly before they hit the main street and make it to East LA, because by then it's gon be a wrap." Will said.

"Yeah," I agreed.

Two more minutes passed before any sign of activity took place. A dark green Lexus ES pulled into the empty alley on the other end of the street. Followed by a black Suburban.

"Get ready," Will said, pulling a duffle bag from the back seat to the armrest between us. In the bag was an AR-15 that Will would be handling and a 12 gauge shot gun and .45 Ruger, that I would have control of.

I made sure the black leather gloves I donned were tight around my fingers. On top of my head, as well as Will's, was a clearish-gray facemask that would obstruct our facial features.

Out of the passenger side of the Lexus, a leggy Hispanic woman of about 30 got out wearing a black, knee length, wrap dress. Her hair was pulled into a tight bun. I could only see the side of her face from the angle in which we sat, but what I seen looked attractive and out of place for the circumstance.

The driver of the Lexus was an average looking, average sized Hispanic man in a dark blue suit. He was the first to step around the car to greet the occupants of the Suburban.

The driver of the Suburban was a large Samoan man in a black and gray pinstripe suit. He wore his hair in a long ponytail, and I recognized him immediately as Sial, the Samoan who worked for ES and delivered the weed and dope to me on his behalf a few years ago. The Samoan, I knew was a Damu (Blood) from Carson as Will had said, but the passenger was not.

Out of the passenger seat of the Suburban stepped Slip, in a dark chocolate colored suit, carrying a black briefcase. I'd never seen him dressed like this before, and immediately I knew he was on business for Big Reck. I looked over at Will disapprovingly.

"You got us out here about to rob Reck's connection?" I asked sourly.

"Reck's connection. Not Reck." Will clarified.

"Fool, you done lost yo mind. You tryna get us killed?"

"I don't know how, Slip ain't about to see it. He gonna be gone by the time we do it."

"Nah, get us out of here," I demanded.

"There go the switch right there," He said, watching Slip hand the woman the briefcase and the Hispanic man hand Sial two briefcases in exchange. "Ready?" Will said, starting the car as the Suburban holding Sial and Slip drove off.

The Lexus started to do a 'k' turn to exit their end of the alley when Will sped towards them before they could make it out.

"Come on," He said, shifting the car to neutral, hoping out, mask down, AR-15 in hand.

I followed suit with the 12 gauge.

We crisscrossed, Will to the Lexus driver side, I to the passenger. "Cut off the car and get out," Will commanded the driver, who obliged the AR-15 trained at his face.

"You get out too," I commanded the passenger, who stepped out with her hands up and an angry scowl on her face. "Open the door, throw me the briefcase," I instructed further. "Try anything stupid and I'ma put a hole in that pretty face of yours," I threatened, which must have hit home for her because she tossed me the case perfectly, with no hesitation. "Now lay on the ground," I said, watching her do so before tossing the briefcase in the Honda's open driver side door.

"You too. Throw me the keys and lay on the ground," Will told the man, who didn't hesitate.

"HEY, FREEZE." Was yelled from behind me.

I spun quickly to see a plain clothes cop behind the door of an unmarked Ford Taurus at the edge of the alley.

'PAP-PAP.' Will fired two quick shots at the man and car, causing him to mistakenly jump out of the doors cover and quickly scramble behind another car out of view.

Another car rolled up with two similar looking occupants as the other officer. BOOM. I let off a thunderous shot at their front tire, blowing it out. The car swerved as the driver and passenger ducked for cover on the inside. "Come on," I shouted to Will, hopping behind the Honda's wheel quickly, foot on the brake putting the car in gear.

Will dived in, his body halfway out when I stomped on the gas, burning rubber around, and almost ran over the woman's leg as she laid on the ground. I swerved around the Lexus, gunning towards the end of the alley. In the rearview mirror I seen the woman hop up, legs spread, gun drawn with two hands, squeezing off four shots. Two of the bullets smashed into the trunk before I hooked a left at the end of the alley and then another quick left before an immediate right on Main, headed into China Town, well into traffic.

With no sign of the Ford Taurus or any other police cruisers, we made it home free onto the 10 freeway. I didn't stop to breathe until we exited on La Brea, down South Central and crossed into Inglewood.

"Come on, this room right here," I said to Will, referring to the motel room to the right of mine.

"What you do? Switch rooms?" Will asked as we entered.

"Nah, but don't nobody know I got this room, but you. This the new stash room."

"No wonder nobody else really be at this motel, you buying all the rooms."

I sat the briefcase down on the neatly made bed. "That was too close, we almost got washed up."

"But we didn't," Will responded quickly.

"Had I known that was Reck's business, I wouldn't have went with yo stupid ass."

"I know, that's why I drove out there," Will said with a triumphant grin.

"No wonder you didn't want Slip to go with you."

"N-E ways." Will dismissed the conversation, walking around to pop open the briefcase.

The inside of the case must've put him in awe as it did me, because we both just stood there a moment, silent, staring at its contents.

Back at home, Gina was seated on the middle couch. The large plasma screen TV was muted, its program she was not paying attention to. Big Reck was out, where? She didn't know. He didn't answer his phone when she attempted to call, which was fine with her because it gave her time to get the details of her trip together.

Msg from W: 'done deal', Gina's cell phone chimed.

'4real', Gina texted back.

Msg from W: 'yep'. Will replied with a smiley face, which peaked Gina's excitement as she shrieked and jumped for joy.

"What you so happy about?" Reck asked, appearing behind her.

"Derreck," she said, caught off guard, "I didn't hear you come in."

"How could you, over all that hoopin' and hollerin'."

"You know I missed you right?" Gina said, throwing her arms around him.

"I'm glad you did, now get dressed, I'm about to take you out to dinner."

"Three hundred and sixty thousand dollars," I said slowly after the last stack of twenties was counted. I was attempting to get my eyes and mouth to convince my brain that that was what the numerous stacks of bills on the bed amounted to.

"Man, $360,000," Will repeated, phone in hand.

"What you doin'?"

"Sending Gina a text."

"Nah, don't do that," I said, clamping my hand over his phone. "That's incriminating evidence. You don't know if Big Reck be going through her phone or not. Tell her when you see her."

"Yeah, you right." Will agreed. "Damn, $360,000, that was a lot more than I thought."

I nodded, "I know."

"A'ight, here's what we gon do." Will grabbed a hefty stack, what I knew was $100,000. "We gon take this hundred stacks and do what I said before, put ya CD out."

I nodded my head, 'no'.

"What you mean, No?"

"We can't be spending no money like that, we gotta be low-key." I answered.

"We are gonna be lo-key. It's just CDs. It's not like we buyin' chains and cars yet. Look, a 100k will get us at least 75 thousand CDs with professional album covers and CD cases. We print a million fliers to handout, internet campaign, and get the lil homies and home girls to sell the CDs at 5 dollars a piece. Shit, that's $370,000 we make back in a couple of months and we in the game."

"Yeah," I said absently, staring into space.

"Yeah? That's it? It sound like you don't want to do it."

"Nah, it ain't that. I was just thinking about something that Ronni said to me."

"What was that?" Will inquired.

"She going to Miami for college, she leaving in like a month. When we was posted yesterday, she told me that she wanted me to go out there with her to stay. I don't know if she was playin or not, but I think she was serious."

"If she was serious, would you consider going?"

"That sounded like a suggestion."

"I don't know, but I've been thinkin' about someplace to go, you know, and Miami seems like an a'ight place."

"You really serious about packin' up and leaving with Gina, huh?"

Will looked at me earnestly before answering, "yeah, dawg, that's why we did this. I wouldn't have had us out there taking a chance like that if it wasn't real."

"Yeah."

"I think going to Miami would be a good idea for all of us. We can start out fresh and not have to worry about the bullshit like out here in L.A." Will continued his pitch.

"Bullshit? You act like you been through a lot. This Inglewood! The city ain't neva been bad to us."

"We gon always be from Inglewood, and let it be known everywhere we go, but at the same time we always talkin' about how we want better, right?" Will asked. I just stared at him. "Now I'm about to be a father and you got a smart girl who loves you and wants to be with you," he went on.

"That may be true, but you just putting it out there because you want somebody to roll with you on the lam," I said jokingly.

"Hell yeah! Why wouldn't I want my dawg with me? We can link up, get a spot, open a business, you know, all that." Will spoke optimistically. "Besides man, I been thinkin' about going back to college myself. Miami could use a good cornerback." He grew somber. Hopefully they won't hold my past at USC against me. I don't know." He shrugged, "maybe I can make the Dolphins, you know, third string or somethin'. Work my way up. What you think?"

"Hey, I think you got game and can do whatever you put yo mind to, for real."

"Yeah," he nodded. "I'm about to go drop off that Honda somewhere. We'll leave the money here in the meantime, right?"

"Yeah, I'll cut open the side of the mattress and put the bread in there and sew it back up."

"Right, we'll catch up later. Finalize those

Miami plans. And take yo ass to the studio and get our product ready," Will said, smiling, before he left.

Chapter 41

The following day I decided to take Will's advice and go to the studio. The album was near completion with only the mastering phase left. I had taken some flicks around the hood for the album artwork, as well as some personal photos with Ronni on the water-docks and piers at the beach.

"I like seeing you like this," Ronni said to me, opposite our exotic dish filled table. We were at, 'Seafood on the Rocks', which akin to its name, sat at the edge of the beach dock on rocks, constantly splashed by the white waves of the ocean.

"Like what?" I asked.

"You know, pleasant, smiling, enjoying yourself."

I flashed another smile, "Well, it's mainly thanks to you. You bring the best out of me."

"Do I?" She asked coyly.

"Of course. You're like a ray of sunshine during the darkest times. I hate to sound selfish, but I'm kind of glad that what's-his-name forgot how unique and precious you are, because had he remembered, I wouldn't be sitting here with you right now."

She blushed before saying, "I'm yours, you don't have to run game on me."

"I wouldn't dare," I answered with a two finger wave around her.

"What'd you do that for?"

"Huh?"

"Huh, the wa-" she started to say but was cut off by six waitresses and waiters singing happy birthday to you.

"Birthday, are you serious?" I barely heard her say over the singing. We both knew it wasn't her birthday.

Grinning, I mouthed the words, "free cake."

"So, baby, where did you say we were going again? I wanna know how I should dress?" Gina asked Reck as he sat fumbling with the DVD player.

"I was thinking," Big Reck said, walking over to guide Gina towards the middle couch, "We should stay in and watch this movie I just picked up. You know, like we use to do."

"Like we use to do?" Gina asked seductively, remembering how they could never make it through a movie before going at it.

"Umm-hmmm," Big Reck hummed, wrapping his massive arm around her shoulder.

Gina pressed up against him, "You know we never use to be able to make it through a movie." She reminded him.

"I know, but this one is good."

"What is it?" She inquired.

"Infidelity 2," Reck said, remote in hand, pushing play.

The video popped on displaying the Radisson hotel's entrance. The video was shot from a side view, evidently from behind the wheel of someone's car like a private investigator. Out of the entrance walked Will alongside Gina, arm in arm to Will's Land Rover.

Gina grew stiff sitting next to Reck, her whole being was overtaken with fear.

The video continued, showing the Rover being followed through traffic to Malibu Castle.

She tried to get up from the couch but Reck's arm wouldn't permit it.

The Video continued, showing Will and Kay's spat while Gina watched from the steps, eventually walking up to comfort Will as Kay and an unknown female sped off.

"Derreck, it's not what you think," Gina said shakily, wiggling out of his embrace.

"Then what is it?" Reck asked calmly.

Gina searched for an answer, but none came.

"Because, while you were out I had a camera set up in that hotel suite of y'all's, watching you flip every nasty little trick in the book. Let me show you," he said, pushing fast forward.

"No," Gina protested abruptly.

Reck pressed stop, lifting and crossing his feet on the coffee table. "Look at you, you don't have nothing to say, huh?"

"Look, baby, I'm sorry. I know I messed up," Gina said.

"You ain't the only one," Reck blurted.

"Yes, yes, it was all me. Will didn't have anything to do with it. I came on to him, please Derreck, believe me." Gina pleaded, knowing the danger Will was in now.

"So it was all you, you just took control over his mind and dick," Reck said, amused.

"Yes, it was me. I swear he didn't want nothing to do with me but I kept coming at him," Gina said frantically.

He waved her off, "Where is he at?"

"Why? What are you going to do to him?"

"The question is, what am I going to have someone do to that lying-ass momma of yours out in New Orleans."

Horrified, Gina gasped, hand over her mouth, "Please, you wouldn't. Reck please."

Reck grabbed the cordless phone and dialed a number that was answered quickly. "Black, how's the south?" He asked, putting the phone on speaker.

"Got the old lady, her other daughter, and some old fool tied up." The person on the other end said.

"Put her on," Reck ordered.

"Gina, Gina I-" The older woman shrieked before the phone was yanked away.

"Mom," Gina yelled, knowing the voice immediately to be her mother's. "Mom," she screeched again, breaking down with racking sobs.

Reck hung up the phone, "You playing with lives. Call him," He barked.

She reached for the phone, "No," Reck knocked her hand away, "Use your cell phone, he ain't answering no other calls."

Gina did as told, hoping that Will wouldn't answer, but her hope failed to materialize when he picked up after the second ring.

"Hello," She said when he answered, watching Reck glare at her. "No, I'm fine ... Where you at? ... Hawthorne, where? Servin' on Lemoli ... No, I can't right now ... Okay, watch your back, I gotta go," She said the latter quickly before Reck snatched the phone away.

He grabbed his phone in turn and placed a call.

Chapter 42

"You know, this whole beach thing is a typical cliché," I said as I walked down the deserted sand alongside Ronni. Farther away from human contact, closer to seclusion.

"Why is that?" She asked.

I shrugged, "Because it's overrated on a date. It's starting to become like the movies."

"Well, maybe it is to you LA natives where almost every main east or west street runs directly into the beach. I've only been three times in my life. This is the second time out here and the first time my feet has touched the sand," she said, tugging my arm to stop. "Besides, I think it's romantic."

"Yeah, it can be," I said, spreading out one of the two blankets I'd brought with me in a backpack.

"Especially on nights like this when there is no one else around," Ronni continued, sitting side by side with me, looking at the small waves dancing on the ocean's surface.

"Yeah, especially on nights like this," I

agreed.

"I can't wait to go to Miami, to get started with college. Just working towards what I want to do with my life."

"Why Miami? Aren't you already in college?" I asked.

"Yeah, community college. This is a big step ahead. I can meet all of my educational needs at a university. Besides, it's always been my dream to go to this school."

"I'm glad one of your dreams is coming true," I said, smoothing back the loose hairs, blown by the breeze, that were starting to block her face.

"The semester begins in September," she reminded me.

"Yeah," I said distantly, my forever reply when I did not have or care to answer right away. In this case it was not having an immediate answer. I didn't have an answer that would satisfy either one of us. September was just a couple of months away and Miami was a thousand miles on the opposite side of the country. A distance like that could have a negative effect on our relationship. I wanted to ask her why she couldn't go to a California university, USC, UCLA, or even Berkley up north would be less complicating than Florida.

"I want you to go with me," she said, cutting my thoughts short. Her head was buried in my chest when she spoke, like she was embarrassed of what she'd just said.

"What was that?" I asked, even though I heard her.

"I said, I want you to go with me," she said with more confidence this time, looking me in the eye. "I mean, um, if you want to."

"Me and Will had a conversation about this yesterday."

"About you going with me?"

"About leaving in general. I mentioned you going to Miami for school purposes. He thought it was a great idea, that maybe he could play football for the university or the Dolphins, possibly. He's ready for a change and feel that it would be best outside of LA." I laughed lightly, "And that we should all roll."

"Sooo?" She said questioningly, "What do you think?"

"I think that you should think about this further. It'll be kind of like deja vu for you, right?" I said, referring to her past situation of moving out here with Ricky.

"I have," she said, looking at me before turning her focus to the restless ocean. "I've thought about it for some time now. One day I just woke up and realized that I want to be with you, no matter where I'm at. I know the person you can be." She returned her focus to me, "I know how special you are."

Remaining silent, I held her stare for a moment before looking up at the paleness of the moon, and then the blackness of the ocean.

"I feel that it will be real good for you. A change of scenery, a fresh start. You should think about it. It'll be good for the both of us."

"Okay," I answered, not sure if I was completely willing to commit to this proposal of the two of us moving to Miami together, however at the moment it didn't sound like a bad idea.

"Okay?" Ronni asked in return, not sure if I was saying okay to thinking or going.

"Okay, I'll go wi-" I started to say but couldn't finish when she pressed her lips against mine fiercly, then giving me a series of pecks.

His mind was heavy as he drove down the night drenched street. Heavy with childhood memories, a time of innocence. A time when the only thing a boy thought about was video games, sports, and riding bikes with his buddies. A time when having money and responsibility wasn't king. These were times that he shared with Will.

He stopped at the red light on Lemoli and Rosecrans, knowing that Will was stationed on the other end of the block at a spot that the two of them controlled along with Kay.

The light turned green and Slip cruised stealthily through the intersection like a panther in the black on black Expedition. The other end of the small apartment lined street was nearly empty except for a couple in their late teens hanging out. Slip sailed up slowly, rolling by the spot, he spotted Will and a young homie he knew from Compton standing on the steps. "Ay, Slip." He heard Will yell as he drove by. He stopped and contemplated for five seconds before reversing, watching as Will jogged up to the side of his SUV.

"What's up? What you was just gon keep driving?" Will asked through the window.

"Nah, I was on my way to retrieve somethin'." Slip answered. "How the money been?"

"Slow. I been over here all day with the lil homie. We probably made like $400 bucks and that's off of solid customers. Where you bout to go?"

"Around the corner. I got swooped on by the haters earlier. I threw a whole pack of dope out the window before they pulled me over." Slip lied, "You gon help me find it?"

"Man, that shit probably gon by now."

"I doubt it. That's a thousand dollars worth of work I threw out the window. We need to get that back."

"A'ight, let me grab my shit. I'll tell the lil homie to close up shop." Will jogged off.

Me or him, me or him, Slip breathed to himself mantra-like, knowing the task he had to carryout on one of his best friends. Me or him.

"Where you throw it at?" Will asked, climbing into the Expedition.

"The river," Slip said, referring to the large

concrete bridge drain that ran under 147th Street.

"The river, damn, it might still be there if it's kinda dry."

Veronica crossed her leg over mine, sitting on my lap as she lifted the satin blouse she wore over her head. Which left nothing but the strapless, see-thru, black lace bra cupping her breast. I moved my hands slowly, but slightly firm, up and down her sides as our tongues continued to slowly tango with one another. She lifted the shirt over my head as well. I traced my fingers around the edge of her skirt, and then the opening, running my hands along her smooth thighs and butt and then up to her lower back when she started to unbuckle my pants. Together we worked them down to my knees before she took me in her hand, reverse joystick, lifting herself up to put me inside. Her pussy felt like a warm, thick, glove of honey as she slid down slowly, second after second, until she reached the end of my shaft. Being in her this deep caused me to rise and thicken to my fullest potential, which was a little more than she could handle as she adjusted herself up about two inches from its base before rhythmically gyrating up and down.

"We should've brought some flashlights. I can't see nothing out here," Will said, walking under 147th St. that made the bridge of the river drain he and Slip were standing in.

"Keep looking, if it's out here it'll be around this area," Slip said, hand in his waist band, not far behind Will.

"Yeah, I'ma use the light from my cell phone," Will said, flipping open his Motorola, scanning it over the half-dry ground.

"Ay, dawg, remember that time in the 9th grade when we got caught ditching school by the sheriff's and we ran down here to get away from them?" Will asked, reminiscing.

"Yeah, yeah," Slip said with a smile at the thought. "You talkin about that time when Kay ass fell all in the shitty rain water and got caught." Slip laughed.

"Yeah," Will shared his laughter, "The homie ain't got no wheels, he got caught as soon as they started chasing us. Ay, his white Tee was all brown when they caught him."

"Ay, yeah, blood somethin' else, he was all gettin' shit on the police tryna wrestle with 'em," Slip continued hysterically. "Remember what he said when he got back to the hood?"

"Man, why y'all niggas leave me." They imitated simultaneously, breaking down with laughter.

"Like he wanted us to get caught with him," Slip went on.

Will laughed before pausing, "What's that for?" He asked, regarding the .40 glock Slip was holding.

"Huh?" Slip said, almost forgetting he had the piece while caught in the moment. "You already know." He sighed glumly, raising the gun.

She had began to quicken the pace, her tight, erotic slick insides gripping at me with each stroke. She wrapped her arms around my neck, placing her chin on my shoulder to brace herself as she rode harder, panting and moaning the whole way through. I pulled her closer, going deeper, farther, wanting to be one. Helping her, pumping harder.

"Kay, Kay," She breathed, "I-I." She started to say when she reached a trembling climax, blessing the moment with a wave of wetness.

"You what?" I asked, placing her on her back, reentering, not quite finished yet.

"I love you," she pulled me down to say in my ear. "I love you, Kaeshon," she mumbled as I began to stroke some more.

"We been knowing each other since kindergarten, and this is what it comes down to?" Will asked Slip, who held the pistol trained at his chest.

"Will, you hardheaded man, always have been. I told you, Kay told you. You seen what happened to ES and you still wanted to sleep with that rat," Slip said.

Will's phone rang. He lifted it to answer.

"Put the phone down," Slip demanded in a menacing manner.

Will obeyed, lowering the phone to his side but not before noticing the number as Gina's. Which reminded him of the life she carried within. "Of all the people he could send, he sent you. My own homeboy," Will spat, solemnly.

"Damn, Will, if you only would've listened. You put my life on the line too ... It's either me or you." Slip spoke regretfully.

Hearing those last words made Will realize that negotiating was pointless. Slip brought him under the bridge to kill him. He lunged at Slip, hurling a right-cross at his chin, reaching for the gun with his left. 'BOWW.' The pistol went off at the same instance as the punch staggered Slip. Will was hit in the left quadricep, but fueled by adrenaline, he continued his charge, this time seizing Slip's gun wrist before he could regain complete balance. 'BOWW, BOWW.' Two more shots echoed into the air as the struggle of strength ensued, hands on top of wrist, the firearm being pointed in every direction up. Will jolted a knee in Slip's groin area, missing by inches, hitting his inner thigh, causing a slight buckle. Slip countered with a crashing headbutt that connected with Will's left cheek, and another at the bridge of his nose, causing Will to blink rapidly, consciously losing his grip on Slip's wrist, doubling back.

"Slip." Will huffed pleadingly. "Jason, come on man." He said, using his real name, hands up in surrender. "It's me, it's Will."

"I know," Slip said remorsefully, pulling the trigger.

"You know I love you, right?" Ronni asked, arms wrapped around my waist and my arm around her shoulder as we walked back through the sand.

"So I've heard," I said playfully.

"Have you?" She said, giving my ribs a squeeze.

"Yeah, I love you too." I admitted.

Will lay slain in the large concrete river, face down with his pockets turned inside out, their, contents missing. The next day his body would be discovered by a group of kids playing football in the drain. His murder would be deemed a robbery-homicide.

Chapter 43

I woke up on the wrong side of the bed. Despite all of the enjoyment from the previous night, I still didn't feel too chummy this morning. Maybe it was all of the tossing and turning that Veronica did last night. Her restless night affected mine slightly. But that I could deal with. It was something else in my core that had me not feeling right.

After drifting to the bathroom to handle my morning business, I felt somewhat better. Seeing that Ronni was awake added to my better mood. She sat on the bed with her legs folded, Indian style, in my burgundy Roca-Wear shirt. Her hair was put up in a loose ponytail, looking domestically gorgeous. I became aroused, but held off because her eyes were closed and lips slowly moving as if she was in prayer or meditating.

"Good morning," she said to me with a light smile after opening her eyes.

"Morning, sunshine," I said, sliding her further down the bed so I could lay on top of her.

She giggled. "I'm glad it's morning."

"I know, you had trouble sleeping last night."

"Yeah. I had that dream again."

"What dream?"

She sighed, "The bad one I told you I had about you."

Puzzlement crossed my face as I tried to recall her mentioning a bad dream about me.

She went on, "The one where you hop in the car with the masked guy and he pulls a gun on you and you get out and run and he shoots you three times in the back."

"It's just a dream, nothing to worry about." I said, mixed with a reassuring smile.

"I know, but ..." She hesitated.

"But what?"

"I don't know, I guess I'll just be glad when we're far away from here."

I nodded agreeably, "Let's go get something to eat."

"I think those guys are trying to get your attention." Ronni said, referring to a couple of thugs in a late 80's model, black, Buick Regal. Two of them, both I knew to be from the bottoms of Inglewood.

I rolled down the window, "What's brackin' red?" I greeted them both.

"You know, B, just another day in the Wood." The stern faced passenger, whose head was covered with a black and red Boston Red Sox cap said. "But look, I just heard and I send mines in regards to the homie B-Will."

"A'ight," I responded reluctantly, not quite sure what he meant.

"When y'all find out who did it, let me know so me and the homies can smash." He concluded flashing a 'B' sign, before the car peeled the corner.

"Wait, what?" I said, looking at Ronni, but really talking to myself.

A look of concern stretched across her face.

The light turned green and the car behind me leaned on their horn as I thought to myself absently. My phone rang, as if on cue. I drove through the intersection and over to the parking side of the road on Crenshaw.

"Yeah," I answered.

"Kay," Slip's voice came in, followed by a heavy sigh.

"Slip, I just ran into some-"

"I'm at the park, how far are you from the park?"

"I'm just leaving the In and Out, about 15 minutes."

"I'll get at you when you get here," he said before hanging up.

When I arrived at the park, Slip was sitting on the steps alongside the recreation center. About 30 or so homies were in and around the back of the building. At 10:30 in the morning with no function to speak of, by itself, spoke volumes. That feeling of uneasiness from this morning started to reemerge.

I stopped in front of Slip, he stood up when I did. "Slip, what happened homie?"

"It's Will, they found his body this morning. The homie got killed," he said, his voice breaking.

"What?" I waved him off naively, "Which Will you talkin bout?"

"The only Will we fuck with," he continued solemnly.

I nodded in denial, "Nah, you bullshittin. The homie down the street at his uncle's or his mom's. Matter-of-fact-"

"They found him in Hawthorne around the corner from the D-spot. In the gutter. Murder-robbery."

Reality hit me like a ton of bricks and I was at a loss for words. I reached out with one hand and grabbed Slip's shoulder and the rail beside the steps for balance.

"I got my ear to the street. We gon ride," he said, as serious as can be.

When I sat back down in the car I was overwhelmed with a mixture of anger and frustration. Which turned into instant depression. I could tell that Ronni had overheard the conversation by the mask of sorrow that covered her face. She reached over to touch my arm. I didn't feel like being touched. I didn't feel like being bothered. I moved my arm to show my discomfort and started the car up to drop her off at home.

Chapter 44

Growing up throughout Los Angeles county, I've heard of and have seen my share of death, have been close to death myself. All drug and gang related. When it has nothing to do with you or anyone you're close to, you don't really pause to reflect on the why and how. You keep going on with your life as if nothing happened, because the clock doesn't stop for one person. When it happens to someone you're close to like a best friend or brother, then that perspective takes on a whole new meaning, and a brief pause becomes long beats. You look at how their life turned out, you study the why and how, and then you look at your own life and from there you decide who you are and what you want to be.

I decided to go to my mother's house and spent the next four days between Will's funeral there. The majority of the time I was locked away in my old room; which was now shared with Corey. I didn't say much, I didn't eat much. I just did a lot of thinking and my mother and siblings respected my space. Especially after numerous attempts to cheer me up failed to pan out.

Ronni called and sent me text messages everyday. Sending her condolences and leaving messages stating how Will was in a better place and in God's hands, that I shouldn't let it get me down and how she loved and missed me. All of her messages went unanswered. I didn't want to talk to her right now. I didn't know when I would want to talk to her again. At the moment I felt she was better off without me.

I kept receiving calls around the clock from a private number I refused to answer. The caller left no text or voicemail. I had a hunch it was Gina.

"You look nice," My mother said, appearing behind me as I stood adjusting my tie in the bathroom mirror. "I can't remember the last time I seen you in a suit."

I glared at her reflection in the mirror, "You forgot my brother, your son's funeral, eight years ago." I said with a little more attitude than I should have.

She stormed off. I thought about going after her to apologize, but decided against it. Who was really at fault?

On the hour drive from my mother's house in Rancho Cucamonga to the Inglewood cemetery, I insisted on us taking separate cars. Me and Rayona were in mine and her and Corey in hers. The reason being, I didn't plan on returning with them.

"Kay, is it true that ghost live at the cemetery?" Rayona asked as we neared the Crenshaw exit off the 105 west. "Because Corey told me they do."

"You're not going to see any ghost."

"But do they live there?" She asked, smart enough to know I didn't answer her question.

"No, there are no such thing as ghost. They're not real."

"But dead people are, am I-"

"No, you're not going to see any dead people." I said, beating her to the punch.

"Are you sad? Mom said you were sad."

I sighed and remained silent, knowing she would know to leave me alone.

"I'm sorry you friend died." She said in her tiny voice, reaching her little hand up to pat me on the shoulder.

*   *   *

We were among approximately 160 people who attended Will's funeral. Along with his mother and other relatives, my family, Ronni, Jessica, Slip, Big Reck, Gina, and a number of Will's former teammates were the only ones actually dressed for the occasion. Everyone else in attendance, which made up the majority, were gang members from most of the numerous gangs in Inglewood. Even a few ese's were in the mix. All wore either white, black, or red t-shirts, and none made any secret of their affiliation.

Ronni chose to stand next to me during the entire service. She held my hand, even though I chose not to interlock my fingers with hers, that didn't stop her from keeping hers clasped around mine.

Almost every woman present cried and none stood out like Will's mother, but the tears rolling down Gina's face were significant. And because of Will, I felt for her when I looked at her stomach. She had just lost a lover and her unborn child's father.

"I got a call yesterday, I have to go up to El Camino to finalize some paperwork and collect my transcripts." Ronni said to me when the service ended and everyone was making their way through the manicured grass to the parking exits.

"Is that right," I said, uninterested, looking around her at what Slip was doing. I knew he had some information for me.

"Yeah, are you doing anything tomorrow morning?" She asked.

"Don't know, can't make any promises," I answered plainly.

"Hi Ronni," Rayona said, approaching with my mother and Corey.

"Hi Rayona." Ronni gave her and the others a hug in turn.

"Excuse me, I'll be right back." I said, walking off in Slip's direction, towards the chain-link fence after he signaled.

"I just got word," Slip said as I approached. "Remember them rips we got into it with at Jessica's party?"

"Yeah, I remember."

"Well, come to find out, they kick it right around the corner from where Will got hit. Him and the lil homie ran into them at the liquor store on Rosecrans the day before and drew down on them, but didn't buss. You already know how that goes." Slip said.

I looked past him and noticed Gina staring at me.

Slip continued, "I got word from one of the hoodrats over there that them niggas been braggin' about how they caught somebody slippin' and came up on a sack. The same sack they servin' on the block right now."

"Is that right?" I asked, my blood starting to boil, "We about to get rid of they ass tonight."

"You already know," Slip said, extending his hand, giving me a handshake with our index finger and thumb looped around one another to form a 'P' symbol.

I walked out to my car to retrieve a package from the trunk, before heading back towards my mother and Ronni. On the way back I seen Big Reck and Gina making their exit. Big Reck was wrapped up in a phone conversation, while Gina continued to stare. I made eye contact with her, and her eyes widened a bit as she nodded a stiff 'no' and tapped the phone on her hip with her index finger before breaking eye contact to climb into the Hummer.

What was that about? I thought as I continued my stroll.

"Mom, I need to talk to you real quick," I said, leading her out of earshot.

"I need to talk to you too." She started before I could. "You need to stop acting like you don't care about that girl."

"What? What are you talking about?"

"Ronni. You need to stop blowing her off. That girl really loves you and wants to be with you."

Ignoring her, "Look, I need you to keep this," I said, handing her a padded manila envelope. "It's for you."

"What is it?" She asked, her hands pulling at the flap.

"No, don't open it here."

She opened it anyway. "Un-un. Boy why're you giving me all this money? Where'd you get this from?"

"Don't worry about it. That's forty-two thousand dollars. You keep that for a rainy day."

"No," she tried to hand it back. "Put this toward your studio."

"I'm done with that," I nodded, not taking the envelope back, instead, I held out a key.

"Here, take it."

"What's this for?"

"That's a spare key to my car."

"For what?" She said abruptly, panic starting to peak through her exterior.

"Just in case-"

"In case what," She cut me off. "Kaeshon?"

"Look, you put that money up, and keep that key," I said as I back-pedaled away from her. "I keep my car around Arbor Vitae and La Brea."

"Kay, what are you going to do? Kaeshon," she called in the distance as I jogged off.

"Kay!" Ronni called as well, but I continued to the Impala.

"What's going on?" Ronni asked.

"I don't know. I think he about to do something that he shouldn't."

"Oh no," Ronni said, almost to herself.

"He acted like this, last time, when his brother Keith died. But this time is worse because he knows what he's doing now."

"I'm going to go after him," Ronni said, turning to run, but was stopped by Cheryl's arm across hers.

"Ronni," Cheryl said before looking down at Rayona and Corey's little faces, "here, take this," she said, handing her the key to Kay's car.

They embraced before Ronni jogged off to where Jessica was waiting for her in the parking lot.

Chapter 45

That night, I went back to the cemetery and stood at Will's grave. I stood staring at the headstone that read, "Here lies William Bryman, star athlete and son. Dec 22, 1982- July 23, 2004." At that moment our life together played in my mind like a short film, unedited and only in portions by scene. Will was my best friend, not homie, because there is a difference between the terms. He was my friend before gangs, before dreams of success in sports; or music, before all of the bullshit, he was my friend.

Of course I was angry, and revenge was inescapable. Whoever killed Will would soon join him. It was only right according to the laws of the street, an unwritten rule in every murdered man's will, and I was executor of the estate.

"Kay, Kay," was yelled from a distance. I turned and seen Veronica running towards me. "Kay," she breathed as she stood in front of me, throwing her arms around my waist. I didn't raise my arms to hug her back.

"What are you doing here?" I asked without warmth.

"I-I was looking for you because," she broke her unwelcomed embrace, "I was worried about you."

"It's 10:30, get home, you got a meeting at school in the morning," I said, looking down at my watch.

"Are you coming with me?"

"Come on, I'll walk you to the car," I answered, evading the question, looking in the distance at a pair of headlights that I knew belonged to Jessica's vehicle.

"Kay," Ronni called as we trampled by one headstone after another, walking towards the car.

"Yeah?"

"I need you," she said pleadingly, "I need you Kay. Please don't do anything that'll take you away from me, please."

I sighed.

"Kaeshon, please listen to me," she continued, grabbing my arm.

"I heard you."

"But are you listening?"

"Come on," I said, pushing forward and noticed she wasn't walking with me any longer. "Look, I'm not going to play these games with you today. Come on."

"What am I supposed to do, huh?" She asked, even though I didn't completely understand the question, I had an answer for her.

"Move on," I said. "Go home to aunt Marie's, gather your things for Miami and when the time comes, leave. Don't worry about me or anything else. There is nothing here for you anymore." I concluded, stepping through the mortuary's bar gate that had permitted us entrance originally.

"But."

"But nothing. What don't you understand?" I paused to say. "This is me, this is what I do, I'm a street nigga, nothing more nothing less. What, you thought you was gon change me?" I asked, raising my voice. I could see that my words were affecting her. "We can move to Miami, New York, or Puerto Rico, and it ain't gon make no difference because I'm still gon be the same Kay that you met." I pushed forward once more, sliding through the gate.

"And what Kay is that, huh?" She wailed, "You don't even know who you are."

I didn't respond, Slip pulled into the cemetery's parking area in a G-ride, a black 95 Caprice with matching tent. Opening the door, Slip could be seen with a red NY cap on, a black long sleeve shirt and a red flag tied around his neck that would be pulled over his mouth at the convenient time.

I had on a black long sleeve as well and pulled the black rag from my pocket as I hopped in the car, but not before hearing Ronni yell, "What about your brother? What about your mother? You want to do that to her again ... Another funeral." And then we were off.

"Where we going?" I asked as we rode down Crenshaw Blvd.

"Hawthorne. I got word of the block they slangin' on out there." Slip answered.

We continued the rest of the trip in silence. It was only a 15 minute drive, but seemed like forever. The entire way, I kept thinking about the last two months and everything that had taken place within them. I thought about the day with Ronni at the motel, the night she showed her true feelings towards me, the night we first became intimate. I thought about what my mother had said to me earlier when she told me how much Ronni was in love with me. Then I thought about Will, my friend, my brother, his life, his potential, his loyalty. Anything I needed, he would help provide. Any situation I found myself in, he would help me find a way out. Whatever the cost, he would kill for me, and I for he.

We banked a right on Rosecrans. I thought about the night of Jessica's party, and that of the situation with ES at the strip club. Gina ... Gina, she's pregnant. Big Reck, Slip, Gina. We banked a left on an apartment filled street. There was about 15 or so people out, Crips, smoker types, teenagers. Slip slowed down, hit the lights, which garnered the attention of all as they strained to see into the stopped car. A look of horror crossed their faces when they spotted the flame red hat and bandana on Slip's face and that of the black bandana on mine.

'SKUUURRR.' The tires screeched and everyone took off running as Slip gunned the Caprice forward.

My thoughts continued to race; repeating, Big Reck, Slip, Gina. I hung out the window with the pistol-grip pump trained on a man who looked to be in his mid-twenties, one of the gang bangers I noticed from Jessica's party. Big Reck, Slip, Gina ... The strip club, ES murder. Gina, Will. Gina at the cemetery ... Warning. I lowered the gun from the running man's head to his midsection. "Shoot." I heard Slip say. I lowered the pump once more, training the shotgun on his legs. "What that Murda One like!" I yelled before the shotgun's explosion, toppling the runner over midstep. He didn't kill Will, so I didn't kill him, just knocked the pep out of his step for a while.

'Whooom,' the Caprice zoomed as we rounded the corner quickly on 147th flying east past Crenshaw into Gardena. It was there that I trained the .45 I had in my lap on Slip.

Chapter 46

The room was dim, the single low wattage table lamp glowed miserably. The TV was off, the bed was made and the carpet clean with exception of two items. On the opposite side of the bed, farthest from the door, rested a 12 gauge shotgun and medium sized duffle, its mouth open revealing hundreds of thousands of dollars. Stack upon stack held in place by rubber band. On the same side of the bed was a nightstand, a grey .45 Smith&Wesson sat on top of it, its orifice facing the cushioned-back chair I was stationed in.

I slumped down in the chair further. My left arm was wrapped around the chair's arm to prevent me from completely falling. In my other hand was a half empty bottle, a 5th of Hennessey. I sat there drunk, completely wasted, cursing myself, cursing life, the world and everyone in it.

With every swig I took, I became more convinced that a miserable existence wasn't worth living. That this miserable existence wasn't worth living.

"Ronni, it's after midnight. I'm getting tired, we've been driving around all night and we don't know what they've done or where they're at," Jessica complained.

Ronni sighed, "I know."

"We've been all over Hawthorne and the parts of Inglewood they hang out in ... I don't know where to find them. They're probably at some hiding spot." Jessica concluded.

"The only spot I've heard mentioned was the motel." Ronni added.

"But we've already stopped by, Kay's car isn't there."

"Okay, well it's on the way back home, so we stop by there again. Maybe his car is somewhere else. If he's not there then we call it a night."

"Alright." Jessica said, zooming down La Brea.

I picked up the gun from the nightstand and examined it, lacing my fingers and palm around its rubber grip. Moving my arm in a sweeping gesture, I aimed it every direction within vision around the room. I don't know how long this carried on before I lowered it back to my lap so that I could take another swig. Memories of the misdeeds I'd done came rushing back headlong. Memories of my brother, watching him get shot, watching him die. Memories of Will, who got killed while I was out with Ronni. I should have been there for him. Thoughts of Slip crossed my mind, that treacherous snake, I cursed recalling our last moment together ...

"Kay, what you doin'?" Slip asked as I held the gun to his head while he drove down 147th facing forward, stiff necked with fear, peering at me out of the corner of his eye.

"What you think I don't know? Pullover the car," I shouted, "PULLOVER."

He obliged, pulling over on the dark residential street between Crenshaw and Van Ness. "Know what? What you talkin' about?" He said, slowly lowering his hand.

"Keep your hands on the wheel," I commanded. "Don't play me like I'm stupid," I said, my heart rate starting to elevate.

He sighed, "What you want me to say?"

"You killed the homie," I accused, unbelieving at first, and then another time to myself as it set in.

"Reck found out. Reck sent Black to follow him and Gina. He got it all on tape. Them at the hotel, at Malibu Castle, he knew everything. It was a wrap."

"And you wrapped it." I spat bitterly through gritted teeth. "Will, somebody you been knowing all yo life."

"Kay," he said, trying to turn and face me but was stopped when I shoved the gun into his temple. "You gotta understand the situation I was in. How-how many times did we warn Will? How many times did we tell him not to step out with that rat?"

"Regardless," I spat.

"Regardless of what?" He raised his voice, "What would you have done?"

"I would have protected my dawg. I would have killed Reck. I would have died telling him to kiss my ass. I would've killed myself before I killed one of my loved ones," I barked.

"So, what you gon kill me now? Ain't I one of yo loved ones? You gon kill me, Kay?"

I retightened my grip on the pistol, gripping anger and fear. "Get out of the car," I said, watching him do so while keeping the gun trained on him. "I'm not you," I said, slamming the door, driving off, and leaving him standing in darkness.

Ronni sat back in the passenger seat of Jessica's Camry as it idled in the small, deserted, motel's parking lot. She let out a sigh of frustration, realizing that she was running out of options.

"Not here, huh?" Jess asked what seemed to be obvious.

Ronni scanned the small row of windows next to the rooms. All were dark except for one, room 4, to the right of Kay's room. The beige curtains glowed from the inner light. This brought to mind a conversation her and Kay had during her first visit here, 'actually the room next door is where I clear my mind when I don't want to be bothered.' His voice echoed in her head. 'What about you car?' She asked. 'There's a commercial parking garage two blocks west of here,' His answer bounced back into her head.

"Maybe he's at his mother's house," Jessica said ideally, cutting off her thoughts.

"No, hey, pull out and make a right on Arbor Vitae. There's a parking compound I want to check out."

"Okay," Jessica breathed, ready to call it quits.

I couldn't remember how long the gun had been at my head. Excessive drinking equates short term memory loss. The barrel of the .45 felt comfortable against the numb skin that covered my skull. In my liquor soaked mind there was no dueling voices, no right and no wrong. Only one voice ... And that one whispered, do-it, do-it. Had I been sober I probably would've cried holding my own weapon to my head, but tears were no longer a part of me.

The truth was, I hated myself. I hated the way everything in my life had gone. My brother was dead; the one with promise. My father was gone. And now Will ... What is life? This long suffering for us born without privilege. What makes it worth living?

"BOOMP." I heard somewhere, "BOOMP," Again, this time louder, causing me to open the heavy lids covering my eyes. I stared, stupefied, at the door guessing it was just my imagination--"BOOMP," When Ronni shouldered in, almost falling through the door.

"Oh my God," She said, pausing to observe the state I was in.

"What're you doin here?" I asked, which sounded fine in my head, but came out slurred.

"Oh God. Kay, Kay, put the gun down," she said, worriedly, taking steps forward with both hands out.

In her hand was a small pocket knife, which I recognized from my glovebox. She had used it to jimmy her way in while ramming the door with her shoulder. I cocked my head to the side, looking at the blade. She stopped in her tracks, noticing my focus, folded the blade and put it in her pocket before taking another step forward.

"Hey," I blurted, unconsciously lowering the gun from my head, pointing it at her, prompting her to stop again.

"Kay, please put the gun down," she pleaded softly.

"Leave."

She nodded, "No, not without you." Taking another step forward.

"Heeey-hey," I crowed, wagging the gun, dropping the nearly empty bottle of Hennessey

311

Akil Victor

on the carpet which I looked down at a moment, contemplatively, only to look up and find Ronni two steps away from me. "Hey. Hey," I said for lack of better words and swung the gun back up to my head.

"Kay, please don't do this. I'm sorry that-"

"For what? You-you sorry for be-being with me when Will died? When I could have been there, huh?"

Tears began to line her eyes.

"It's my fault he died."

"Kay, you can't blame yourself for what happened to Will."

"Will- Keith, Keith," I cried, "My brother."

"No- Kay, don't," she cooed.

"YOU DON'T KNOW." I shouted. "I wasn't there," Sorrow lowering my voice. "He came looking for me and I wasn't there."

"Please," she tried to get a word in.

"We got into it with some marks- I bragged to him about it." I babbled solemnly. "he didn't care, said leave the bullshit alone-stop hanging out, stay away from them- they ain't ya homies. They'll get you in trouble."

"I called him a busta, a coward. I told him that jail had made him soft," I went on.

"Kay," Ronni said, slowly advancing a step closer, focused on the gun.

"I was mad. I took a swing at him and ran. I ran to the hood, to the park. He followed me," I continued, choked up. "He stopped in front of the park, looking for me ... And they came ... They came." I wailed. "They should've got me," I said, my vision beginning to blur as the levee broke, overwhelming me with a stream of tears escaping down my face.

"Please, baby," she cried, "Just hand me the gun, please."

"No," I nodded, the barrel bumping my temple, "Leave."

"I can't, because what happened to Will wasn't your fault. What happened to your brother wasn't your fault. I won't leave," she declared. "Not without you. I need your strength, your mother needs your strength. Rayona and Corey need you. There is no one else for them, for us. Please." She spoke, reaching out. "Please." She gently clasped her hand around the gun, moving it away from my head.

"Leave," I said one last time, defeated.

She took the gun away, holding it outward to eject the clip, which fell to the floor between the shotgun and liquor bottle. She looked around the room and then picked up the currency filled duffle bag and walked out.

Moments later, the door reopened and with it the room was swept by light. A light that shined bravely like it didn't come from the Impala's halogen headlights, but from God himself.

When she entered again, I didn't see Veronica Tomez, but an angel extending her arms. With her a whole new world, with her,

Akil Victor

warmth and hope, and at that moment I needed both.

Chapter 47

It was 11:20 a.m. when I opened my eyes the next day. I adjusted my vision to what, at first, was an unfamiliar setting until I realized that I was in Ronni's room at aunt Marie's. I didn't remember arriving here last night, I didn't remember walking through the door and ending up in this room. However, I did remember, in parts, the incident that led to my being here.

Ronni wasn't present in the tidy room. I put on my shoes, needing to piss badly. I wanted to wait until Ronni came back into the room. I was nervous not knowing if aunt Marie was home and knew I was here. Seven minutes later, my bladder felt like it was about to burst. I wasn't going to wait any longer.

After using the bathroom, I walked in to the living room and found aunt Marie sitting on the couch reading the Los Angeles Times. "Good morning," I greeted.

She looked at me over the rims of her glasses, her eyes and smile warm when she replied," It is indeed. I have some breakfast for you in the oven." She got up and went into the kitchen. "And I'll make you some coffee, you look like you need it," she called back.

"Thank you," I said when the bacon, eggs, and toast breakfast was placed in front of me.

"No problem dear," she said, giving me a light shoulder squeeze on her way back to the couch. "Veronica went to school to pick up some paperwork, She should return soon."

"Okay." That answered one question I had in mind.

Ronni returned a minute later, walking over to give aunt Marie a kiss on the cheek before signaling for me to follow her to the room.

We were silent. I leaned on the room's closed door, she sat on the bed looking at the paperwork she came home with. It was awkward, I didn't know where any conversation we would have would begin. What do you say to someone who witnessed your most vulnerable moment? A moment, whether you knew it or not, whether you wanted it or not, you needed help. Sometimes a simple thank you isn't enough, but's that's where I started.

"Thank you."

She shifted her focus away from the documents and off to the side contemplatively before rising, taking a step forward and wrapping her arms around me tightly.

"Thank you," I repeated for my own benefit, hugging her back firmly.

She gave no verbal response, just nodded her head into my shirt, which had begun to moisten.

"Hey, um, I'ma go back and freshen up." I said after a while.

She took a step back, wiped away any traces of tears, reached into her pocket and held out the Impala's spare key.

I closed her fingers around it, "Keep it."

"I put all your things from the original room in the car already."

"Did you? Last night?"

She nodded, "I don't- you shouldn't stay there anymore."

"I know."

The backseat was filled with my belonging just as she had said. One suitcase and two duffle bags filled with shoes and clothes, a fourth; smaller, sports bag, the one filled with money was in the trunk. Out of habit, I looked through it.

"I disposed of the gun last night," she said over my shoulder, "Both of them."

I nodded, no need to respond.

When I crossed over to the driver side door, she said, "You could shower here if you want. You already have all of your belongings."

I glanced over at aunt Marie's house.

"It's okay, she wouldn't have a problem with it," she said, just about guessing what I was thinking.

"Right now I wouldn't feel comfortable." I opened the door, she stood there looking like she just lost her puppy. "Hey, it's okay," I said. "I'm all good. You don't have to worry about nothing else like last night happening again. Hell, I don't think I'll ever touch another drink again, either."

"I'm going with you," she said, settling into the passenger seat.

"Just as long as you know I don't need supervision." I said, adjusting my mirror before backing out.

"I know, but the feeling in my stomach hasn't subsided yet."

When we arrived back at the motel room, the place was in tatters. The blankets, on the ground. The mattress was overturned, and there was a fist sized hole in the wall next to the bathroom door.

"It was like this when I grabbed your things last night."

I didn't respond, just stood in the doorway staring into the blackness of the hole, knowing whose fist had been there.

"What's that?" She asked, pointing down at a letter caught under my foot.

The letter was made out to Kay, and had the motels address and room number on the envelope. It was stamped and post marked, actually sent through the mail. The handwriting on the envelope was neat, feminine, but had no return address.

I tore open the letter, which read:

Dear Kay,

I hope that this letter finds you in time and before its end, you'll find it in your heart to forgive me.

First off, my heart bleeds for Will, for our loss...

The letter began with words, and the lines they were on, slightly smeared by what looked to be a dried wet spot, tears? I noticed before I continued reading...

I want to let you know that if it had been possible, if it were up to me, I would have been the one laid to rest instead of Will. Kay, I truly loved Will with every fiber in my being. Regardless of what anyone thinks or say, and this child that I carry within is his. I <u>have not</u> been with Derreck or anyone else sexually but Will for a couple of months.

Derreck had us followed by a couple of people, one of them I found out to be Slip. He revealed this to me through a video tape that showed me and Will together. I don't know who did what, but I know that Slip was involved with what happened to Will. I also know that they've given everyone false information about who killed Will, and that you need to seriously watch your back. You can't trust none of those

319

niggas from y'all area.

Right now, I am being kept under lock and key. My phone and everything I do is monitored, and he had somebody take my momma hostage. I honestly think something is about to happen to me. I haven't told Derreck that I'm pregnant. I don't know what to do. Kay, please stay away from them because I know that they know you knew what was going on.

Beside the motel, I don't know where to find you, but … I tried to call you a few times but you didn't pick up. My number was private because I can't chance nobody calling me back. I don't know what's going to happen to me, but I have to get out of here.

I want you to take care of yourself and please be careful.

Gina.

The letter ended with shaky handwriting.

I stood there a minute, letting the missive's words soak in. Everything she wrote, I'd already came to the conclusion of. But her taking the time to write it showed that her stated intentions and feelings were genuine.

"Who is it from?" Ronni asked, standing beside me, she hadn't been reading along, but making an assessment of the room's damage.

"That girl Will was seeing, Gina."

"Is she okay?"

"I hope so," I said without thought. The words rolled off my tongue naturally.

My eyes must have been readable, because hers seemed to be of understanding.

She looked around the room once more, "Wow, Kay."

"You said it was like this last night?" I asked.

She studied me a second before asking, "You didn't do this?" When you were mad last night? Because I thought you did. I didn't-"

"Oh yeah," I chimed in, "You know last night was a blur to me." I said, untruthfully. I could tell she wasn't completely satisfied with this answer.

I stepped outside of the room into the bright sunlight, smell of pollution and the sight of medium traffic on La Brea. I decided to take the four steps to the room next door so I could shower. Upon entrance, Ronni paused at the door as if seeing some unseen force. More than likely revisiting last night's occurrence, which I knew was more unnerving to her than it was to me.

"I'll just be a few minutes, if you want to wait in the car and listen to music." I offered, to which she turned heel and did so.

The room was clean, except for the jagged circular Hennessey stain on the carpet. The only remaining evidence of my presence here last night.

The 10 minute shower I took was relaxing and refreshing. Clothing wise, I decided to go with a beige Dickies khaki suit over classic white Air force's. After apologizing to Ronni for my neglectful, careless behavior over the last few days, I decided to put it all behind me and keep moving forward. Plans unchanged.

The day came and went quickly as the three of us sat in aunt Marie's living room, with me sandwiched between the two of them taking a trip down memory lane in their memories vehicle. Collectively, I looked at photo albums and scrap books put together by the two of them. Ronni's told the story of a proud New Yorker of Puerto Rican heritage who was hardworking, determined, and ambitious. There was educational ribbons, certificates, and her diploma in there along with many adorable photos. Aunt Marie's was the story of a strong willed Mexican-American woman from a deep rooted lineage with an insatiable appetite to succeed. Regardless of gender and racial injustices.

Inside of aunt Marie's scrapbook was also a number of old newspaper articles, photos, and clippings along with letters from various individuals she had mentored throughout the years. One letter in particular had been headed: To Mrs. Marquez, from Keith Anthony.

"I was so proud of him during this time." Aunt Marie said as I stared at the letter. "I felt like he was my own. I kept it on my refrigerator for two months, until ... Well it was hard to look at afterwards. But I never planned on parting ways with it. That is, until now," she said, reaching over to take it out of its plastic covering.

"Oh, no, Mrs.,-aunt Marie." I said, starting to protest.

"Oh, hush, it will be better in your possession, and it has a strong message regarding the change your brother was going through."

"Thank you, ma'am."

"You're welcome," she said, standing to excuse herself. I stood as well. "You two have a goodnight. I'll see you kids in the morning," she said, leaving the room.

I stared down at the letter in my lap, my brother's handwriting.

"What does it say?" Ronni asked.

"Dear, Mrs. Marquez: You once told me that a man is measured by his deeds," I began reading, picturing my brother's 17 year old handsome face as he wrote this letter. "And no bad deed goes unpunished, especially for a man of color. I reflected on that as I sat in jail for the second time looking out of the small rectangular window at steel and concrete.

It's been six months since that day, and in two months I'll be graduating from high school. Which is a day that I thought I'd never see come. It's all thanks to you taking the time out to really show me that you care. To really counsel me and point out the error of my ways and what I could do to change. I know it seems a bit premature to be celebrating right now, but my mother is so proud she won't let me or her friends think of anything but my success right now. I'm trying my best to make my little brother Kaeshon see things the same way. Right now he's fascinated with street life, obsessed with the way I was living before I opened my eyes.

I have to be the man of the house and if not me, then him. He looks up to me so much that I believe the way he is is partially my fault. Mrs. Marquez, I've been doing a lot of thinking into the college situation as well, and I want you to be the first to know that I've been thinking of joining the Air Force. I figure I can kill two birds with one stone. I could train for a career and enroll in college while being in the service. The money I'd be making I could send to my mother to help her out. Also me stepping up like this, being a man and taking care of my responsibility and looking out for the fam, I'm sure my brother will respect that. Hopefully, just like he was influenced by my negative actions, he'll be influenced by my positive actions and follow suit.

Thanks again.
Keith Anthony."

"He really wanted to help you all out. He sounded like a great guy." Ronni said when I finished reading the letter.

"He was," I said, more to myself than her.

Ronni's phone vibrated, buzzing between

both of our legs. "Excuse me," she said before answering. "Hello, Hey Jess ... Kay?" She looked in my direction, I nodded a quick 'no' to whatever it was, she continued, "Why do you ask? I don't know. I guess he doesn't want to be bothered ... Okay, you too, bye."

"What did she want?" I asked.

"She didn't say, but I think Slip is looking for you."

"I didn't hear or feel my phone ring."

"Are you two okay?" She inquired.

"We're strangers."

Chapter 48

We ended up falling asleep on the couch before being untangled by the aroma of aunt Marie's cooking; chorizo, cheese, and scrambled egg filled breakfast burritos.

"Good morning you two." She sang cheerfully, placing the dishes on the table.

"So, Kaeshon, how's the music coming along?" Aunt Marie asked as we sat at the dining room table.

"Good actually. I just finished the album completely. Which reminds me, I have to pick up the final copy of the mastered version today."

"That's great. I can't wait to hear it. Veronica how does it sound?"

"The song that I heard was good," Ronni answered.

"Oh I can't wait," aunt Marie sang happily, "Can I have a copy before you two move."

"You sure can." I smiled, her joy was infectious.

"Have you thought about what you're

going to do with your music when you get to Miami?"

"Um, briefly, they have a pretty good market out there. Plus the internet is always in my favor to reach a wider network."

Aunt Marie nodded, "Well, since you two are leaving in a couple of days, I want to give you some advice."

"Okay," I said.

"One; prepare yourself in what you want in a career and life. Remember that neither is a brief hiatus. Two; learn and grow from first hand experiences. And three; be decisive and open to change, only if it's for the better. and always, always have a back up plan." She paused to look at the both of us, stopping on me, "Got it?"

"Sure do," I answered.

"Are we going to pick up the CD?" Ronni asked as we traveled east on Marine.

"Yeah, but first I want to stop somewhere else." I answered, hooking a left on Prairie.

"Where?"

I hesitated a moment before answering, "To talk to Will."

"Okay," she said, reaching up to briefly rub my arm.

"So, what did aunt Marie mean by we're leaving in a couple of days?"

"Oh yeah, about that. Remember my auntie I mentioned that lives out there?"

I nodded.

"Well, I also mentioned that she was in real estate, and she already has a place for us. So I was thinking the sooner the better, so we can get situated and familiar with the city." She paused for effect, receiving none, she continued, "What do you think about that?"

"When exactly do you want to leave?"

"I was thinking the beginning of next week, Monday."

"Monday? Today's Friday, that's only three days."

"If you, if it's too early and you want to wait a few days-"

"Nah, it's cool. Besides the summer is still fresh, we can always come back in a month to kick it with our peoples," I said.

She nodded, "Yeah, we can, and every chance we get as well."

We crossed into Inglewood on Prairie, floating past Imperial. Ronni fumbled with the CD player, it roared to life blaring a loud rock melody, which gained the attention of the passengers in cars on both sides of us.

I turned down the music, "Woman, what're you doing?" I asked as we passed ran down streets full of seedy motels, liquor stores, and Mexican markets.

"What do you mean?"

"I mean, this is the hood. We can't be bumping that kind of music loud around here."

"You're the one who left the volume turned up so loud," she retorted.

"Not my CD, so I can't agree with you," I countered.

"Who cares what they think," Ronni said, skipping songs until she found one that suited her. Madonna of course. Her favorite song, the one she was listening to when I first met her.

She turned it up a bit, its melody drifting out of the open windows. The light on Prairie and Century turned red as Ronni began to sing along. I looked to my left, noticing a tough looking brother staring over at us with a look that bordered amusement and read, 'your girl's running the radio.' I put my hands up with a shrug, he threw his head back and laughed.

Ronni turned my face toward hers and sang along with Madonna, 'I looked into your eyes/and my whole world came tumbling down.'

The light turned green, I reclaimed my face, cruising by a very busy Hollywood Park Casino and then an empty Great Western Forum, behind moderate traffic.

"You're the devil in disguise," she sung before looking back-over her seat, clearly distracted by something.

"What?" I asked.

She nodded, "Just somebody driving crazy back there."

'To know you is to love you-' The song continued.

I looked into the rearview mirror, catching a glimpse of a large sedan jumping three cars behind me, and then quickly back into the lane it came from. A large black taxi-like 95 Chevy Caprice.

"What the fu-" I said, staring into the side view mirror, unsnapping the panel on the driver door that served as a secret compartment. Watching as the car sped up and swerved around a horn blaring Honda, speeding up still ... before, for me, the slow motion hit.

The car was nearly side by side with mine, and quickly advancing. I dug for the 9mm I had stashed in the panel with my less capable left hand, lifting it quickly as possible when the first shot rang out. 'Boom,' it thundered and crackled, piercing through the metal of the door jamb between the windshield and driver's window, coming from a scowling Slip who aimed around me for ...

I lunged forward instinctively in an attempt to cover Ronni as the second thunderous crackle and then a third shot clamored our way before I could return two shots of my own at the tail of the speeding away Caprice.

My ears were hot and heavy, the sound of my heartbeat drumming wildly within them. I looked over at Ronni who sat panting wide-eyed. The left half of her shirt was stained crimson with spreading blood. I scanned the opposite side of the road, the traffic becoming lighter do-to the red-light at Prairie and Florence. I seen Daniel Freeman hospital to my left and banked a hard 7-shaped turn, cutting through the intersection and three approaching cars that leaned on their horns as I flew into the crowded parking lot of the hospital stopping in front of the sliding doors. Moving as fast as possible, I got out and ran to Ronni's side, threw the door open, unbuckled her seatbelt and grabbed her in my arms amid several onlookers and ran into the hospital.

She clung to my neck as we entered the lobby, "HELP, GUNSHOT, HELP." I yelled frantically at the nurses and receptionist in view. Their response was swift. Half a dozen nurses jogged over along with a waiting paramedic with a gurney.

"What's her name?" One of them asked, helping position the gurney.

"Ronni," I blurted.

"Ronni, you're going to be okay," The woman went on to say, placing an oxygen mask over a hyperventilating Ronni. As they began to wheel her off, she held steadfast to my hand nodding, 'no.' She breathed, "Don't do anything, don't leave," she nodded as they wheeled her through the double doors of the ER, my stop.

"Sir, you're bleeding," The paramedic who stayed behind with me said.

I followed his focus to my rotator cuff, my white T-shirt was sticky from blood that

I thought was Ronni's but the hole at the top of my arm said otherwise. With the awareness came the pain, a sickening wave of burning and stinging sensations that rendered my arm immobile.

"We've got to get you some help," The paramedic said, reaching out for me. I jerked back and headed for the exit quickly.

I jumped in my car, fueled by anger and a thirst for revenge. I zoomed into light traffic, one arm holding the wheel, the other nearly paralyzed, clutching the pistol. Pain is as much mental as it is physical, I kept telling myself as I drove, wincing.

I had an idea where he was heading, at least to stash the car. I made a left on Beach traveling down past Hyde Park to a set of duplexes where the homies hung at. There were 10 of them congregating out front when I pulled up, no sign of Slip.

I hopped out of the car, gun in hand, receiving immediate attention.

"Kay, what's up? What happened dawg?" One of them, a light-skin, ponytailed individual a few years older than me asked.

"Where Slip at?" I asked in turn through bared teeth.

"SKUUURRR," Got our attention and answered my question as Slip braked abruptly at the corner of Hyde Park, lifting his firearm, "BAP BAP," Squeezing off two shots, causing everyone to duck and reach for their weapons instinctively, before Slip hauled ass again.

I ran back to my car as at least a dozen more homies came running up from the rear of the duplexes.

The chase was on as I emerged 25 yards behind him, gunning down the residential streets across a God given green light at La Brea, crossing on to Plymouth. The streets that ran this, the northwestern end of Inglewood, would be confusing to anyone unfamiliar with the area. They all wrapped around in semi, half, and full circles. Which in the past gave us the ability to dispose of and easily elude any enemies and cops.

Slip made a quick, hard right on Edgewood, startling kids playing on the sidewalk as he rounded the semi-circle with me close behind. We were almost bumper to bumper as we flew down the street at 85 miles plus and increasing. A quick left was made on Warren Lane, with the Caprice he was whipping drifting too wide, *BOOOOM* Hitting a parked bucket hard as he rounded the corner, bouncing off the car, steering right, then left, swerving, smashing into another Chevy parked in front of a ran down ese building. This time the car was stopped completely with a sickening crunch.

No motion came from inside of Slip's Caprice as I got out tearing down the blood soaked T-shirt I had on, which clung around my waist as I approached. Half a dozen or so Mexican gang members stood watching from their stoop. Three more were on the sidewalk behind me. Other Hispanic and Black families either peeked out their windows or watched from their yards briefly before tearing their attention away and dragging small children inside the house.

A couple of cholos started to step forward as I moved briskly towards the Caprice, but were stopped by a hand put up by one of their OG's.

Slip began to stir, climbing over the seat and forcing open the passenger side door. He fell out with a grip on the .40 Glock he'd been terrorizing with. I jogged forward and kicked it out of his hand and into the gutter as hard as I could. He forced himself to his knees, clearly hurt. I booted him in the stomach and then the mouth, which flipped him over. He stared up at me from his back and bared bloodied teeth, a twisted smile that was a mixture of pain and amusement.

"Damn, all this over a bitch," Slip let out a gruff chuckle.

I trained the gun on him. Heard a series of sirens in the distance. All of the gawkers began to disperse.

"Nah, it's all over you," I said, reaching down to cock the gun.

Slip laughed again.

The sirens grew closer.

POP.

Chapter 49

After receiving treatment myself, I went over to Ronni's hospital room. When I arrived at the opened door, aunt Marie, Ricky, and Melissa were at her bedside. At the sight of them, I hesitated, not for Ricky or Melissa's sake because I hardly knew them, but I was nervous about what aunt Marie would think. She had left such a good impression on me, and after an incident like this, I wasn't sure what her opinion would be about me.

I started to turn back and return at a later time, but was noticed and motioned over by aunt Marie, who met me at the door.

"Are you alright?" She asked in a lower tone than normal, referring to my left arm that rested in a sling.

With my head lowered, I nodded and answered, "Yeah."

She reached for and wrapped her two small hands around my free hand, "Okay, we're about to leave. I'll see you a little later."

On the way in I avoided eye contact with

Ricky, he did the same as he was walking out.

"Hey," I said when I stood at the side of her bed, which was angled 35 degrees so that she could partially sit up.

"Hey," she said back. She looked tired, which I knew was because of the pain killers. "Where are my flowers?"

"Uh, do you want me to go get you some?" I asked, ready to do so.

"No." She smiled lightly.

I took a seat next to her bed, "How are you?"

"Well, half an hour in surgery. They removed a bullet that was lodged right above my breast and right below my collar bone. What about you?" She motioned to my braced arm.

"Just my upper arm," I said. "Ronni, I'm sorry that you had to go through this. I'm sorry I put you through this."

"Stop," she cut in, "Don't blame yourself. You didn't do this."

"I know but-" I started to protest.

She cut me off, "The police were here."

It's routine for hospitals to notify the proper authorities when gunshot victims arrive without paramedics.

"They asked about the incident?" I inquired.

"Yeah, I told them it was a blue car, the reason why, I don't know. Is my boyfriend a gang member? No. I think it was mistaken identity.

No, I didn't get a good look at the shooter, it happened so quickly." She answered, giving me a brief playback of her answers to the questioning.

I nodded when she paused. I knew she wasn't finished.

She continued, "They asked me where you were at, said you had been shot but refused treatment and left abruptly. I thought you were here. I didn't have an answer for them, but right when they were prodding, their radios went off. The dispatcher said something about shots being fired, two cars racing through the streets, one chasing the other a few blocks from here." She paused for effect.

"Sounds like you're forming a question," I said.

She looked at me a second longer before breaking eye contact to stare down at her fidgeting fingers. "I have to stay overnight, they ran some test, blood work, urine, routine stuff. I should be discharged first thing tomorrow. The doctor said I could use the rest. I think we should leave sooner."

"Here? Now?"

She nodded negatively, "I'm talking about the state. This situation just proves everything I was talking about."

Silence, within the room that went on for several beats. The only sounds to be heard were those beyond the door.

She continued, "I don't mean to throw

anything in your face."

"It's alright. You were right completely, but we both overlooked one thing."

"What's that?"

I searched for the right words, treading lightly. "I can't go with you."

She sat up, a bit of pain from the swift motion evident on her face, but her focus more clear. "W-what?" She stammered.

"Don't hurt yourself, you gotta relax," I said, regarding her condition.

"No, no. What do you mean you can't go?"

"Come on Ronni, look at you, you're in a hospital bed. You just got shot as a result of being with me."

"And," she interjected.

"Put the facts together. Me in the motel room, how I was feeling, what I might've done. And before then, that money, where do you think I got the money from?"

"Give it away." She blurted.

"You don't understand."

"I do understand, you're leaving me."

"No, I'm stepping back so you can leave and get on with your life. I'm not right for you, you can do a hell of a lot better than me."

"Can you do better than me?" She asked.

"Of course not."

"Am I not right for you?" She reached for my hand.

"Perf- you don't even have to ask a question like that."

"Then why quit? After all we've been through, we're almost there, a whole new environment. This shouldn't stop us, all we have to do now is leave. You promised me you would go with me, remember?" She asked, her eyes bored into mine, searchingly.

"Yeah," I stood to give her a peck on the forehead. She was notably growing weary, "Yeah," I repeated.

"Pick me up in the morning." she said, with lazy lids.

I smiled at her, a smile weary in its own right. "Get some rest." Another kiss before sitting back down to watch her fall asleep.

Have you ever met someone with so much passion and charisma, such an uncanny lust for life that it scares you, motivates you, and inspires you, all at the same time? People like that you admire, their company you don't want to be without. Their characteristics can go unmatched for a lifetime. They are respected, loved, and never forgotten.

For me, her name was Veronica Tomez, Ronni. As I sat there watching her sleep, I knew that some promises had to be broken. Regardless of intention, but for the greater good. The flame that she possessed would engulf any fire of mine and she deserved to be without burden on her life's journey. A journey she had all figured out. I had yet to discover mine.

Chapter 50

"Hello, Ms. Tomez." The doctor said, chart in hand, after entering Ronni's hospital room.

"Good morning," Ronni replied. The morning bringing with it relief now that yesterday was officially in the past.

"Good morning, I have some test results for you," The doctor said, her face accompanied with a smile.

"Does that smile mean good news?"

"It means you can relax on your way home. You are completely healthy."

"Thank you."

"One more question," The doc said.

"Yes," Ronni said in return, expectantly.

The doctor smiled once more, "How do you feel about children?"

"Come on Kay, pick up." Ronni said to herself, walking through the hospital's sliding doors. "Pick up." This time with a sigh as the voicemail answered instead.

She disconnected and immediately

pressed the redial option, stepping to the curb before the parking lot, watching as aunt Marie became visible through the rows of inactive cars before her. Slowly, she lowered the phone from her ear. The expression on her face equally downcast as she looked out onto the busy street of Prairie at the traffic drifting by. "He's not coming is he?" She asked, realization setting in as the older woman stood in front of her.

Chapter 51

I made myself unavailable over the next couple of days, well mainly to her, screening calls from both Ronni and Jessica. It was hard to even listen to the voicemails she left. Which weren't of anger, but confusion. She cried on one of them and called me a commitment dodging liar. It hurt to know that I had hurt her, and I realized that I'd broken two promises to her.

Monday morning, I received a call from aunt Marie, detailing how she had seen Ronni off to the airport. That whether this new chapter in her life would be better with or without me, only us two would know.

Later on that night, I received an emergency call from Gina.

When I arrived at the home Big Reck and Gina shared in Westchester, just looking at the outside, one could tell that the inside was a mess. I took a seat next to her on the porch after entering the iron-wrought gate. The window to left of where we sat was broken with a large jagged hole through its center like a soft-ball sized rock had been thrown through.

The EMTs, police cruisers, and the coroner had left prior to my arrival. From the looks of Gina's condition; a wrapped wrist and bruising around her neck and jaw, she should have left with them.

After our initial greeting on the porch, we sat in silence for the next 15 minutes. Big Reck had been found dead in the living room of their trashed home from a single shot to the torso. Gina's wrist, neck, and face told the tale of self-defense, which was the reason she wasn't sitting in jail instead of on the steps with me.

"You know I got your letter, right?" I said, attempting to eradicate the silence. "Thank you."

She nodded, still silent for a moment before saying, "He bailed Slip out the other day ... A half a million dollar bail so Slip could go on the run. That gun he had was the same gun that he used ..." She shied away, blinking away tears, shivered.

I wrapped my arm around her shoulder. She didn't have to continue her sentence.

"I thought you'd been gone by now," she went on to say.

"Nah, Miami wasn't in the cards for me."

"You don't plan on staying out here, do you?"

"What you plan on doing?" I asked instead

of answering her question.

"I'm going home, to Louisiana," she answered slowly.

"You need some money?"

She met my eyes for the second time since I arrived, "No, you keep it. Take it and get as far away from here as possible."

"You know, when me and Will did that, he was doing it for y'all future."

She faced forward, looking off into the distant night, "He also did it for you."

"But-" I started to say.

"I've found some of Reck's money. This house is in both of our name and the cars. So, I don't need anything, but ..." She paused, looking down at her belly and then back to me. "My child is going to need a Godfather and me and Will wanted that to be you."

My phone's ring tone kicked in. I held it out, the glowing display reading Ronni, before I turned it off.

Gina looked at the phone, seeing the display before I cut the power, "Kay, you have so much ahead of you. Take that money and do something positive with it."

I nodded as we sat there in the light-chill staring off into nothingness.

Chapter 52

6 weeks later ...

"Hey mom, how you doing?" I asked after entering her home.

"Fine, Kaeshon, just fine," she said in between chopping tomatoes, sounding a bit frustrated.

"What's wrong? Where Rayona and Corey?" I asked, leaning on the counter, not far from her.

"They're outside playing." She placed the knife down on the cutting board. "What are you going to do, Kay?" She asked, still bothered.

"About what?" I asked, not knowing her problem.

"Have you called that girl back?"

"No," I answered plainly. It had been two weeks since Ronni's last call or letter, before then, her and my mother had been speaking regularly.

"Kay, that girl really loved you," she went on. "You could've been in college with her right now."

"Come on mom, we've been through this before."

"And we'll go through it again," she snapped.

"What's your problem?"

"My problem is I don't want to lose another son."

"What are you talkin' about? I haven't been to the hood in weeks."

"What, are you taking a vacation? Neither did your brother and the moment he went back out there, what happened? And I don't know Will's story, but I know it wasn't too different." She paused for a breather, "You think I don't know what you do to get money?" She continued, turning the volume back up while walking towards her room.

I stood there as she stormed off.

"You think I don't know what you do out there?" She said, returning with an arm full of red and burgundy clothes, tossing them at me. A litter of shirts, red belts and flags, khakis, Chucks, and various baseball caps. "You think I don't know," she said, heading back towards the room once more.

I followed her this time, watching her snatch the remaining items out of her armoire. When she noticed me standing there, she started throwing them my way, hitting me with a burgundy Inglewood FUBU football jersey I remembered losing five years ago.

After exhausting herself, she sat on the bed. I stepped over to the armoire, kicking out of my way a blue bandana that belonged to my little brother, and picked up the old picture of me and Keith, when I was seven and he was ten. After studying the picture a beat longer, I took a seat next to my mom.

"I'm planning on checking into school for sound engineering. I've been looking into it lately," I said.

"Where at?" She asked.

"Well, there's a film and audio institute not too far from here," I said. "I figure I wouldn't be too far away in case you need me."

"In case I need you! Boy, I'm not an old woman. I can take care of myself. I'm your mother, you're not my father."

"I know, but when it comes to Rayona and Corey."

She nodded her head in the negative, "Don't use them as an excuse. I've been raising my kids by myself ever since I had them." She got up and started collecting the clothes.

"Nah, it's alright. I got it. I'll take them to the Salvation Army," I said.

"Kay," she called, stopping in the doorway before exiting the room, "like every other mother, I just want what's best for my kids. I want to watch them grow and become something in life."

Before my father's absence, before his presence became burdensome, he always stressed the importance of what it meant to be a man. At a time when I didn't understand what a man was beyond a boy progressing into adulthood. He told me what a man was vocally, which made sense logically, although it wouldn't be clear if his example always followed his words. From him I knew that a man had to stand for something, especially if he was Black. He had to stand for what he believed in, for what was right. I was told that a man should be decisive, strong in his word and actions. A man should have a clear sense of himself and his family. A man knows hard work and exercises loyalty and above all else, responsibility.

Before Keith's passing, he understood all of this. It was evident in the letter he wrote to aunt Marie, he had found himself and wanted better. He knew what he wanted in life and he knew what he wanted for his family.

I pocketed the picture of me and my brother, gathered all of the clothing and after a Salvation Army trip, I drove.

I drove past city limits, counties, farmlands, booming towns, and rural areas alike. Night and day, through light, moderate, and heavy traffic, with the intent of clearing my mind, a revelation clear. It was time to find myself and what I considered would make me whole. So I continued to drive.

Chapter 53

Ronni sat in the leather button-back chair, on the opposite end of an old mahogany table facing the U's dean of admissions and financial aid. The room was filled with plaques, certificates, and degrees. Accomplishments, and she felt accomplished just sitting there.

"And next, we come to tuition." The stout, scholarly man said, reviewing Veronica's file. "Usually it cos-," he cut his sentence short, scanning the documents in front of him. "It looks like your tuition has already been covered in full," he said with a smile.

Ronni looked over at her aunt, her late mother's sister Valencia, who sat all-business in the seat to her right. Valencia shrugged and nodded a quick no to Ronni's silent question of, 'did you pay it?'

"Does it say by whom it was paid?" Ronni inquired of the dean.

"No, it's blank. Cashiers."

Miami's sunlight poured over them as

they walked through the university's vast parking lot.

"Do you have any idea who sent the check?" Valencia asked as they strolled between the rows of cars.

To the right of them an alarm deactivation double chirped, a sound of nostalgia for Ronni who looked in the sounds direction. "Yeah," she answered, her focus on the back of a lean brother whose left arm was held by a blue sling as he walked towards a black Chevy Impala. Ronni's heart skipped a beat when she paused, butterflies entered her stomach as she headed in his direction. "Hey," she said, gently grabbing his shoulder, turning to face her was a startled, unfamiliar face. "Sorry," she mumbled, disappointment evident as she continued on with Valencia, who looked confused. "Someone I thought I knew," Ronni shrugged as they neared her aunt's BMW.

"Looking for me?" She heard behind her, the voice causing a complete stop and turn. "I didn't forget the flowers this time," I said, holding out the colorfully assorted bouquet.

She stared at me for a moment, a look I couldn't read. I walked to her, arms outstretched and wrapped them around her. It took her a couple of second to fully return my embrace, but when she did, I felt her arms squeeze me with what seemed like all the power she could muster.

"I know I owe you a thousand apologies ... I'm sorry."

She craned her head back and looked at me, the warmth in her eyes once more, "you plan on staying?"

"Yeah," I answered.

"Then I forgive you," she responded without hesitation. "Um, aunt Valencia, remember the guy Kay I was telling you about?"

"Nice to meet you," Valencia said, flashing a beautiful smile as she extended her hand. "You plan on attending school here?"

"Yes ma'am."

"It was long overdue," Ronni chimed in as we started walking together. "Oh, one more thing," she said, pulling my ear down to her lips, "I'm pregnant."

Now it was my time to be excited.

Continue reading for a sample of Akil Victor's next book: Wantonda

Wantonda

By

Akil Victor

Akil Victor

WANTON:

ˈwänt(ə)n/

adjective

1. **1.**
(of a cruel or violent action) deliberate and unprovoked.

"sheer wanton vandalism"

synonyms:	deliberate, willful, malicious, spiteful, wicked, cruel; More

2. **2.**
(especially of a woman) sexually immodest or promiscuous.

synonyms:	promiscuous, immoral, immodest, indecent, shameless, unchaste, fast, loose, impure, abandoned, lustful, lecherous, lascivious, libidinous, licentious, dissolute, debauched, degenerate, corrupt, whorish, disreputable
	"a wanton seductress"

Chapter 1

Linda Asami stood at the window of the Imperial Hotel suite she and Malcolm were secluded in. It was a beautiful night in Tokyo with a view of the luminous yellow, white, and red lights of the many buildings lined along Hibiya Park. She battled conflicting thoughts as she stared down at the continuous flow of life. People with simple worries, like their kids behavior and paying bills. Worries she'd happily trade for the ones consuming her at the moment. Her worries held someone's life in the balance; literally.

She felt Malcom's presence, his strong arms wrapping around her. The scent of his Polo cologne drifting up to her nose. She felt at ease in his arms, a warmth that was as foreign to her as the man himself. She looked down at his arm, covered in a silk long sleeve shirt. His chocolate-hued hand across her stomach and under that of her light tan hand made a stark contrast, which she found all the more beautiful. He nuzzled into her neck, sending chills up her spine and warmth in her nether region as she felt the rise of his strong erection. To say she didn't love him would be a lie.

His hand slowly rubbed across her stomach, pausing, "I love you so much. I can't wait to be a father," he said, as she assumed he imagined the very small life forming within her.

She turned around to face him, a light smile lifting her lips. "I love you too," she said in her accented English.

His hands went to her face, and he kissed her with those full lips that threw everything that she was supposed to do in question. She knew his role, but he didn't know her's. He was an American businessman and Senator. A personal friend of the vice president and of the director of the C.I.A. He knew things that people only dreamed of knowing, and the nightmares the simple world wished weren't true. To him, she was the daughter of a business associate that would act as a liaison when he was in town, whom he just happened to fall for along the way. But there was more to the story, so much more to the story. And Malcolm, like many other successful and powerful men, thought he was too smart and couldn't foul up. He wasn't as arrogant as most, which she liked, maybe even gullible in his love for her. But he had fell victim to his lust like many men before him. And although she'd never been a victim to anything, she found herself hesitant at her circumstances and feelings. How did she allow herself to get pregnant? With a Black American's baby at that.

"Let me prepare you a drink, honey," she said, hand on his chest, lightly pushing him back to the large canopy bed. He smiled that smile of his, the one that lit his deep brown eyes and accentuated his full lips. The smile that had always given her pause.

She went to the little wet bar in the suite. Watching his reflection in the mirror behind the bottles of expensive liquor. Paying attention to his mannerisms and movements, keeping an eye on him as he removed his tie. She grabbed the Cognac, his favorite, discreetly peering at him as she plucked a little vial from behind a sliding panel on the mirror. She upended it's powder in his drink, stirring it with a straw as she prepared a cyanide free glass for herself.

She spun around, opening up the flap of her peach tone, silk, robe. Exposing the black lingerie covering the special places of her lithe toned body. Which garnered his attention, like always. He stood there, gazing at her in admiration. Providing her with a reverence that she loved. Walking to him, she sidled between his legs, one hand on his broad chest, the other putting the drink to his lips. Instead of sipping, he clasped his large hand around hers and the cup. Giving her heart a brief start at the suddenness of it all.

"Did I ever tell you how much I love you," he said.

She relaxed, smiled. "I love you too." Looking at his lips instead of his eyes, she said, "Drink, baby."

He obliged, grabbing the glass and taking a strong sip. She kissed his stubble-free jawline. Assisting him with lifting the glass once more as she lowered her mouth to his neck, her tongue tracing a line on its nape. He had one arm around her, it tightened as his body went rigid and the glass slipped from his other hand to the lush carpet. Bouncing just once as the poison laced cognac spilled out and seeped into the thick fibers.

He tried to talk, the words coming out in strained gurgles as he loosened his hold on her and his hands shot for his heart. His eyes were wide with fear and confusion. He reached for her again as he began to sink to his knees. She took a step back, looking down at his stiff fingers as they clawed at the air for her. She found it hard to look at him in that moment but forced herself to. It was her duty after all, her current role in life. He fell over sideways, sweating profusely and struggling to breathe, she noted his strength, admired it even. His hand went to his trouser pocket and pulled out a small suede jewelry box, it fell from his rigid fingers. She reached for it, opened it and gasped at what it held. The most beautiful diamond ring she'd ever seen, it's colors illuminating radiance under the dim suite light. She felt weak. The ring box fell from her hand. She raised her hand to her mouth in panic as she looked down at him struggling to breathe and hold on for dear life.

She rushed to the bathroom, digging through the medicine cabinet until she came upon a little tube of sodium thiosulphate crystals. An anti-agent for cyanide poisoning. Something all in her profession should have handy. She sprinted across the room for her purse. In a bottom secret compartment were two syringes amongst other small death inducing things. One syringe was filled with more poison however, the second one was empty. She grabbed the empty one and raced back to the bathroom. Getting it open to drop a few crystals in and fill the rest of the tube with water. She shook it up frantically, watching as it dissolved and ran to his side.

She kneeled beside him with slightly trembling fingers. Faintly aware of this being the first time she was nervous since her service began 15 years prior. Taking a deep breath, she injected it, pressing the contents into his bloodstream. Hoping the antidote would beat any potential neurological problems from the cyanide possibly cutting off oxygen to his brain. His breathing eased up a bit. His eyes on her with, wonderment, worry, fear. She looked down at him from her knees. Exasperated as she leaned back on her calves. She knew her whole world was over and life would never be the same for either of them. She was pregnant with his baby and he wanted to marry her and... *No one has ever made me feel like this...I love him,* she thought and was overtaken with an abject fear.

Scrambling to her feet, she helped him to a sitting position at the end of the bed. He stared up at her, gone was all of the emotions in his eyes, replaced with a look she could not read. She touched his face gingerly, her eyes softening before reaching down for the ring box. She opened it and slid the beautiful diamond home on her finger. Mesmerized by how it looked and made her feel. Then, the phone rang. It's blare cutting through the silence with a shrillness that put her on edge. She went to it, lifting it off it's cradle and heard, *Your service is no longer needed,* in Japanese.

She closed her eyes, shutting them tight to clear her mind and sweep away any irrationality, just like she was disciplined to do since youth. She knew that they had hidden cameras in the suite somewhere. She knew her decision to let Malcom live would possibly forfeit her life, but she no longer cared. What he showed her and offered was a realization that she could be more than some secret government organization's tool. Moving quickly to the bar, she felt alongside its outer wooden edge until her fingers felt a panel, she pushed it, the wood sliding to the side to reveal a cache of weapons. Various guns and fighting knives.

Throwing off her satin robe, she strapped on a leather cross-strap belt around her shoulders and torso that held two PPK handguns. Beside and behind the cross-straps were loops for two small tanto daggers and katana swords, she slid them in. After a quick thought, she grabbed a 9mm, held it to her side and walked toward Malcom. He looked up at her, his breath still a bit ragged but continuous. "Can you move?" She asked.

He attempted to do so, the effort great and accomplishment small. "Yeah," he rasped, which was an understatement.

She held out the gun to him, he regarded it for a second before slowly reaching out to grab it, his face showing the strained pain the entire way.

"You know me as Miako Mitamoto, daughter of a hotel magnate. My real name is Linda Asami.

I am an information extractor and assassin for a Japanese organization I will not name. You," she paused a second to visually scan her surroundings and choose her words, "Your love, way of being, and treatment of me has compromised decisions. And because I choose to let you live, we must defend ourselves. We don't have much time." She said, noticing his focus was on her ring finger, the diamond he had given her. When his eyes met hers again, she'd seen the return of that love that she'd longed for. The door exploded open, and before her eyes quickly left his to look in that direction, she'd seen the fear.

[A1]Sample edit ends here.

Made in the USA
Monee, IL
11 December 2020